Brown Paper Bag

a novel by

Venus Mason Theus

_Priority_ONE
publications

Detroit, MI USA

BROWN PAPER BAG
Copyright © 2006, 2011 Venus Mason Theus

All scripture quotations are taken from the Authorized King
James Version of the Holy Bible.

ISBN 13: 978-1-933972-25-1
ISBN 10:   1-933972-25-4

Author's Note

This is a work of fiction. Any references to actual events, real
people living or dead or to real locales are intended only to give
the novel a sense of reality and authenticity. Other names,
characters, places and incidents are either the product of the
author's imagination or are used fictitiously and their
resemblance, if any, to real-life counterparts, is entirely
coincidental.

Cover design and photography by Juan Roberts
Interior design by Christina Dixon
Editing by Tenita Johnson

Printed in the United States of America

Acknowledgements

I could not begin to give thanks and acknowledgements without first honoring Jesus Christ - my Lord, my Savior, my Jehovah Jireh (provider), my Jehovah Shalom (peace), my Jehovah Rapha (healer) and El Shaddai (the Almighty). You gave me victory over every heartache, illness, injury, and fiery trial I've ever encountered. Thank you for every mountain's peak and every valley's floor, because in each situation, you've shown your power and majesty. I love you because you loved me first. Thank you for creating me, loving me and calling me to serve you. Thank you for unmerited favor. Thank you for showering me with genuine love from family and true friends. I commit this, and all the work that I do unto you, my awesome heavenly father.

In loving memory of my maternal grandparents/surrogate parents, George and Mattie Jordan-Wright, without whom, where would I be?

To my mom, Mary F. Clinkscales, the epitome of character and grace. You are my champion and my *s/hero*.

To my dad, William Anthony Mason, and my *bonus mom* Litha Ruth Mason, who have shown me that it's never too late.

To my spiritual shepherd, Bishop Charles H. Ellis, III Greater Grace Temple - Detroit, Michigan, thank you for keeping-it-real, for believing in me and keeping me encouraged during my *many* storms.

To my phenomenal First Lady Crisette M. Ellis, Proverbs 31:10-31 in the flesh.

To my church family at Greater Grace Temple in Detroit,

To my surrogate mothers, Lady Wilma Ruth Ellis-Johnson, who taught me to always have hope, seek wisdom and show compassion. To Mrs. Shirley Armstrong-Kite, Evangelist Marcia Norton, Mrs. Sue Smith, Cousin Nancy Liggins and Delores "Mom" Winans.

You've all shown me kindness and given me encouragement beyond measure – always on time. You each possess qualities that make me want to be like you *when I grow up.*

To my Got-Your-Back Girlfriends, who have endured innumerable hours praying, purging guilt, dismissing shame, wiping tears, coaching, consoling, celebrating, and of course sipping tea with me...Denise Smith – *who talked me down from the ledge too many times to tell...* to Jackie Baptist – an amazingly gifted graphic artist, I'm privileged to have you as a friend, *you're an angel always there when I need a "quick favor,"* to Pat Broughton – *my buddy and one-woman fan club,* to Bernadette Hardy *thanks for the tea pot purse,* to Vickie Stuckey – *my twin spirit,* to Cheryl Smith, *thank you for the generous seed!* Also to Margaret "Tudy" Dunton – *a powerful and phenomenal woman,* Victoria Johnson, and Jackie Woodland, - *thanks for all the prayers, hugs and kisses-and for keeping me beautiful,* to my neighbors, Ann Winston, and Joann Martin – *it really does take a village, doesn't it?*

... To My Friends-Since-We-All-Had-Waistlines (Over 30 years) Bernice Stephens-Moore, Kimberly Reed-Thompson, Anna J. Knott, Anita Robinson-Norwood, and Karen E. Gaskill, Thomasina Seaborn (ok, so you still have a waistline). *Who needs sisters when I have all of you?*

Who Says a Woman Can't Have a Male Best Friend? I've been blessed with two testosteronic best buds...Minister Wollie Stuckey, and Erwin Norwood. *Love you guys to pieces!!!!!!*

I would like to thank the following Christian Fiction writers for their encouragement and inspiration: Kim Brooks, Dara Nicole, Valerie Coleman, Kendra Norman Bellamy, Stacey Hawkins Adams, Sherri Lewis, Tia McCollors, Tiffany L. Warren, Vanessa Davis Griggs, Sharon Ewell Foster and Marilynn Griffith.

I also want to thank authors Sylvia Hubbard, Minister Mary Darlene Edwards, Jackie Moore, Minister Barbara Smith, Versandra Kennebrew and Monica Marie Jones for imparting their literary wisdom and generously sharing their crafts with aspiring writers.

Many thanks to Tenita C. Johnson for calming my paranoia with her editing tips.

Thanks to Pam Perry for countless hours of PR coaching, mentoring and just plain sister love – you are the epitome of Agape.

Special thanks to Christina Dixon, PriorityONE Publications for entrusting Brown Paper Bag to blaze the trail as its first fiction title.

To My Reasons Why…

My sons Jerome A. Theus, Jr. and James G.L. Theus (#15), my daughters Cherise Theus-Miller, Lakeisha Theus-Stiff and Jessica Theus, my Son's-In-Law Roderick (Naiari) Miller and William Stiff, and to *Na Na's little Princes and Princesses*…Ericka, Jerome III, Diamond, Isaiah, Joshua, Naiyana, Israel, Ramiyah, Ishmael, Zoe, Odyssey, Arielle, Jordan and Madison. Use your gifts for God's glory - I expect greatness tempered with humility from each of you.

To all of my Linwood Avenue "Homies" - Detroit, Michigan…Cliff (Jr.) and Stevie Moore, Larry Russell, Debra McCaughan, Freddie Sims, Anna J. Knott, Linda Pickett, Cynthia; Thelma, Charlene and Charles Stewart; and the entire Stephens family. *In memory of William Wimes, Aaron and Barron Floyd; Rhonda Oliver, Thelma Stewart and Weslon Gray.*

Last but certainly not least, to my husband, Jerome A. Theus, Sr., my best friend, my lover, my soul mate, my confidante, my encouragement, my inspiration, the high priest of our home…you're the best earthly thing that ever happened to me, I love you eternally.

Foreword

*B*rown *Paper Bag* captures the collision of values within the African American culture of the United States during the 1950s through the mid-1970s. Theus gives a snapshot of the conflicts between the blue-color working class and the elite.   Much like *Pieces from Life's Crazy Quilt*, written by Marvin V. Arnett, Theus tells about a subculture that few African Americans discuss; but is still alive today.

Dr. Martin Luther King, Jr. had a dream that one day everyone would be judged by the content of their character; and not by the color of their skin. He was referring to the black/white issue. *Brown Paper Bag* uncovers a mindset embedded within the African American community since the days of slavery.

Theus skillfully illuminates the struggles through her characters' daily interpersonal relationships. Just when the ripples of discord seem to cease, a new wave of disunity begins.

This novel took me down memory lane, re-opening old wounds and then closing them again through the love of God and redemptive power of Jesus Christ. Weeping may endure for a night, but joy comes in the morning.

Denise A. Smith, Author
Back from Sanity's Edge

I am not my hair
I am not this skin
I am not your expectations (no)
I am not my hair
I am not this skin
I am the soul that lives within

– India Aire,
Testimony: Vol. 1, Life & Relationship (2006)

Prologue

Be not forgetful to entertain strangers:
for thereby some have entertained angels unawares.

Hebrews 13:2

1986 ~ Baton Rouge, Louisiana

Albertina hovered above the inanimate form that was her own body. She heard unintelligible voices and the sound of several sets of shuffling feet approaching. A sea of white coats with hands that held clipboards and pens stood at the foot of her hospital bed. Five, no six white coats.

One of them spoke as the others listened and scribbled notes. She willed her eyes to open but they disobeyed. She tried to speak but was unable to make her lips part. Her mind was screaming. She wanted someone to pull out all of the tubes and wires. Tubes that pushed oxygen in and out of her lungs. Wires that made her heart beat. Tubes that nourished and hydrated her... drained her body's waste. Wires and tubes that enabled her to live.

The white coats formed a semi-circle around her hospital bed. A gray-haired white coat asked questions of the others. Two of them answered. The gray-haired one scowled and shook his head. He impatiently waited for the obvious correct answer.

Finally a medical student with topaz-colored eyes gave him the answer he waited for. The corners of Gray-hair's mouth turned upward as he nodded approvingly.

Albertina observed as the white coats continued to violate her. Gray-hair lifted the thin cotton sheet that covered the remnants of her dignity, pointed and asked more questions. Again, the girl with topaz colored eyes answered correctly.

Albertina sensed a familiarity with the bright intern. Neither she nor her young benefactor was aware that their past – and future were entwined.

Somebody lied. Somebody died.

                    The obvious is sometimes obscure.

Chapter One

Lover and friend hast thou put far from me,
and mine acquaintance into darkness.

Psalm 88:18

1958 ~ Detroit, Michigan

"Who's that baby's daddy?"

"Are you drunk or something? Why would you ask me that?"

A deafening clap of thunder tore open the late-night sky and released sheets of April rain.

Gregory shouted over the thunder, "I just had a talk with Thomas."

"What has Thomas got to do with our baby?"

"*Is* it our baby Natalie? Do you even know who the father is?"

"Gregory you know I have never been with anybody but you – that one time! I can't believe you even fixed your mouth to ask me such a question."

"Liar!" He slapped her - hit her so hard she was sure she'd bitten right through her tongue. Bewildered by his sudden attack, Natalie tasted her own blood – not knowing whether the bleeding was from the tongue bite or the split in her rapidly swelling lips.

She ignored the excruciating pain and reached for him, pleading for an explanation. "Why did you do that? What did I do to deserve that?"

He grabbed her shoulders, shaking her. "I'm not falling for that innocent act any more Natalie. You played me for a fool - big time. I can't believe I almost married you."

She wrenched herself free of his grip and instinctively pushed him so hard he stumbled backward - barely missing the porch steps. "This isn't you talking Gregory. Your mouth is moving, but Albertina Baptiste is talking."

Another back-handed blow to her mouth sent Natalie crashing against the house - jabbing her back into the doorbell. The intensity of the blow against the doorbell shot a wave of pain into Natalie's spine that traveled up to her neck, back down to her tailbone and into her right leg.

"You keep my mother's name out of your filthy, lying mouth."

A crowd of curious neighbors carrying umbrellas and wearing rain slickers had gathered in front of the house. Block Captain Elijah Nelson yelled into the crowd, "I'm calling the police!"

The neighbor's comment fueled Gregory's anger like gasoline doused on a flame. "This is a private matter. You people need to mind your own business." He returned his attention to Natalie.

"What are you planning to do about that baby?"

"You seem to believe it's not your baby, so it's not your business."

"Don't get smart with me." He shoved her against the house, clutched her throat with his left hand and raised his right fist.

The screen door slapped against the house. Hattie Jordan burst onto the porch wielding a meat cleaver. "Boy, if you hit my daughter you gon' draw back a bleedin' nub!"

Her husband, Dallas, stumbled out of the house carrying a shotgun and wiping sleep from his eyes.

"Whas' going on out here? Natalie, did this boy put his hands on you?"

Hattie answered, "Look at her mouth Dallas. This fool had her pinned 'gin the house." Natalie's face was twisted from the pain that radiated from the center of her back.

Dallas snatched his daughter away from Gregory's grip and leveled the barrel of the shotgun between his brows.

"Look-a-here, Mama's Boy, you get yo' tail off my prop'ty 'fo I blow yo' head clean off."

"Daddy no!" Natalie sobbed into her father's shoulder.

A black and white squad car pulled up in front of the house. The driver shined a light on the porch and yelled to Gregory. "What's going on here? We got a call that a lady was being assaulted at this address."

Dallas eased the shotgun back in the house while the officers focused on Gregory.

One of the officers exited the squad car. He thought he recognized Gregory and yelled over his shoulder to his partner.

"Hey Jake, ain't this the guy we pulled over just a few minutes ago?"

Jake looked at Gregory, then his '56 Chevy. He yelled back.

"Yeah Mel, one and the same. What's going on up there Mr. Baptiste?"

Gregory answered, "Just a little lover's quarrel. Sorry if we disturbed anyone. We didn't mean to cause any trouble."

Officer Jake got out of the car to break up the crowd.

"Alright everybody, show's over. Go on home, there's nothing else to see here."

The reluctant crowd dispersed. Several people returned to their homes to peer through the windows of darkened rooms. A few of the more defiant neighbors congregated with Elijah Nelson on his front porch – hoping the entertainment would continue.

Officer Mel walked over to the bottom of the stairs and surveyed the scene. Natalie hid her face from the policeman's light.

"You folks sure there is nothing going on that we need to know about?" He directed his attention to Natalie, "Young lady, are you hurt?" From the shadows, she wiped a trembling hand across her face and tried to speak normally but her voice and her bulging lips betrayed her. "N-no thank you officer. I'm ok."

A quick assessment of the scene and judging from the swelling and bruises on Natalie's face, his suspicions were confirmed. He'd witnessed this scenario on countless weekend calls. He shrugged his shoulders and said, "Well, we can't make you turn him in." The officer raised the collar of his raincoat and spoke to Gregory. "So this is where you were in such a hurry to get to huh?"

Gregory stared past him - at Natalie. Then his acid-churning stomach sent him into a fit of violent convulsions and dry heaves.

The policemen exchanged looks. "Tell you what Mr. Baptiste, me and Officer Tyson there will give you a ride home." He motioned for Gregory to start moving toward the squad car.

Gregory imagined the hissy-fit Albertina would have if her son was brought home in a police car.

"No thanks, I'm alright. I can make it."

Officer Jake propped his foot on the bottom step and leaned forward. "Young man, I don't think you understand. Officer Tyson and I *insist* that you accept our offer."

He scowled. "And what am I supposed to do about my car? I can't just leave it here."

"In light of the circumstances, I plan to give this house special attention all night. I'm sure nothing will happen while it's parked in front of the Jordans' house. You can arrange to take care of it in the morning." He placed his hand on the young man's shoulder. "Come on now. Get in the squad car son."

Dallas put his arm around his daughter's slightly protruding waist and gently guided her toward the warmth and safety of their home. She looked over her shoulder and saw Gregory glaring at her from the back seat of the police cruiser. Natalie's tears mingled with the rain and splattered onto her cheeks as she watched her baby's father disappear into an envelope of darkness.

Chapter Two

The Lord is a refuge for the oppressed;
a stronghold in times of trouble.

Psalm 9:9

The skin underneath Natalie's engagement ring was swollen and raw from absently pulling it off and forcing it back on. The ring's luster was dulled by tear-drenched eyes. She had never seen Gregory like this. So angry, so filled with rage, that a stranger would have mistaken it for hatred. But Gregory didn't hate her, he couldn't possibly hate her. He loved her. Everybody knew Gregory loved Natalie – whether they liked it or not.

She sat at her parents' kitchen table trying to make sense of what had just happened.

"Mama, I don't know how Gregory could accuse me of doing that. What would make him think I would *ever* do such a thing? Who could have filled his head with that pack of lies?"

Her mother answered, "Baby, I think we both know who's responsible for that. But Gregory's a grown-tail man. He's got a mind of his own."

"But how could he think I'd do that with his own cousin? Thomas was supposed to be our Best Man. I just don't know what happened. One minute we're making wedding plans, the next minute he's accusing me of things I'd never dream of doing!"

"Go rinse your mouth out with some salt and warm water. It's gon' hurt like the devil but it'll take that swellin' in your tongue down. It's just a blessin' you didn't bite it clean through."

Natalie retreated to the bathroom to nurse her injuries. She turned on the light and was frightened by her own reflection. The swollen area around her mouth and nose was covered with spotty purple and blue bruises.

When she returned to the kitchen, Hattie gently placed a beef steak on the side of her daughter's face then gave her a cup of warm milk and honey. Natalie made an attempt to sip from the cup but the injuries to her mouth forbade it.

"Try to get some in ya with a spoon. You need somethin' to calm your nerves so you can get some rest."

"That's alright Mama. I'm so upset I'd probably just vomit it back up anyway. Gregory's upset too. I've never seen him like this before. Never."

"I don't care how upset Gregory is, he ain't got no right to whup on you."

"It's my fault for being so stupid. I never should have trusted Thomas. I shouldn't have been spending so much time with him like that. It's no wonder people thought we were messing around. I just don't understand why he would lie. Even if for some reason he couldn't stand me, why would he want to hurt Gregory like this?"

"First of all, it ain't your fault. Irregardless of what anybody else think, Gregory s'posed to know you better than that. You was marrying him – not people. You give them folks they ring back and get on with your life."

She nodded her head slowly as she devised a plan for reconciliation. "Right, I'll tell him to come get it tomorrow. Then when he gets here we can talk and get this mess straightened out."

"No you don't tell him to come get nothin'. Understand what's happening here baby, he just might come back here beggin' and actin' all sorry for now. But sho' as you born, the next thang you know he'll be goin' upside your head again - and again – until both y'all get used to it. I done seen too many womens go through that; but not none of the women in this family.

No Ma'am, don't you get that stuff started. Your daddy said that boy is never to set foot on this prop'ty again and I know he meant it. He can take them peoples they ring over there tomorrow and let that be the end of it. Now try to get some of that milk and honey down and go to bed. You needs your rest."

She pointed at Natalie's stomach. "Don't forget you got a little baby growin' in you."

Hours later the cuckoo clock in the next room announced that it was 2 a.m. Hattie had long since gone to bed, realizing that only God could comfort her daughter.

Although she was still wide awake, Natalie dragged herself upstairs and dropped onto her bed. The otherwise cheery hues of yellow throughout the room seemed to have paled to a nauseating grayish color. The room was shrinking. The walls were closing in on her; she struggled to breathe.

Menacing lightening and shadows from the lights of passing cars outside her window created specters that taunted her with the night's ordeal.

Sleep eluded her for several more hours. The tiny baby inside her womb fluttered and stirred incessantly. It must have sensed its mother's agony as she mentally reenacted the melodrama.

It was daylight when both she and the baby finally surrendered to fatigue. But there would be no rest, no sweet dreams. Only hellish nightmares of the circumstances which led to this very moment.

By the break of day, Natalie had taken a journey to places and events she had locked away in the deepest, darkest crevices of her mind.

Chapter Three

*I snatched you from the power of Egypt
and from the hand of all your oppressors.*

Judges 6:9

Moving to Detroit was to be Natalie's passageway to freedom from a lifetime of imprisonment. She hadn't been bound by simple captors such as bars or locked doors. She was tethered to the unremitting subjective mindset of ignorance, intolerance and cruelty because she looked different. Different from her own people.

The summer of 1954 was her last in Sweet Water, Georgia. The fourteen-year-old experienced a growth spurt as she blossomed into womanhood.

At 5'10", she averaged a full head taller than the girls and even several of Sweet Water's boys. Curves and embellishments had sprouted in all the right places as Mother Nature graced or as some would say, cursed her with womanly attributes. Everyone – man, woman, boy and girl, took notice of her at first glance.

Natalie's confident stride and exotic beauty were mistaken for flaws. Her skin was the color of rich, semi-sweet chocolate. Her full lips, prominent nose, cheekbones and even her exceptional height were evidence that she was an undeniable descendent of the African Motherland.

However, the people of Sweet Water saw anything but beauty in Natalie. *"That girl would be kinda good lookin' if she wasn't so black...and so tall."*

"The way she walk with her nose always up in the air, she look like a stuck up, black giraffe."

Sweet Water was a town plagued by shallowness and indifference. The dusty little hamlet consisted of slightly less than 200 people. A few of them were domestics and entrepreneurs.

The rest of the inhabitants worked for the area's largest employer, the Sweet Water Carpet Mill.

Among Sweet Water's commercial residents were Lester and Sons Texaco filling station, the Bijou movie theatre, Simpson's Home for Funerals, Ezee's Greasy Spoon, and last but certainly not least - Miss Delphine's Exquisite Dress and Millinery Boutique. The only church for colored people, Pure Word Church of the Living God, sat on the outskirts of town.

Nearly everyone in Sweet Water struggled to make ends meet. Hattie worked as a cook and housekeeper for a white family in Haslette, a larger town with more prominent citizens.

Dallas worked eight to ten hours a day at the carpet mill. Then another four or five hours a week doing handy work for old man Simpson at the white folks' funeral parlor.

The children of Sweet Water seldom enjoyed the luxury of playtime and frolic. Most of them only attended school until the third or fourth grade. Some stayed through the eighth grade and an exceptional few were fortunate enough to attend a year or two of high school.

All of them, including Natalie, were required to work in fields or inside the Haslette or Northbridge houses after school and on Saturdays.

From the tender age of eight, Natalie contributed to her family's income by washing and ironing white folks' laundry on Friday evenings and Saturdays. Her only friends were her cousin Bernadette and her German shepherd mix, Black Gal.

On rare occasions, they were able to enjoy themselves as carefree teenagers; the two girls chattered about movie stars and cute boys. All the while, Natalie fussed with Bernadette's hair –

copying the hairstyles of their cinema idols Lena Horne, Eartha Kitt and Dorothy Dandridge.

From the first day she attended the Sweet Water School until the last, Natalie was subjected to the cruelty of the other kids because of physical attributes over which she had no control.

No matter how hard she tried to fit in, she was isolated and subjected to the heartless insults of the other children.

While most Negroes in the United States were embroiled in the struggle to gain racial equality and white America's social acceptance, Natalie's mahogany complexion and distinct ethnic features provoked merciless verbal attacks and vicious pranks from her people within her own race.

One day, as she prepared to recite the Preamble in front of the 8th grade class, she was mortified when Arnie Blacksmith yelled out, "Dang, look at them big ol' shoes. Her feet big as my daddy's!"

Everyone in the classroom laughed, including Miss Tucker. Instead of calling the class to order, twenty-something-year-old Amelia Tucker chimed in. "Natalie, did your parents buy those shoes or did they have somebody build 'em for you?"

To her horror, the class exploded with laughter. From that day on, Natalie was nick-named Stompers. She would never have mentioned a word to her parents, but Bernadette told her own mother about the incident. In turn, Baby Sis told Hattie at church the following Sunday.

First thing Monday morning, Hattie visited the school to have a few choice words with Miss Tucker. That evening at the dinner table, Hattie told Dallas how she came real close to putting her religion on the shelf.

"I told that woman if she didn't put a stop to them kids' ridiculing my child, she would have to answer to me."

However, the version that Miss Tucker gave Mr. Pringle, the head teacher, was that Hattie had made threats against her because she had *disciplined* Natalie for refusing to recite the Preamble. Consequently, he suspended Natalie and told Hattie not to send her back to *his* school unless she was willing to respect authority like the other students.

Dallas dipped a soda biscuit in a bowl of red-eye gravy as he listened to Hattie's recount of the ordeal at the school.

"What we gon' do Dallas? It just ain't fair for that gal to be left outta school while them hoot'lums parade in front of this house every day to get they learn'in."

He reached for another biscuit. "Let me study 'bout it." Tuesday passed; Dallas neither said nor did anything. Then Wednesday and Thursday – still nothing. Hattie was growing anxious but knew better than to pressure him.

Finally, on Friday morning, dressed in his suit and Sunday hat, Dallas walked the five mile trek to the school and had a man-to-man talk with Odell Pringle.

Pringle listened to Dallas recount Hattie's description of the incident while sitting on a tree stump in back of the weather-worn schoolhouse. "Now Dallas, I realize you and me have known each other since we were boys, but I have to tell you up front that I don't play favorites. As a matter of fact, I had to suspend my own nephew last year when he..."

Dallas held up his hand. "First off Odell, I ain't askin' for nothin'. I come here to *tell* you to let my gal back in school come Monday morning. If I thought for one moment that Natalie sass-talked the teacher, I would stand by what you done – but I know better than that. Truth is, I'm sho' you do too."

Pringle shook his head vehemently. "No sir Dallas. Not a chance. Rules are rules."

"Rules are rules huh? Well, lemme ask you this Odell, what kinda rules yo' wife got about you runnin' 'round with young women – Oscar Tucker's gal in particular?"

Pringle raised his eyebrows. "Dallas Jordan, are you trying to accuse me of something?"

"No sir. Not accusing you of anything. I just wonder what your wife would think if she know'd you and that girl been doing more than grading papers after dem kids leaves the schoolhouse."

"You trying to blackmail me Dallas Jordan? Do you honestly think my wife would believe your speculations?"

"No. I don't think she would b'lieve no 'spec-a-lations. Pauline always struck me as havin' a good head on her shoulders. But I'm sho' she'd b'lieve what somebody told her they seen. She'd b'lieve me if I told her I seen you comin' outta that gal's house every Wednesday night on my way home from the funeral parlor." Dallas scratched his chin. "That's s'posed to be your regular poker night at Slim Taylor's ain't it?"

Pringle lowered his eyes. "Alright Dallas, I guess maybe I see your point. Natalie is kinda shy. Maybe Amy - Miss Tucker mistook her shyness for impudence." He looked at Dallas. "I'm glad we had this talk. I'll speak with Miss Tucker. I'll put a stop to everything today - before things get out of hand."

Dallas extended his hand to Pringle. "Odell, I'm glad we could clear this up - I'd hate for anybody else to get hurt over this misunderstanding."

When he returned from his *meeting* with Odell Pringle, Dallas called Natalie to him. "You go back to school come Monday morning, ya hear?"

She stood dumbfounded waiting for details. She and Hattie had hoped for a blow-by-blow description of what had taken place, but Dallas never uttered another word about the incident.

"Did you hear what I said gal?"

"Yes sir."

"Alright then. What's for lunch Hattie?"

Natalie didn't know what to expect when she returned to school on Monday morning, but she was sure there wouldn't be a welcoming committee waiting for her. To her surprise, both Mr. Pringle and Miss Tucker apologized to her in front of the entire class. The children had all been instructed not to tease Natalie any more, about anything.

Natalie wished her parents had left matters alone though.

Now the kids imposed a school-wide exile upon her, with the exception of Bernadette. They wouldn't speak to her and made amplified efforts to avoid touching her or even making eye contact. The silent treatment and the behind-the-back whispering were even more painful than the taunting.

Black Gal eagerly waited for Natalie in the schoolyard at the end of each day. After the exile was imposed, she and Black Gal detoured from the main road to linger among the graves of Sweet Water Memorial's more prominent citizens. Natalie found solace among the headstones.

On Friday afternoon, Fannie and Sula Mae Justice diverted from their regular route home from school. As was customary on Fridays, Jessie Mitchell and his younger brother James plotted to pull yet another devilish prank to start their weekend.

The boys had dared Fannie and Sula Mae to take the back road past the graveyard. Most of Sweet Water's girls wouldn't set foot near that graveyard even if you paid them. But Fannie and Sula Mae were not like most girls – especially Sula Mae who was unnaturally ruthless.

The mischievous pair stumbled upon Natalie's place of refuge. She was sitting on the ground propped against Emmanuel Pruitt's four-foot monument, singing her own rendition of the Star Spangled Banner. She would soon realize that her classmates' cease-fire was limited to the school's property.

Just as she reached the high notes, *o'er the land of the free...* she heard giggling come from somewhere near the Brightmoore family's plot. Fannie and Sula Mae sprang up from behind *Beloved Wife and Mother, Millicent Brightmoore's* headstone. Sula Mae started chanting a song of her own. "Grave digger, Grave digger Natalie is a Grave digger..." Fannie and the boys joined in.

Angered and humiliated, Natalie sprang from the ground and lunged at Sula Mae. She grabbed the girl's skinny neck and began choking her and flinging her around like a rag doll. The rascally bunch was unaware that Black Gal had been lying in the grass beside Natalie.

Sula Mae's posse attempted to rescue her but Black Gal held them at bay. The hair on Black Gal's back stood on end. She growled and bared her teeth - ready to attack upon Natalie's command.

The frightened pranksters huddled together.

"Call your dog! Natalie, get your dog!"

She commanded, "Y'all quit messin' wit me!"

"Ok! We was just playin'. Natalie just call yo' dang dog!"

Natalie released the vice grip she had on Sula Mae's throat and shoved her to the ground. "I'm sick of y'all messin' wit me all the time. Why you cain't just leave me alone?"

The puny ring-leader fell limp onto the ground – coughing and gasping for air.

"Black Gal. Down. Come here girl." Natalie patted her thigh and her obedient rescuer retreated.

Jessie, James and Fannie took off running. James hollered over his shoulder. "Grave digger!"

Fannie called to Sula Mae. "Come on girl, let's get outta here, it's spooky."

Sula Mae lay on the ground glaring at Natalie.

"Ain't you got no place to go Sula Mae?"

"Yeah, I got some place to go and you do too. You going straight to the devil. You and your mangy dog!"

Sula Mae stood slowly, brushing Georgia's rust-colored dust off her legs. She inspected the new gingham pinafore her mother had purchased from Miss Delphine's boutique.

"You better be glad my new dress from New York City ain't tore." She stuck her finger in Natalie's face and made an ominous threat. "From now on Natalie Jordan, you better sleep with one eye open."

Chapter Four

Ye thought evil against me; but
God meant it unto good.

Genesis 50:20

Dallas was the first to notice that Black Gal hadn't run up to greet them when the family returned home from prayer meeting. "Black Gal must be out in them woods chasing a rabbit or something." He whistled. No Black Gal.

Natalie tried calling her. "Blaaack Gaaal. Come on here girl." Still nothing.

Hattie rushed toward the house. "I got to get outta this girdle – quick! I'll see y'all in the house. Honey, I'm going to make some hot water bread and get the rest of the food on the table."

"Sounds good Sugar Lump. I'm starvin'."

"Daddy, where you think she at?"

"I don't know. She don't usually stray off too far. She'll be back fo' sun down." Dallas followed Hattie into the house while Natalie scouted out back for her dog.

A few moments later, a chilling shriek assaulted the evening's tranquility. Hattie and Dallas ran to the wooded area behind the house and found Natalie on the ground. Her dress was drenched with blood. She was hugging and rocking Black Gal's lifeless body.

"Why would somebody do this to Black Gal? She didn't hurt nobody!" The dog had been savagely bludgeoned to death. A bloody lead pipe was conspicuously lying next to the spot where Natalie found the dog's body.

"Get Natalie in the house Hattie. I'll take care of Black Gal."

Inside her bedroom, the heartbroken girl clutched a chew toy that Dallas had made when Black Gal was a puppy.

She wept uncontrollably. "Mama why do people hate me so much? Somebody did this just to hurt me."

"I don't know baby. I don't even think the people that hate others know why."

"Mama when I find out who did this, I'm gon' take that pipe and beat the mess outta them. They need to pay for what they did to Black Gal. She didn't do nothin' to nobody."

"Shh, hush talking like that. It ain't our place to get revenge. The Lord said He will repay evil doers. They did terrible things to the good Lord Jesus too baby. His only crime was that he loved all of us. Even mean, hateful folks. And we have to do the same thing. The good book says we have to love folks that hate us, treat everybody right. We even have to pray for our enemies."

The girl tearfully replied, "I don't think I can do that Mama. Other than Bernadette, Black Gal was my only friend in the whole wide world. It feels like they killed a part of me too."

Hattie wrapped her arms around the grieving girl. "I know baby. You have a right to feel like that. You just hold your head up when you at school. Don't give 'em the satisfaction of knowing how bad they hurt you."

"I ain't never going back to that school Mama. Everybody there hates me – even Miss Tucker."

"Staying home from school ain't gon' hurt nobody but you. You got to get your schoolin'. You goin' all the way through high school. After that, who knows? You might even go to college. Just trust the Lord. He'll give you peace while you sitting right in the midst of your storm."

Hattie hugged the teen again and kissed her forehead. "Sweet Pea, God can turn this awful situation into something for your own good."

"Even losing somebody you love?"

"Yes darlin'. Even losing somebody you love."

Chapter Five

...Get thee out of thy country, and from thy kindred,
and from thy father's house, unto a land that I will shew thee.

Genesis 12:1

Dallas' brother Houston sent word that Ford Motor Company was hiring in masses. He said that men were making money hand over fist. Within a week of Houston's phone call, he and Otis Brown had loaded the Brown family's pickup truck and left for Detroit.

After standing in line outside Ford's Rouge assembly plant for seven hours, then answering a few routine questions, both men were hired on the spot.

Dallas and Brown rented rooms at the YMCA where they would stay until they could find suitable dwelling places for their wives and children. Houston had offered to let Dallas stay at his house until he got on his feet, but Dallas declined. Hattie wouldn't hear of him staying one night under the same roof with "that woman."

Two years before, Houston had abandoned Baby Sis, his *real* wife of 17 years and their *real* kids to live with a 21-year-old mother of three small children. Juanita, Houston's common law wife, was six months pregnant with the fourth. This time Houston was the father – *perhaps*.

Dallas had been in Detroit for nearly a year when he finally sent for Hattie and Natalie. On their last Sunday in Sweet Water, the congregation of Pure Word held a send-off fellowship for them. To her surprise, many of Natalie's schoolmates hugged her and wished her well. Sula Mae Justice remained distant and silent as her sister Fannie tearfully bid Natalie goodbye. She was too busy making plans for life in the city to try to evaluate the sincerity of her sudden well-wishers.

Bernadette was happy that her cousin was going to live in a place where she could finally find friendship and happiness. But at the same time, she was sad because she was losing her best friend and being left behind in a dusty old town that offered nothing but bleakness and despair.

"Maybe your mama will let you come up to Detroit and stay with your daddy sometimes."

Baby Sis overheard the teens talking and yelled back. "Ain't no child of mine staying in the devil's den with that woman and her mixed-up chirrens. Ain't none of 'em even got the same daddy."

Natalie whispered, "Well I know she'll let you stay with us."

Following the church fellowship, Baby Sis and her three children drove Hattie and Natalie home to load up the few belongings they were taking with them. She surprised them each with a tin foil-lined shoe box filled with fried chicken, rolls, homemade sugar cookies and a thermos full of ice cold lemonade.

Bernadette's oldest brother Ray Jay drove them to the Greyhound bus station. Baby Sis and Bernadette rode along to see them off.

The girls chattered excitedly about starting high school in the fall. On the heels of the U.S. Supreme Court decision in *Brown vs. the Board of Education of Topeka, Kansas*, Bernadette and four other Negro students were selected to participate in Haslette High School's pilot integration program.

Natalie looked forward to going to a big city high school where she could make lots of friends; go to sock hops, track meets and football games. Bernadette told her, "I bet you catch a boyfriend the minute you step off the bus." Natalie giggled, "I hope so. You'll probably start going with somebody as soon as you get to Haslette High too."

"Are you kiddin' me? Ain't but one colored boy gon' be goin' to Haslette High - that old frog-eyed Clarence Franklin. I ain't that desperate."

Natalie teased, "Then I guess you'll have to go with one of them cute white boys."

"Now you talkin'. I'll make sure I get one with the bluest eyes and the blondest hair in the whole school. Then we'll get married and have us some high-yella babies with good hair."

The girls shared a belly laugh at the ridiculous notion.

As Ray Jay's station wagon approached the bus terminal, Bernadette and Natalie embraced and smooched each other's cheeks.

Bernadette crooked her baby finger and said to Natalie, "Pinkie swear that you'll write me every single week."

Natalie nodded and locked pinkies with Bernadette, "Pinkie swear."

She exited the station wagon then boarded the bus with her mother. Hattie gave Natalie the window seat in second-to-the-last row of the bus. She searched the crowd of people who were outside seeing loved ones off until she spotted Bernadette's gloomy face and blew a kiss to her beloved cousin.

A few miles into their road trip, Hattie nudged Natalie and pointed to the window on the opposite side. "Look-a-there Sweetpea. Thas' one of them Justice gals runnin' one of them Mitchell boys ain't it?"

Natalie looked just in time to catch a glimpse of a muddy shoe print embedded in the center of a bed sheet that Fannie had apparently just hung on a clothesline. She was chasing after Jessie Mitchell with his own shoe while his brother James rolled on the ground laughing.

"Yes Ma'am. That's Fannie runnin' Jessie again. Them two always at it."

"Think you gon' miss this place Sweetpea?"

"No Ma'am, I don't believe I will."
"Me neither Sweetpea. Me neither."

Chapter Six

In my Father's house are many mansions:
if it were not so, I would have told you.

John 14:2

The Jordans' new home was a cramped, four-family flat. Sharing a bathroom with three other families required patience and strategy. The landlord had created a ridiculous schedule which was biologically impossible to adhere to. Fortunately, all of the tenants worked together to make the best of the situation.

The men from two of the families worked at the Ford Rouge Plant along with Dallas and Houston. A fourth family was headed by a grandmother raising her deceased daughter's two children. Two of the wives did "day work" for families in northwest Detroit's Palmer Woods subdivision. The woman from the flat adjacent to the Jordans told Hattie about a family who was looking for a *girl* to cook and clean for them.

Hattie and Rhoda Feldman developed a warm relationship from the beginning. Mrs. Feldman babbled continuously as she guided Hattie on a tour of her late-1920s English Tudor Revival. The lavish home was surrounded by an acre of luxurious landscaping and boastfully included a courtyard in the front, and a sunken floral garden, a tennis court and a 14 x 28 foot swimming pool around back. The flooring was primarily rich hardwood with imported rugs from Turkey and India. The house was swollen with amenities such as carved wood moldings,

Pewabic tile, a winding front interior staircase and sparkling chandeliers that looked like suspended clusters of diamonds.

To Hattie's delight, the spacious kitchen was equipped with an abundantly stocked pantry and every modern appliance and gadget imaginable.

Each of the nine bedrooms was elaborately decorated with European imports. The master suite included an onyx fireplace, a Greek-inspired bathroom and a balcony overlooking the swimming pool.

Mrs. Feldman was a chronic name dropper. "Now I'm not one to brag Hattie, but the architect who designed our house is a Japanese guy by the name of Minoru Yamasaki. I hear he's only designed a few houses in his entire career. Yamasaki's specialty is industrial buildings.

My cousin Moishe is a very successful jeweler in Manhattan. He says Governor Rockefeller and some of the other big wigs in New York have their heads together on a project to build some huge complex where big shot business deals can take place."

Hattie smiled and nodded as if she cared. Mrs. Feldman chattered on. "I don't know if it'll fly though. I hear Yamasaki designed a matching set of towers for the project. Mind you now, my cousin is a big mover and shaker in Manhattan and he's privy to lots of important information. So he should know about these things, right Hattie?"

"Yes Ma'am."

"Anyway, according to Cousin Moishe, the nay-sayers are worried that those Twin Towers would ruin New York's skyline and put a strain on the Port Authority. But if they do approve this project, it will really put this guy on the map. It won't hurt Mr. Feldman and me either. We figure that would make our house much more valuable than the other houses in the neighborhood should we ever decide to sell - not that we plan to. We hope to stay here until our grandchildren have grandchildren. God willing we should live to see the day..."

Hattie had stopped listening to Mrs. Feldman several minutes ago. She was visualizing herself masterfully running the Feldman household. She was especially anxious to get started in Mrs. Feldman's kitchen.

"Well, Ma'am, I don't know nothin' 'bout that architect fella, but I can tell you this certainly is the most beautiful home I've ever been inside."

Rhoda beamed with pride and continued name dropping. "We had the entire house done by a very exclusive French interior decorator, Monsieur Yves Vincennes." She snorted an obnoxious sounding laugh. "Sounds like a woman's name doesn't it?"

Hattie nodded, "Yes Ma'am."

Snort, Snort. "Nope, Yves is a man. It's not E-v-e, he spells it Y-v-e-s but the s is silent... Mrs. Feldman waved her hand, "I tell you Hattie, I've *nevah* understood those foreigners with all their fancy names and titles."

After touring the second level of the home, they climbed another set of stairs, which led to a modestly decorated studio apartment. "Mr. Feldman and I sometimes *en-ta-tain* until the wee hours of the morning so you may want to stay *ovah* Hattie. This is your room." Mrs. Feldman pointed out the apartment's amenities. "There is a furnished bedroom with a sitting room and a full bathroom. There's a built-in shower too." She excitedly added, "See? You even have your own radio to listen to Hattie.

You can redecorate this room if you want to. We'll give you some money for that. Well, *I* will anyway." She winked at Hattie. "Mr. Feldman doesn't need to know everything. The other girl and I had an understanding that way." She sighed, "I hope you'll work out as well as she did. Evelyn got sick with the *can-sah* and couldn't work anymore – the poor girl."

"Yes Ma'am. I hope so too."

"Hattie, we'll need you to work five days a week from 10 to 4, and at least once a month at night for our *pah-ties.*

We'll give you Wednesdays and either Saturday or Sunday off. You probably want to go to church on Sundays don't you?"

"Yes Ma'am. Me and my family, we goes to church on Sunday."

"Yeah, I thought so. You look like the church-going type. No big deal. I won't have you work on Sundays. Any questions for me so *fah* Hattie?"

"Yes Ma'am. I saw some rooms fixed up like some kids stay in 'em. How many chirrens you got?"

"Oh. Didn't I mention my boys?" Mrs. Feldman placed her hand over her heart. "How could I forget my sweet little angel faces? Yes, we have two lovely sons, Eddie and Freddie. The boys have a nanny. We *might* have to ask you to look after them on a rare occasion though. Maybe you'll have to pick them up from school once in a blue moon. Hampton Elementary is only a few blocks from here. Hattie, you'll just love the boys."

"They twins?"

Mrs. Feldman snort-giggled again. "So one would think. They were born *exactly noine* months apart – to the date. Mr. Feldman was anxious to get right back in the saddle *afta* Eddie was born if you know what I mean." She winked at Hattie. "You know how men are."

"Yes Ma'am. They' do get anxious."

Snort, snort. "Well Hattie, that's pretty much all I have to show you. I'll give you $6.00 a day plus *cah* fare." She reached in her pocket and pulled out a key ring with two keys. "Here's your very own set of keys to the house. These go to the back and side doors." She side-glanced Hattie. "I can trust you not to take anything without our permission - right?"

"Oh yes Ma'am. I'm a Christian woman. I wouldn't take nothin' didn't belongst to me."

"Alright then." She pointed at Hattie, "I was thinking Hattie, if you do a *really* good job, maybe I'll see if I can get Mr. Feldman to let you have your dry cleaning done for half off."

Chapter Seven

I am come that they might have life,
and that they might have it more abundantly.

John 10:10

Mumford High School was mammoth in comparison to the four-room schoolhouse back in Sweet Water. Natalie was overwhelmed by the number of kids there and pleasantly surprised to see that there were several other girls who were her height, some even taller. She was shocked when she discovered several other Negro students as well as a few staff members were there – some were even teachers.

On the first day of school, all the ninth graders were required to attend an assembly so that the administrative staff could welcome them and give them an orientation of what they could expect during their high school career. They were also informed of what was expected of them... good citizenship, good attendance, good grades and lots of school spirit.

The counselor and assistant principal lectured them on the importance of striving for academic excellence. However, the principal's address to the class of '58 encouraged them to show up in full force for the track meets, football and basketball games. He told them the Mustangs stood a really good chance to go all the way to the championships this season.

The ninth graders were each given a pledge card to sign, promising to do their best in all areas. In exchange for the signed pledge cards, each student was given a Mumford High School lapel pin to wear with pride.

After the assembly, the students were to choose lockers from a section designated for ninth graders. Natalie selected a locker directly across from the ninth grade counselor's office.

She was fiddling with the combination of her new lock when a diminutive girl who looked like she was barely old enough to be out of grade school came up behind her making

claims on the locker. "What you think you doing? This is my locker."

Natalie was certain that the locker was empty when she chose it. "Oh, I didn't see anything in here so I thought it was available."

"Well it's not. It's mine so you need to find another locker!"

Having only been up north a few weeks, Natalie took great pains to quell her heavy southern drawl and to command the proper use of the King's English.

"Miss Thompson said we could use any of the empty lockers along this corridor. First come, first serve. You didn't have nothin' – I mean *anything*, in the locker and you didn't have no, *any* lock on the locker – so *you* are the one who needs to move!"

The pixie-like girl slammed her palm against the locker door, jutted her chin upward and shouted at Natalie.

"Look you big ole, country girl. You don't know who you messin' with. I'm gonna tell you one last time - find yourself someplace else to hang."

A crowd quickly gathered around the two girls. Natalie couldn't believe this was happening on her first day of high school.

She immediately had flashbacks of the persecution she endured all those years back in Sweet Water.

She saw images of the Mitchell boys and Justice girls in the faces of the jeering crowd that had formed.

Black Gal wasn't there to defend her and the outcome of this incident would define the next four years. Natalie wasn't about to play the pitiful victim like back in Sweet Water. She said to herself, "I left that sniveling coward on the Greyhound bus."

She was bombarded by recollections of the incident at the Sweet Water Memorial Park, holograms of the kids taunting her in the graveyard and Miss Tucker's heartless comments. Finally, images of Black Gal's lifeless body spun before her.

Without warning, Natalie unleashed all the rage she'd suppressed for most of her fourteen years in Sweet Water.

She snatched a handful of the girl's hair, slammed her into the locker and pounded the girl's face with her fist.

Then the pixie knee'd Natalie in the stomach hard – causing her to double over. The girl took a swing at Natalie, but she ducked and the punch hit another kid.

The crowd began to chant, "Fight! Fight! Fight!" The girls walked around each other in circles, each waiting for the other to throw the next blow.

Someone pushed Natalie into the girl and the two were engaged in an all out brawl. Each of them took several good hits to the face and torso.

The girl reached back to deliver another blow when someone grabbed her around the waist from behind and picked her up - arms and legs flailing about.

The principal, Myron Beresh, had intervened and pulled the opponents apart. "You two, in my office! Now!" He pointed toward the school's administrative wing. "The rest of you kids go to your classes before you all get detention." The disappointed crowd scattered.

Mr. Beresh caught up with the girls and led them past the main desk and into his office. "What on earth could the two of you have to fight about on the first day of school?"

Silence.

"I'll rephrase the question. What were the two of you fighting about... and don't tell me nothing."

More silence.

"Do you even know each other's names?"

The girls each shook their heads.

"Well, let's start there, tell you what – how about you at least exchange names, then we'll go from there."

He turned the two visitor's chairs in front of his desk so that they faced each other. "The two of you will stay here until you know each other's names and somebody can tell me what you were fighting about. Keep in mind, you have to make up any assignments you miss while sitting in here sucking up each other's air. So the sooner you talk – the better. I don't care, I got all day."

While the girls continued their silent vigil, Mr. Beresh turned his attention to the neglected pile of files, memos and letters in his wooden inbox.

After about 10 minutes, he rose to leave the office. "I have to leave for a short time. I suggest that you two collaborate on a story before I get back, it's almost fourth period."

Mr. Beresh had been gone for about five minutes when the other girl finally spoke up. "Gwen."

"What?"

"My name is Gwen Brewster."

"Natalie Jordan."

"You talk real country. Where you from?"

"I am from Atlanta, Georgia. Well, near Atlanta – kind of. Where are you from?"

"Where you think I'm from dumb bunny? I'm from here – Detroit!"

"Well it's hard to tell since you were not using proper English."

"Oh now I know you not trying to cap on *me* 'bout the way *I* talk!" The girls locked eyes for several seconds then burst into a fit of laughter.

"You should see your hair. I got you good, Gwen."

"I got in some good licks too, Natalie. You look like the bride of Frankenstein."

Once they'd cleared the air, Natalie noticed that were it not for her wild looking hair and potty-mouth, Gwen could be a knock-out. Her flawless skin was the color of corn meal; she had an angelic face, and a curvaceous petite frame. But her unkempt, sandy brown hair begged for attention. Natalie offered to "do something" with Gwen's hair as a peace offering. Gwen eagerly accepted.

The two were chattering and laughing when Mr. Beresh returned to his office. "Well I see we've made some progress here. I was just about to request a United Nations summit."

Gwen had no idea what he was referring to. "Huh?"

Natalie began to explain. "The United Nations is a group of countries who work together to…"

"Aw I was just playin'. I know what the United Nations is. Dang, how dumb do you think I am?"

"All right ladies, never mind about the U.N. I'm just glad you two have cleared the air. Now will somebody please tell me what this is all about?"

Gwen began, "I ain't… I mean I haven't been able to find a locker any place else in the school. People took all of 'em. Them kids in summer school musta claimed lockers already."

Mr. Beresh told her, "I'm afraid at this point, you'll have to have a locker partner; many students are doubling up this year. We've had a significant increase in the student population. A lot of families moved here from the south over the summer because of all the new job opportunities in the auto plants.

Since you two seem to have cleared the air, I suggest that you share the locker you were, um negotiating."

Gwen looked over at Natalie. "You kiddin' me, right? You want me to let *her* hang in my locker?"

Natalie's eyes pleaded with Mr. Beresh, "Do I have to?"   "I think you'll both be pleasantly surprised. Who knows, you might wind up being friends. Stranger things have happened."

Chapter Eight

Oh, that you would bless me
and enlarge my territory!

1 Chronicles 4:10

During the ride home from work, Dallas noticed a house on Linwood with a For Sale sign in the front yard. He quickly surveyed the block. Floral gardens, manicured lawns and oak trees adorned the front of each house. The trees on both sides of the street bowed to each other and formed a picturesque archway along the half-mile avenue, making the neighborhood appear cozy and inviting.

Two men struggled to load a deep freezer into a moving van in front of the house.

"Looka there Houston."

"Yeah. What about it?"

"I think I'll buy that house, that's what. Pull over!"

"Man you crazy. Them white folks ain't gon' sell that house to you."

"It don't hurt to ask."

Houston shook his head and pulled over. "I'll stay in the car. I don't want to see you get embarrassed."

"The Bible says we have not because we ask not. Ain't nobody gon' be embarrassed." Dallas cautiously approached the men.

"S'cuse me, can y'all gentlemens tell me who own this house?"

A short, stocky white man with no neck eyed Dallas and continued working without answering.

The other one, a tall bald-headed man with a red beard sat his end of the load down and arched his back. "Whew-eee! That son-of-a-gun weighs a ton!"

He turned to Dallas, "You wanna know somethin' about this house?"

His partner spoke, "Come on Fred, quit foolin' around. We ain't got no time for this!"

Fred ignored his impatient co-worker and continued, "From what I understand, they put the old man in a home. His granddaughter is taking care of his business affairs. She's in the house now."

Dallas asked, "Did she sell the house yet?"

"You lookin' to buy it?"

"I just might be."

Shortie snatched a grimy bandana from his back pocket and mopped his face. "For Pete's sake, Fred!"

"Aw keep your shirt on Mack, the girl said she's in a hurry to get rid of it."

"Yeah but she didn't say she wanted to sell it to no nig—"

"You want to talk to me about this house, mister?" A young brunette woman joined the threesome. She stuck out her hand to shake Dallas'.

The grouchy short man motioned for Fred to get back to work. "Break time's over pal."

The girl took a step closer to Dallas. "My name is Greta Liggins. My grandfather owns this house."

Dallas pointed to Fred. "The man there says you might be looking to sell."

She smiled. "The man there told you right. I'll be getting married and moving to San Francisco soon. We're taking my grandfather along so we can look after him. I'd like to get everything settled before then. Maybe we can work something out."

"Well, I need to see if my wife likes the house first."

"Of course you do. I'd have a fit if Lyle brought me a set of keys to a house sight unseen. I'll tell you what. Lyle and I will be here packing all day Sunday."

"Why don't you bring your wife over, say around 1:30?"

"Thank you Miss, I'm pretty sho' we can stop by after church."

"It was nice to meet you. Oh, I didn't catch your name."

"I'm Dallas Jordan. I'll bring Hattie and my daughter Natalie over on Sunday."

"I'm looking forward to meeting the rest of your family. See you then Mr. Jordan."

"Yes Ma'am, we'll see you then."

Chapter Nine

...And ye shall possess their land,
as the LORD your God hath promised unto you.

Joshua 23:5

After a tour of the house, the Jordans were sold – even Houston. Greta told Dallas that a man named Aaron Martin from the real estate company would be handling everything after this. Dallas gave her Houston's phone number and left instructions for him to set up an appointment whenever and wherever the realtor said. Houston was still skeptical that his brother would ever actually move into the house; however, he accepted his assignment.

One week later, Dallas and Hattie could hardly contain their excitement as they sat across the desk from the loan officer at the Detroit Bank and Trust.

They had a steady work history, the money for the down payment, a tidy savings account, and reliable references. Everything was in order and as far as the realtor could tell, it was just a matter of Old Man Liggins' acceptance of their offer.

Greta was excited for the Jordans. "My family spent many happy years in this house. I'm sure you'll be happy here too."

At the nursing home, the old man was just about to sign off on the deal when the realtor casually mentioned how the Jordans would be happy to know that another family of Negroes had recently moved into the neighborhood.

"What's this you say? You're selling my house to a bunch of coloreds? Oh no! The day a one of them heathen moves into that house, I'll be cold and sleeping in my grave!"

Martin tried to reason with the stubborn old man. "But sir, they're willing to pay more than your original asking price, the house has been on the market for months and you have no other offers."

The old man ripped the paperwork in two and threw the pieces at the realtor. "Martin, are you hard of hearing or just plain stupid? I said no deal and I mean it. Tell that pack of baboons to stay with their own kind and leave decent human beings be!"

Hattie was heartbroken when Dallas delivered the bad news. They had been so sure they would own the house.

"I don't understand what happened. We had all our business in order. We even offered to pay the man more than he asked. That Mr. Martin talked like we had everything all sewed up."

"I know honey, it ain't over yet. If God wants us to have that house, ain't no devil in hell that can keep us from buying it. We just have to wait on the Lord – and believe."

Chapter Ten

Psalm 84:11

Houston was unusually quiet during the ride home from the plant. His brother asked him, "Cat got your tongue today boy? You ain't been this quiet your whole life."

He swore. "Women! Yeah. I gotta tell you something I know you ain't gon' like."

"What is it man? Spill it."

"That dang Juanita took a phone call from that real estate guy 'bout a week or so back. Only she didn't say nothing to me 'bout it 'til this morning. Man I tell you I cussed her out good. I woulda kicked her tail if I wasn't runnin' late for work."

"Houston. Ain't *no* man, got *no* business, putting his hands on *no* woman."

"Yeah I know, but sometimes she makes me so mad..."

"Aw scratch your head and get glad. Now tell me 'bout this phone call. Was it Aaron Martin, the old man's real estate agent?"

"Yeah that's who it was." Houston raised his hips and pulled a crumpled slip of paper out of his pocket. The paper had the real estate agent's name and phone number scribbled on it.

Dallas anxiously took the paper. "Pull over to that phone booth. You got a dime?"

Houston sifted through the ashtray and produced a coin bearing President Roosevelt's image. "Here you go bruh."

Dallas examined the coin briefly, "Man can you believe it cost ten cents to call somebody on the phone now?"

"Everything's high these days man. Gasoline done went up to 25 cents a gallon! Come on. Let's see what this man is talkin' 'bout." This time Houston didn't stay in the car.

"Metropolitan Realtors, this is Trudy Merriweather speaking, may I help you?"

"Hello? I'd like to speak to Mr. Aaron Martin please."

"Yes sir, may I tell Mr. Martin who is calling?"

"Tell him Dallas Jordan is on the phone, please."

"Thank you, I'll see if he is available."

A few moments later Aaron Martin answered. "Good afternoon, this is Aaron Martin speaking."

"Mr. Martin, this is Dallas Jordan, you know, I tried to buy the house on Linwood last year."

"Oh yes Mr. Jordan! I've been hoping to hear from you. Have you bought a new home yet?"

"We have our eye on one." He didn't let on that he was talking about the Linwood house.

"Well before you make a final decision, let me give you some new information."

Dallas winked at his brother. "I'm listening."

"The old man died recently and left the house to his granddaughter. She got married and moved to California. She said she wants you to buy that house if you still want it."

"I see. Sorry to hear about the old man's passing."

Martin continued, "I have to be honest with you Mr. Jordan, I didn't like the way things were handled before but of course, it wasn't my call to make. I'll say this, I'm a firm believer that things have a way of working themselves out. Miss Liggins, well Mrs. Yates now that she's married, has authorized me to do whatever I have to do to put your family in that house. Do you and your wife still want it?"

"Well, I'll have to ask the Mrs." He winked at Houston again.

"Tell you what Mr. Jordan. Suppose you tell your wife that we'll knock $500 off the original asking price to sweeten the deal?"

Dallas forced his voice to sound calm, but he was shaking with excitement. "I'll have to see what my wife says. If she still want the house I'll call you back."

"Fair enough. Will you do me a favor? Will you call me as soon as you talk it over with Mrs. Jordan?"

"I can let you know one way or the other in a day or two Mr. Martin."

Dallas replaced the receiver and grabbed his brother by the shoulders shaking him. "What did I tell you boy? What-did-I-tell-you? My God can do anything but fail! Come on. Hurry up and get me home so I can tell my girls."

Dallas filled his brother in on the details during the drive home.

"Man, you can take that $500 and get you a sharp ride!"

"I'm way ahead of you man."

Chapter Eleven

She sets about her work vigorously;
her arms are strong for her tasks.

Proverbs 31:17

Shortly before graduating, Natalie enrolled in an evening course at Fleming's School of Beauty. Her goal was to own a full service beauty shop by her twenty-first birthday. She planned to name it *Graceful and Glamorous Beauty Salon.*

Natalie had a natural flair for creating beautiful, trendy hairstyles – and she had what the folks down south called a *growin' hand.* She had already built a client base of about 20 regular customers.

By the spring of 1958, the Jordans had finally finished remodeling and redecorating. Dallas, Houston and several other men from the plant installed plumbing and electrical fixtures for Natalie's beauty salon in the Jordan's basement.

Natalie was weary from alternating between cramming for high school finals and studying for a bleaching and tinting exam. She had just dozed off when Gwen burst into her bedroom yakking a mile a minute. "Girl, I finally saw that new boy at the filling station!"

Wiping sleep from her eyes, Natalie asked, "What new boy at the filling station?"

Gwen tried to pry Natalie's textbook away from her. "Girl, do you ever come up for air? Put those books down so I can tell you all about my future husband."

"I thought Tony Moore was your future husband."

"I ain't studdin' Tony Moore."

Gwen pushed herself onto the bed next to Natalie.

"There's a new boy working at the Sinclair station. He's so fine I could just sop him up with a biscuit then lick the platter." Gwen's eyes danced as she described the latest object of her affection.

"He's real light-skinned, you almost can't tell he's colored. And he's got good hair and dreamy light brown eyes..."

"If he's that good lookin' he's probably not worth a dime. I wouldn't trust him any farther than I could throw him."

"Oh, you're always so negative. You could at least go look at him and see what everybody's been talking about."

"What about Tony? Aren't you supposed to be going to the prom with him?"

"I quit Tony. He needs to find himself a new date for the prom. Hey! Why don't you go with him?"

Natalie looked at Gwen as if she'd sprouted antennae.

"Ok. Now I know you've lost your mind." She held up her index finger. "Number one: Who told you I wanted to go to the prom?" She added her middle finger. "Number Two: *If* I wanted to go, who says Tony would want to take *me*? I have never seen him with nothin' but light-skinned girls." The ring finger went up. "Number three: You haven't even met the boy at the Sinclair station – so how do you know he'll take you to the prom? If he's as fine as you say, I'm sure he already got a girl – or two."

Gwen never had problems getting guys to fall head over heels for her – even the so-called pretty boys. She waved her hand. "I ain't worried about none of that. Let's just say I'm confident."

"We'll see."

"Yeah, we'll see."

Natalie drove up to the second pump at the Sinclair station. Immediately, she knew what Gwen had been making so much noise about. The guy she had made such a fuss over was melt-in-your-mouth fine. He was long-legged, lean and muscular. The forest green uniform fit his athletic physique like it was tailor made.

Gwen watched hungrily as the muscles in his back and upper arms rippled when he stretched to wash Natalie's windshield and check the oil. She rolled down her window and started in on her prey. Batting false eyelashes, she spoke in a lustful tone. "You're pretty good at that. Do you make house calls?"

The young man gave Gwen an obligatory smile then crossed in front of the car to talk to Natalie.

"Um, Miss I noticed that your oil is about a quart low. Would you like me to take care of that for you?"

Natalie wished her heart wouldn't beat so loudly. His lyrical voice and honey-colored eyes gave her goose bumps.

"No, thank you. But I'll let my father know."

Gwen reached across Natalie to pass him a slip of paper on which she'd written her name, address and phone number. He accepted Gwen's note without taking his eyes off Natalie. For the first time ever, Gwen's charm and beauty had failed her.

Flashing two rows of perfect pearly white teeth he asked, "Is there anything else I can do for you Miss? Do you want me to check your tires?"

Natalie returned the smile. "Thanks for asking. I think my tires are fine."

He winked. "I think so too." Gwen observed the exchange. He was flirting with Natalie!

Natalie paid him and spun off before she made a complete fool of herself. She didn't tell Gwen but in her rearview mirror she saw him throw her note in a trash bin.

Natalie should have been studying for her Home Economics quiz but instead, found herself daydreaming about the boy from the Sinclair station.

Gwen had easily conceded defeat and reconciled with Tony Moore, although he never even knew they had broken up.

⚮

Natalie's daydream about the boy from the filling station was interrupted by her mother's call.

"Nat-a-leeee. Somebody's here to seeee you."

She couldn't imagine who it could be. She ran a brush through her hair and dabbed on a layer of Raucous Red lipstick - just in case. As she tiptoed down the stairs, she recognized that lyrical voice talking to her father. *It couldn't be the boy from the fillin' station.* She tried to peer into the room unnoticed, but her mysterious visitor caught sight of her and stood flashing his endearing porcelain smile.

"Hello there!"

Natalie sheepishly entered the room.

Her visitor said, "Sorry to barge in on you unexpectedly like this. I got your address from my boss, Mr. Gus - he said he and your father are friends. I hope I'm not in trouble."

Natalie's face felt hot. "No, that's alright. I guess." She looked to her father for approval.

Dallas nodded and said, "Well young man, I got to go water my grass. Maybe I'll take you up on going to that ball game at Briggs Stadium with you and your daddy sometime."

The young man was still standing. "Yes sir, I'm looking forward to that. Maybe when the Braves come to town."

Dallas told him, "Now you're talking." He turned to his confused daughter. "Natalie ain't you gon' offer your guest a seat? See if he want somethin' to drink."

"Oh, sorry. Would you like to have a seat?" Natalie sat on the loveseat opposite the young man and stared at him. She nervously clasped her hands and kept pinching herself to make sure she wasn't still daydreaming. Finally she spoke again, "Can I offer you a Coke or some lemonade?"

"Oh, don't put yourself to any trouble. I'll have whatever you're having."

"It's no trouble. I'll be right back. Make yourself comfortable."

She padded into the kitchen and eased the receiver off the wall phone to call Gwen. She whispered into the phone, "You won't believe who's sitting in my living room!"

"What? Why you talking so low?" Gwen shouted as though that would enable her to hear Natalie better.

"Shhh, quit talking so loud. Guess who's in my living room?"

"Natalie my hair is wet, I ain't got time to play Twenty Questions with you. Now tell me who's in your living room?"

Natalie pried ice cubes out of a metal tray. "Nope, I ain't telling you. You HAVE to guess."

Gwen was irritated. "I don't know, Eartha Kitt."

"No, silly. Anyway, it's a guy."

"Alright then, Harry Belafonte."

"Now you're just being a smart aleck."

"Look girl, if you don't hurry up and tell me I'm hanging up on you."

Natalie peeked around the corner to check on her visitor. He seemed fascinated by Hattie's coo-coo clock. She called out to him, "I'll be right there." She cupped her hand around the mouth of the receiver and told Gwen that it was the fine boy from the filling station. "His name is Astor Gregory Baptiste, Jr."

Gwen squealed. "Sounds like his parents have money, girl you hit the jackpot!"

"Shhh! Don't talk so loud!"

Gwen thumped the phone pretending it was Natalie's head. "He can't hear me over the phone dumb bunny."

"Hmph. If his parents are so rich, why is he pumping gas and washing my daddy's windshield?"

"I don't know. Rich people do stuff like that sometimes so their kids don't turn into spoiled brats. Anyway girl, I gotta go. I got vinegar water dripping in my eyes. Look here. Astor Gregory Baptiste had better been gone when I come over there for my press and curl. You hear me?"

"Yeah, yeah, yeah. Bye."

Chapter Twelve

Thou hast ravished my heart, with one of thine eyes,
with one chain of thy neck.

Song of Solomon 4:9

Natalie looked like an ebony fairytale princess in her peach colored tulle and lace prom dress. She styled a human hair fall into a sophisticated upsweep with ringlets framing her face. A peach and cream colored corsage from Schelberg's Stems and Blooms had been delivered to her earlier that afternoon.

She could hardly contain herself when her prom date arrived. From her bedroom window, she could see that he looked more handsome than ever in his black formal wear.

Friends and neighbors crowded the Jordans' house and even spilled out onto the front lawn to take pictures of their neighborhood princess.

Five years ago when Gregory was a senior at the all boys University of Detroit Jesuit High School, most of the guys dated Immaculata High's debutants. Back then, he thought proms and Immaculata's girls were too high brow and refused to attend. Now a recent college graduate, Gregory was as excited about attending Natalie's prom as she was.

Natalie was the envy of all the girls at Mumford High's senior prom. The more aggressive girls winked, blew kisses and one actually slipped him a note right in front of her own date *and* Natalie. But Gregory ignored their futile attempts to get his attention.

The undeniable chemistry between the two of them thwarted any hopes the desperate girls had of capturing his heart. Gregory only took his eyes off Natalie for a brief moment, when all eyes were on Gwen and Tony as they were being crowned Prom King and Queen. Natalie would later write to Bernadette that the prom had been more than she could ever have hoped for.

Albertina Baptiste was more than a little curious to learn what her son found so captivating about this Natalie person he had been rambling about. He had been dating her exclusively for over a year. Gregory hadn't given any girl that much attention since the seventh grade crush he had on Vanessa Underwood.

She said to her husband, "Gregory really seems to like this Natalie girl, don't you think?"

"If that's the case, it's a good sign. It's about time he slowed down and quit chasing after everything in a skirt."

"I'm surprised to hear a father talk that way. I thought men encouraged their sons to sow their wild oats."

"I think our son has already sown more than his fair share of wild oats. Maybe he's ready to settle down and get married."

"How can we be sure we want him to marry that girl? We don't even know what she looks like or where she comes from."

"You afraid we'll have grandchildren that look like gargoyles or something Tina?"

"The thought of grandchildren frightens me period, let alone ugly ones."

"I'm sure you have nothing to worry about. Have you ever seen Gregory with an ugly girl? Anyway, as long as she doesn't drag her knuckles on the ground when she walks, I don't care what she looks like."

"That kind of talk is what scares me, Astor. We don't know a thing about this girl. There is a lot to consider when talking about marriage my dear."

"Why don't you just speak your mind Tina? Why don't you just admit that you're really afraid the girl might be too dark?"

"You said it, not me."

"I know you. You thought it."

"Be honest Astor. You don't want any little beady-haired spooks running around calling you grandpa either. Now do you?"

"Tina, all I care about is character, not color. How can you be so obsessed about skin color when your own mother was a lovely shade of brown? Ma Mere was beautiful until the day she died."

"Ma Mere's brown skin and nappy hair held her back from many opportunities she was more than qualified for. That's why she constantly reminded us of how fortunate she was to have married Papa. Granted, it wasn't often that she was able to benefit from their union because she was too dark, but we children did." She turned and looked at her husband. "I shudder to think what our lives would have been like if Ma Mere had been the one with dominant genes. She told us that herself - and she encouraged all of us to marry well also."

He teased her. "You telling me, I didn't win you over with my charm and wit?"

"Oh, you know what I mean Astor." She smiled. "I realize I struck it rich when I married you."

"Well, be that as it may, let's not forget that we're still colored – and we also have limitations. We've had our share of challenges to overcome as well. We still do."

Albertina clearly understood the socio-economic advantages of having fair skin and wanted her children, and the generations to come, to be afforded those same advantages. It was her life's mission to ensure that her bloodline was *uncompromised*.

Her offspring didn't fully understand why certain friendships and alliances they tried to form were strongly discouraged. But they would eventually learn.

Albertina's parents had done the same with her and her siblings. They were taught the art of making proper friends, proper courting and ultimately - proper breeding.

After scrutinizing Astor's background and family, Mr. and Mrs. LeFleur encouraged the relationship between their youngest daughter and Astor Rene` Baptiste when they met in high school.

Later, they both attended Xavier's College of Pharmacy in New Orleans. And with the blessings of both sets of parents, they were married during their freshman year.

By the time they were seniors, they had two small children. Even with all the grueling demands on their time, energy and resources, they both graduated as scheduled then moved their family to Detroit.

They moved into a modest home and immediately executed an aggressive business plan to become the first Negroes in the north to own and operate a chain of pharmacies.

The plan was for Astor to take a job as a counter clerk at Cunningham's drug store. He would gain the trust of his employer, which would give him complete access to the vital administrative and operational procedures he and Albertina would later use for their own business ventures. Albertina worked as a bona fide pharmacist at McKinnley's Emporium, which was owned by a black family.

Astor and Albertina celebrated their seventh wedding anniversary with the grand opening of the Motor City Pharmacy on Detroit's west side. Two years later, they opened a second drug store on the northeast side of town in a neighborhood known as Conant Gardens.

Albertina operated the west side store, while Astor ran the store on the east side. A year later, the Motor City Pharmacy – Midtown was also in operation.

"By the way Astor, I've got a bone to pick with you."

"What else is new Tina?"

"I want to know why you're forcing my son to work at that disgusting gas station."

"For the hundredth time Tina, *your son* as you put it, didn't want to work at the drug store. He thought I was going to have him filling prescriptions the day he graduated.

He needs to learn every aspect of the business – starting with the counter, like I did. Instead he wants to come in late, leave early and chase skirt tails all day.

I got complaints from several customers when he worked at the eastside store. On top of all that – he expected me to pay him! What kind of example is that for my real employees?"

"Correction, our employees."

Astor was exasperated. "Here's the bottom line... we paid good money to send him to Xavier when he could just have stayed home and gone to Wayne State or the University of Detroit. I hope someday soon he'll be able to put that expensive education to good use. But in the meantime, no able-bodied adult is going to lay around my house, eat up my food and wear out my furniture for free.

As long as he lives under my roof, he's going to work somewhere – even if it's digging ditches."

Albertina planted her hands on her hips and spewed a string of acidic Creole cuss words at her husband.

Chapter Thirteen

Come, my beloved, let us go forth into the field;
let us lodge in the villages.

Song of Solomon 7:11

stor sipped a cup of coffee and read the morning edition of the *Detroit News* while his wife circled the names associated with familiar faces in the *Michigan Chronicle*.

Albertina hoped this week's edition would include the article featuring the Michigan Association of Negro Pharmacists' Annual Ball. She and Astor were the co-chairpersons for this year's affair. Albertina thrived on lime-light and notoriety. "Our picture isn't in this week's edition either Astor. I don't know why it takes them so long. That ball was held over a month ago!"

Before Astor could tell her how much he didn't care about having his picture in the paper, Albertina's golden child stealthily entered the room and hugged her shoulders from behind. Then he planted a juicy smack on his mother's cheek. "To what do I owe this auspicious honor?"

Gregory snatched the half-eaten muffin from his mother's plate and took a bite. With a mouth full of food, he answered. "Can't a guy greet his mother with a good morning kiss?"

Before she could respond, he snickered, "Morning Dad."

Astor peeked from behind the sports section. "G' morning son." Albertina didn't buy his random act of adoration for one moment. She smiled up at the masculine replica of herself. "A *guy* can; you can't. It's altogether out of character. Now why are you trying to butter me up?"

"Well, it's about Natalie."

Albertina gasped. "Good Lord, what is it now?"

Astor put his paper down and peered at his son over his reading glasses.

"Don't get excited guys, it's nothing bad. I just want to have the Jordans over for dinner soon. I'd like for us all to get to know each other better."

Albertina's eyes narrowed. "Why do we need to meet this girl's parents? What do you have on your mind son?"

Astor picked the paper back up and pretended not to listen.

"We're all going to be part of one big happy family. It's time we all meet and get to know one another." He playfully leaned backward as if he expected his mother to take a swing at him.

"You asked that girl to marry you? And she said yes?"

"Not exactly, it's kind of preliminary Mother."

Astor put his paper down again. "Son, what do you mean by *preliminary?* Either the girl accepted your proposal or she didn't." He went back to his newspaper.

"Well, she said yes, but didn't actually accept yet." He realized he wasn't making sense. "She said she wants our families to meet and get to know each other before we start making any serious plans."

Albertina was guardedly relieved. "Of course dear, if it means that much to you, we can arrange a dinner party."

"Great." He leaned over and kissed her again. "Can we have it on a Sunday? Natalie usually does hair on Fridays and Saturdays."

Albertina sucked her teeth. "You mean to tell me you're considering marrying a hairdresser? What do you expect to accomplish if you're linked to a hairdresser Gregory?"

"For now, she does hair in the basement of their home, but she plans to own a salon someday."

Albertina rolled her eyes. "Someday is not on the calendar Gregory. How many times have I heard that from the girls at Gi Gi's?"

Gregory continued pleading his case. "She has quite a clientele - you should give her a try yourself."

Albertina cringed at the thought of going to someone's basement for her monthly henna rinse and wet set.

"She can cut men's hair too Mother. She cut my hair yesterday. See?"

He bent down for Albertina to inspect Natalie's work. She obliged him. "Yes, very nice dear."

"See Dad?"

Astor peered around the newspaper. "I have to admit, that's the best hair cut you've had since you were 15 years old."

Albertina sensed the need to tactfully diffuse Gregory's growing frustration. "Well alright son, your father and I will let you know what we can come up with in a day or so. We wouldn't want to just throw something together if it's that important to you."

"Thanks Mother. By the way Dad, when it's official, I want to give Natalie that ring you always talk about." Gregory gulped down a glass of apple juice, popped his Sinclair hat on his head then bounded out the door whistling *Here Comes the Bride*.

Albertina waited until she heard the sound of her son's Chevy engine roaring down the street. "What do you make of that, Astor?"

"Looks like our son is getting married. I 'spose I'd better get Tallulah out of the safe deposit box."

Albertina touched a napkin to the corners of her mouth.

"That my dear, remains to be seen."

Chapter Fourteen

For out of the abundance of the heart the mouth speaketh.
Matthew 12:34

Sheila couldn't believe the words she was hearing. As he gathered items from the refrigerator, Gregory casually told her about his plans to marry Natalie. *Who does he think he's kidding?* "Do Mother and Daddy know about this?"

He gathered an assortment of deli meats, cheeses and condiments in preparation to make himself a Dagwood sandwich. "Yup." He pointed to the food. "Want some?"

"No thanks. You're saying both Mother and Daddy are ok with you marrying Natalie Jordan?"

He shrugged. "Why wouldn't they be?"

"Has Mother ever *seen* Natalie?"

"Nope, I'm working on getting our family together with hers. Anyway, what are you getting at Sheila?"

"What I'm getting at is that Mother is gonna take one look at Natalie and have a stroke."

"Why would she do that? Natalie is gorgeous. That's the craziest thing I've ever heard Sheila."

In an instant, Sheila's whole face became a kaleidoscope of colors and vicious expressions. "Don't-you-ever-call-me-crazy!"

"Ok, ok, calm down. You don't have to jump down my throat. I just think maybe you're underestimating Mother."

As if her emotions were controlled by some sort of power switch, Sheila's entire demeanor immediately returned to normal. "Mother will never let you marry anybody who can't pass the paper bag test Greggy."

Sheila talked to her brother's back as he spread yellow mustard and mayonnaise on three slices of marble rye bread.

"The what? Paper bag test?"

"You heard me. The paper bag test."

"Sheila, what are you talking about?"

"Come off it Greggy. Don't play dumb. You know as well as I do that there are some rootie toot Negroes out there, your precious Omega Gamma Psi frat brothers for example, who refuse to even casually associate with anybody who's darker than a brown paper bag. You and Thomas were in the thick of it at Xavier. Come to think of it, I believe Mother must have invented the test."

Gregory dismissed Sheila's comments as he stacked lettuce and tomato slices on each slice of the bread. "You don't know what you're talking about. We were just being selective back then, and it had nothing to do with anybody's skin color." He layered thin slices of ham on top of the lettuce. "If we rejected any of those guys, it was because they were losers." Gregory side-glanced his sister as he added slices of Swiss cheese and slivers of shaved pastrami. "But you know what? I think maybe *you're* the one who has a problem with Natalie."

"Oh really? Don't forget I was in love with probably the darkest man on earth. We were engaged remember? That is until Mother broke us up."

He thought for a few moments as he went to the freezer to retrieve a bottle of Coca Cola he had set aside earlier to chill. The image of an espresso-colored man with an incessant smile came to mind. "Wasn't he that insurance salesman or something?"

"He was an actuary, but yes that was Dennis."

He jabbed a straw into the drink which was almost frozen and sucked hard. "Boy that's good. If somebody were to sell this stuff already frozen I bet they could make a mint! Ok, now back to you and Dennis - you guys broke up. What did Mother have to do with it?"

"At first we didn't realize what was going on. Mother sabotaged our plans to get married. She kept switching dates, going behind our backs undoing arrangements we'd made with the florist, the caterer, musicians... it was a nightmare. I guess she thought we'd get frustrated and abandon our plans to get married altogether. Well in the end, she succeeded – as always. Mother never loses."

"That doesn't mean she had anything to do with you and Dennis breaking up. Guys aren't interested in flowers and wedding cake. If this guy really wanted to marry you, he would have insisted that you elope. And as for Mother, we both know she can be overly ambitious. She's like the ultimate socialite. If anything, she may have gone overboard trying to make sure you had a wedding that none of her girlfriends' daughters could top. You know how competitive she is."

"Now who's crazy? Mother had everything to do with our breakup. She literally ran Dennis off because, in her eyes, he wasn't good enough to even *date* a Baptiste. Mother did other strange things to see that Dennis and I never got married."

"What kind of strange things Sheila?"

"Right before the wedding invitations were to go out, Dennis started making all sorts of excuses not to see me. Then one day, he just seemed to disappear off the face of the earth."

"How do you know the guy didn't just get cold feet and duck out on you?"

"Dennis and I loved each other. Before then, he used to tell me he couldn't stand to be away from me, even for a few hours. He'd come over every evening after work. We'd spend almost every waking moment together on the weekends. You don't do a complete 180 degree turnaround when you're in love like that.

At first I couldn't believe Mother was even remotely capable of going to such great lengths to keep us apart, so I dismissed the notion - just like you're doing."

Gregory adjusted his jaws to accommodate his super-sized sandwich.

Sheila looked at him with disgust. "Where do you put it all? You eat like a horse yet you're as skinny as a rail. If I so much as smell food I gain ten pounds."

He winked. "I got my mojo working for me. Now tell me, what proof do you have that Mother was behind all this?" With little effort, he took a gigantic bite.

"You're such a pig. Natalie must not have seen you eat – if she had, we probably wouldn't even be having this conversation." Sheila pushed herself off the bar stool she'd been sitting on and leaned against the double oven. She continued. "After I lost all contact with Dennis for about two weeks, I literally got sick. I couldn't eat, couldn't sleep and could barely manage to drag myself out of bed. I was so worried – I wondered if I had done anything to bring this on myself. I finally used a phone number Dennis had given me to track down his parents.

He must been in a hurry or something when he gave it to me because the man who answered the phone when I called that number said he'd never heard of anyone named Dennis Harvey.

Well one day, I pulled myself together enough to go to his job. At first, I couldn't even get past the receptionist's desk."

Sheila ignored the cynical expression on Gregory's face. "Anyway, Dennis' manager refused to see me so I left. But when I was about to get on the elevator, the receptionist ran in after me. She didn't say a word while we were inside the building, but once we were on the street, she asked if I could join her for lunch. I could tell from the expression on her face that she wasn't just looking for someone to share a meal with."

Gregory was relieved when the telephone rang. He pointed to the moss green unit on the breakfast room wall. "One of us should probably get that." Sheila jerked her head in the direction of the ringing phone, indicating that Gregory should answer it. He hoped it was for either of them so that they could end the outrageous conversation.

To his disappointment, the caller was some old lady who wanted to speak with Prophet Hezekiah at the Temple of Prosperity. He reluctantly returned his attention to Sheila's narrative.

"Ok, so I'm sitting in a booth with Minerva and she swore me to secrecy. She told me that a man had been hanging around the office asking to see the manager without an appointment – this was a short time before Dennis vanished. The guy showed up twice but said Mr. Conley refused to see him the first time. But then she said that when he returned, he told her to tell her boss that Albertina Baptiste sent him."

Gregory's jaw dropped. "You've got to be kidding. Seriously?"

"Seriously. Minerva said as soon as Conley heard Mother's name, he dropped what he was doing and met with the man immediately. She told me that Conley ordered her to have the Personnel Department send Dennis' entire personnel file to his office right away. Then the very next day, Dennis disappeared without a trace. She said it's like he never even existed.

Next thing I know, I'm miles away from home in some kind of rest camp making pot holders and macramé plant hangers. She faced Gregory. "Is that proof enough for you little brother?"

He bit the last of his sandwich tower and licked his fingers. "I just don't know Sis. I grant you that Mother is very shrewd and has connections, but all this just sounds like too much cloak and dagger for me to believe she's as involved as you say. There's got to be some other explanation."

"You mean you don't believe me?"

"It just doesn't add up Sis. When would Mother have the time to meddle in other people's business when she has to run the pharmacy, attend all her social activities, and keep this house spotless without hired help?"

"You think I'm either lying or hallucinating don't you?"

"I wouldn't say all that Sheila."

"Exactly what are you saying Gregory?"

"I'm not saying anything else. I guess I don't know what to say."

"On that note, let me give you a final piece of advice little brother. Elope before something happens. If you don't, I can promise – no guarantee, that the wedding you and Natalie are planning will never take place. Don't say I didn't warn you."

Gregory was heated. "You know what I really think Sis? I think maybe you didn't know that Dennis guy as well as you thought. Maybe he didn't love you so much after all. I mean, if he did, why would he just up and split? Besides, his disappearance might have worked out in your favor. It sounds like this Dennis guy was a real piece of work. If you ask me, you're better off without him."

"Ok, you don't have to believe me. It's just a matter of time before Mother shows her true colors again."

"Sis, I'm really sorry things didn't work out for you. But that's not going to happen to us and I believe in my heart that you'll hook up with a really great guy someday. But for now, when Mother meets Natalie and her parents, she'll be rushing to get us down that aisle. You'll see." Sheila left the room mumbling to herself.

Gregory sipped the remnants of his drink and watched his mother through the kitchen's sliding glass doors. Albertina was donned in sunglasses, a lavender Bermuda shorts set, a wide brimmed straw hat and purple gardening gloves.

She was meticulously pruning her cherished yellow Madame Butterfly rosebush. Gregory scoffed at his sister's accusations.

"That girl should be committed."

Chapter Fifteen

They feast on the abundance of your house;
you give them drink from your river of delights.

Psalm 36:8

lbertina delegated the task of coordinating the Jordan/Baptiste get-acquainted party to Sheila. As a freshman in college, Sheila had studied Interior Design and Decorating in Milan. The following summer, she attended a culinary arts program in Paris before finally declaring Psychology as her major.

Since the event would be held during the Fourth of July weekend, she chose to decorate the rambling backyard, the tables and the gazebo in a patriotic theme. She planned the menu and assigned the purchase and preparation of the food to Astor. He shopped at Eastern Market, an open-air farmer's bazaar located in the heart of Detroit where he bought seafood, porterhouse steaks, slabs of baby back ribs and an array of fresh produce.

Gregory was assigned to entertainment. He brought his hi-fi to the Florida room where he would later serve as disc jockey. Astor had offered to wheel his portable bar out onto the patio and double as bartender, but Gregory informed him that Natalie's family didn't drink alcohol. Instead of the portable bar, Gregory set out a huge tin tub, which would later be filled with ice cold sodas and a couple of bottles of Black Label beer for Astor.

"I don't suppose I'd offend the Jordans if I have a beer or two." Then he joked. "I don't think I trust a man who won't take an occasional drink."

When the Jordans arrived, Sheila greeted them warmly then escorted them to the backyard.

Although Albertina insisted it wasn't necessary, Hattie brought a fruity lime gelatin mold to the get-acquainted dinner. Gregory nervously introduced his father and sister to Natalie's parents.

Astor and Dallas quickly found common ground when they began to compare the Detroit Tigers' and the Atlanta Braves' stats. Sheila entertained Natalie and Hattie with pictures of Gregory from infancy through college.

Hattie commented. "Gregory, you sho' was a pretty baby!"

"Thanks Mrs. Jordan." He whispered to Natalie. "That's a sneak preview of what our babies will look like."

She pinched him. "Hush!" She looked around the yard and asked, "Anyway, where is your mother? I'm dying to meet the woman who gave birth to my earth-angel."

Albertina had eased up the back staircase in order not to be seen in her scruffies when the Jordans arrived. She indulged in a bubble bath then, in keeping with Sheila's patriotic theme, she slipped into a red silk shirt. She clipped on a pair of red and gold earrings then draped her throat with a strand of star shaped red and white beads.

She departed from the customary tight chignon she ordinarily wore. Instead, she allowed her shoulder length auburn locks to hang loosely. Finally, she slid her pedicured feet into a pair of red mules. She admired herself in the full-length mirror and smiled at the image she saw. At age 45, she was, in a word - stunning.

The Jordans had been at the Baptiste house for almost an hour before Albertina finally made her appearance. She made no apologies for her tardiness and just as she planned, all eyes were on her when she entered the backyard.

Gregory made the proper introductions. Albertina shook hands with Dallas and Hattie, then kissed the air next to Natalie's cheek. "So you're the girl who has stolen my son's heart." *Good grief, if my son thinks he's going to marry that Tar Baby, it will be over my dead body!* Natalie felt a warm sensation in her face, a feeling that would recur throughout the evening. She caught Albertina blatantly staring at her on several occasions. She couldn't help but wonder what her future mother-in-law might be thinking.

"So tell me Mrs. Jordan…"

Hattie interrupted. "Just call me Hattie."

"Oh, Hattie." Albertina smirked.

"And please feel free to call me Albertina. I was about to ask you, what line of business are you and Mr. Jordan in?"

"I runs the house for a Jewish family over in Palmer Woods. They owns the dry cleanin' store up on Livernois and some more in other parts of the city too."

"Oh you're talking about Jacob and Rhoda Feldman?"

Hattie grinned proudly. "Yeah, that's them. You use their cleaners?"

"As a matter of fact we do, but they're our neighbors as well."

Hattie looked disappointed. "Naw, they house is over by the park. You must mean another family."

"What I mean is that the Feldmans are our business neighbors. We own the pharmacy two doors down from one of their dry cleaning stores. The one on Clairmount."

"Lordy be. Now that's a real blessin' ain't it? It's so nice to see our people in business. Natalie in business for herself too."

Albertina raised an eyebrow. "So Gregory tells me."

"She's real good. The Lord give her a gift doing hair. Her setup in our basement is real nice and she got a whole bunch of customers. But me and her daddy gon' help get her set up in her own building for a real beauty parlor pretty soon. She'll be able to make money off renting booths too."

"That's very nice," Albertina replied smugly.

From across the yard, Astor saw that Hattie looked like she needed to be rescued and quickly brought over two glasses of iced tea. "Ladies, here's a little something to wet your whistles."

Albertina reached for her glass. "That's sweet of you Astor Dear."

Hattie tasted her tea. "I never tasted sweet tea like this before. I tastes the spearmint - gives it a little kick don't it?"

"Yes, it comes from our garden."

Astor grinned as he watched Hattie enjoy her tea. "It's called Plantation Tea."

"Well it's delicious. You got something in it 'sides spearmint though."

"Astor got the recipe from one of our neighbors at our place up north."

"Oh, y'all have a house up north too?"

"It's just a little cottage in a resort town called Idlewild. We mainly use it in the summertime."

"Sounds real nice." Hattie was more interested in her iced tea than real estate. She sipped again. "I tell you Astor, this is the best iced tea I've ever tasted." She turned to Albertina and asked, "You think it would be alright to give me a sprig of your spearmint so I can root it for my garden?"

"Of course you can. Astor's the vegetable and herb gardener though. My specialty is roses. As you can see, I'm particularly fond of yellow roses. I simply can't get my fill. I've raised six different species of yellow roses back here. Astor, why don't you show Hattie your herb garden?"

"Sure thing. Follow me Hattie." Astor held out his elbow and escorted Hattie to his herb garden. This led to Hattie bragging about the collard greens, okra, and bell peppers in her own garden. "I'll have to bring y'all some so you can put 'em up for the winter. Do y'all do any canning and preserving?"

Astor reached down to pluck a sprig of thyme and inhaled its pungent aroma. "Not any more. My mother and sisters used to do a lot of canning and pickling back home. I grew up in Many, Louisiana. It's part of Sabine Parish.

Nowadays, the closest 'Tina and I come to canning is when we put our leftovers in Mason jars. Sometimes I miss that whole production."

"Well I still puts my vegetables up for the winter. We got a grapevine in the backyard too. I makes my own jelly. I'll have to make sho' y'all get some too."

On the other side of the massive yard, Dallas had Natalie and Gregory cornered. He was telling them tales of his boyhood in the mountains of Columbus, Georgia. "Y'all got it easy these days. When me and Mama was kids, we used to have to cut through the woods to fetch water in pails. You'd better not spill a drop on the way back either. We'd heat our bath water in big iron pots on a wood burning stove. And, we made our own soap too. We didn't have no luxuries like you kids today. No 'lectricity, no television... Yes suh, y'all got it made in the shade in these modern times."

Meanwhile, Sheila buzzed around replenishing glasses, serving plates and emptying Albertina's ash trays. All the while, she kept a close watch on her mother.

Chapter Sixteen

Come with me from Lebanon, my bride,
come with me from Lebanon.

Song of Solomon 4:8

A t dusk Gregory whispered to his sister. "Sheila, help me gather everyone together. It's now or never."

"Ok, I just have a few loose ends to tie up first." Sheila had been working feverishly inside the rented tent blowing up red, white and blue balloons, setting out the dessert dishes and setting up a fountain for punch. She took a step back to admire her work. *Excellent job if I do say so myself.* The Jordans ooo'ed and ahh'ed when Sheila clicked on the power switch, romantically illuminating the entire backyard with frosty red lights. She tapped on a water glass with a butter knife to get everyone's attention. "Time for dessert. May I have everyone gather under the tent, please?"

Natalie was ecstatic when she stepped inside the tent. Astor hugged Sheila and said, "It looks like you actually learned something while you were in Europe. You've outdone yourself sweetheart!"

Gregory agreed. "Yeah Sis, this is really cool!" He motioned for Astor to slip *Tallulah* to him. He cleared his throat and began.

"Ok, can I get everyone to grab a glass and take a seat at the table?"

A heart-shaped cake adorned the center of a round skirted table. The inscription on the cake read *Gregory and Natalie Forever.*

Sheila received even more compliments as the group settled into their seats around the table.

Gregory nervously began. "I don't think it's any secret why we're all here this evening. But before I go any further, I have to thank my parents and my sister for putting all this together." He hugged Sheila and gave her a peck on the cheek. "You did a phenomenal job Sis. Thanks for everything." He raised his glass toward the Jordans.

"Mr. and Mrs. Jordan, thank you for coming tonight and again, welcome to our home."

He took Natalie's hand and coached her to stand next to him. "All my life, I've been afforded a lot of privileges thanks to the hard work and dedication of my parents. Sheila and I grew up in this great neighborhood, we were educated at the best schools, and when it came to stuff, we had everything a kid could ever dream of. Who could ask for anything more?"

Albertina beamed.

"But once I became a man, I realized that there was still something missing from my life. All of that stuff seemed meaningless and I began to feel empty inside. I knew something was missing, but I couldn't put my finger on exactly what it was."

Albertina's smiled disappeared.

"Then one day when I was working at Gus' greasy filling station, the missing element drove right up to pump number two and asked me to fill 'er up."

Natalie's cheeks warmed again as Gregory turned and looked into her sparkling dark brown eyes. "Baby, since you and I have been together, I've been happier than I've ever been in my entire life. I know I would be even happier if I could spend the rest of my life with you by my side, as my wife. And if you'll allow me, I'd like to dedicate my life to making you happy too." He knelt at her feet. "Natalie Rosetta Jordan, will you be my wife?"

The group held its collective breath as everyone waited for her answer.

In a barely audible voice, she tearfully answered. "Yes Gregory, I'd love to marry you."

He stood and brushed her lips gently. Astor cleared his throat.

"Ah, son. Aren't you forgetting something?"

"Huh? Oh, yeah!" He dug into his pocket and produced the Baptiste family heirloom, a blue sapphire and diamond engagement ring. As he placed the ring on Natalie's finger, he fumbled to explain its origin.

"Um, there's a story behind this ring. For as long as I can remember, my dad's been telling me that someday when I got married, he'd give me this for my bride. I think it's a Tallulah diamond or something like that, right Dad?"

Sheila was sarcastic. "Well that's romantic."

Astor jumped in. "Let me help you out son. My great-grandfather couldn't afford to buy a ring for my great-grandmother Tallulah when they got married. Right from the start, Grandma Tallulah started having babies every year until they finally ended up with eleven kids to raise. From what I understand, for years Grandma Tallulah had her eye on a ring very similar to this one in the showcase of a jewelry store in Baton Rouge. She would visit the jewelry store to look at the ring every time she went there. Sometimes she'd even try it on.

My granddaddy promised he would buy it for her someday when they could afford it. Well, with all those mouths to feed, it literally took him a lifetime, but Granddaddy Wilber kept his promise. He presented this ring to my grandma at a party celebrating their 50th wedding anniversary. Look inside Natalie, you'll see he had it engraved to fit the occasion."

Natalie silently read the inscription, smiled and said, "I guess that says it all."

He continued. "My daddy said Grandma Tallulah was so overwhelmed they all thought the old lady was going to have a heart attack right then and there. Well after she got her wits together, she gathered everyone close to her and made 'em listen carefully. She told them all she knew she wouldn't be around much longer so she wanted to start a tradition to make sure the ring would stay in the family. Sure enough, she passed away a short time afterward. Somehow along the way, the family just starting calling the ring *Tallulah*. This ring is to be passed down from generation to generation by way of the firstborn sons to their wives."

Astor's eyes welled, his voice quivered. "Now, my only son is giving it to his bride-to-be." He kissed Natalie on the forehead.

"Welcome to the Baptiste family Natalie."

Sheila and Albertina watched the others celebrate.

Chapter Seventeen

Let's lie in wait for someone's blood,
let's waylay some harmless soul

Proverbs 1:11

Time passed like a whirlwind as Gregory and Natalie made plans for their wedding. Sheila doubled as their wedding coordinator and Maid of Honor. Gregory had been frantically searching for his promiscuous cousin Thomas for several weeks; then seemingly out of nowhere, he appeared. He couldn't believe his eyes when he saw Thomas' custom-painted cobalt blue convertible parked in his driveway.

Thomas and Gregory were thick as thieves until a couple of years ago. With the exception of a few family gatherings, the two hadn't seen much of each other since college. Albertina was relieved that they'd grown apart. She blamed Thomas for a very serious legal scrape he had gotten Gregory got into when they were roommates at Xavier.

Gregory tiptoed to the family's rec-room. He was elated when he saw Thomas bent over the pool table shooting balls into the pockets. Sheila was perched on a bar stool dressed in a tennis outfit. The two of them seemed to be engaged in an intense conversation. Gregory tried to sneak up behind him and thump the back of his head. But Thomas heard him and swirled around just in time to block the would-be assailant's attack. He grabbed Gregory and put him in a playful headlock. The two wrestled to the floor like a couple of eight-year-olds. Sheila jumped out of harm's way. "You two had better stop before you break something." She flung her tennis racket case over her shoulder and grabbed her tote bag. "I'm off to whip the socks off of Debbie Cain - again." She winked at her cousin. "Don't be such a stranger, Thomas."

"Later Gator." He told Gregory, "You better be glad your sister called me off. I was 'bout to put a hurtin' on you boy."

"Only thing hurtin' me is your breath. Dang man, haven't you ever heard of Listerine?"

Thomas waved him off as he watched his cousin reach into the refrigerator behind the bar. Gregory grabbed a bottle of milk, turned it up and drained it in just a few gulps. He set the empty bottle in a crate along with the other empty milk and juice bottles for the Twin Pines milkman to pick up.

"Ooo, Aunt Tina, did you see what your son just did?"

Albertina smacked Gregory's rear end with the back of her hand. "Gregory, please behave like you've had some upbringing. You're not in your dorm anymore."

The young men settled into two overstuffed chairs to catch up. "Cuz, what's this noise I hear 'bout you getting married? I should have known something was up. Nobody can catch up with you these days."

"You're the one who's been acting like an undercover agent. I've been trying to find you for months." His mood sobered. "Now about my getting married... you heard right and I've never been happier in my life."

"No doubt Cuz, I've never seen you look this happy before. It's just hard to believe that somebody finally got the Motor City Playboy to settle down."

"Well believe it. This is real."

"I'll take your word for it Cuz. So when is all this legit' stuff taking place? Am I gonna get an invitation or do I have to crash the wedding?"

Gregory's eyes lit up. "Matter of fact Tom, I wanted to ask you to be my Best Man. That's why I've been trying to find you."

"Best Man? You want me to be the Best Man in your wedding?"

"Yeah you. Who else? You're like the brother I never had."

"Aw man, don't get all sentimental on me now. But yeah, I'll definitely be your Best Man. Just tell me when and where. I'll be there for you and your girl man."

"Your timing is scary. I was about ready to hire a private detective to locate you man. You disappear for a couple of years, nobody, not even your own people can find you – then you show up on my doorstep today like a stray cat. What brings you by man?"

Thomas tilted his head back and pinched his forehead pretending to have a supernatural experience. "I'm psychic. I had this vision of you sitting in your bedroom crying your eyes out because you ain't got no Best Man."

Gregory laughed. "Yeah right. Seriously though, is this just a coincidence or did somebody from the family contact you?"

Thomas' face darkened. "Well man, matter of fact, I got this little situation. I owe this guy a lot of money and..."

Albertina reappeared. "I thought you guys might like a little snack. I set out sandwiches. Why don't you run up to the kitchen and help yourselves."

"Thanks Aunt Tina, I'll take you up on your offer. You coming Cuz?"

Albertina was stretched out on her chaise lounge in front of their Philco television set when they returned with their refreshments.

"Thanks for the snacks Mother."

"You're welcome. Now don't mind me fellas. Finish catching up.   Bill Kennedy is showing Bette Davis' movie, *Now Voyager*."

Chapter Eighteen

They repay me evil for good, and hatred for my friendship.
Psalm 109:5

Gregory had convinced his father to re-hire him at the pharmacy. He arranged to leave work early so that he could pick Natalie up from the beauty school. Then, he'd return to work and stay until closing.

One evening before leaving, Albertina called him into the tiny office above the drug store. She showed him a pile of ledgers, invoices, and other documents. "Son, I hate to dump all this on you, but Mother has a splitting headache. We have to meet with the tax attorney in a few days and I'm afraid we won't be ready. Can you spend a little time to see if you can reconcile these figures?"

Gregory surveyed the massive pile of books and papers.

"Mother, you've got to be kidding! This is going to take all night – at least."

"Darling someday you'll take over the business. Your father and I think it's important that you learn every aspect of the business.

I'm afraid this is the side of entrepreneurship that isn't very glamorous and now is as good a time as any to learn about it."

"Mother, don't think for one minute I don't know what you're up to."

"What do you think I'm up to son?"

"You're trying to set things up so you and Dad can retire. I heard you two talking about moving back to Louisiana the other night. You want to groom me so that I can gradually take over."

Albertina smiled. "Yes, dear. I guess you saw right through my little plan."

"A blind man could see through your plan Mother. And you're not nearly as tough as you try to make people think either."

"You're right son. My intentions are often misunderstood."

Gregory patted his pockets for his car keys. "Anyway, let me get Natalie home then I'll be back to dive into these books for you."

"No, no dear, let me take care of Natalie. This is going to take a while. The sooner you get started, the sooner you'll get home."

"Really Mother? *You'll* pick Natalie up tonight?"

"I'll see that she makes it home safely. Just give me the address to the beauty school. Don't worry, Mother will take care of your precious fiancée."

Natalie was bewildered when she found Thomas leaning against his car in front of her beauty school.

"Hey Natalie."

"Hey Thomas. What are you doing here?" She peeked inside Thomas' sports car looking for Gregory. "Where's your cousin?"

"Cuz couldn't make it this evening; had to work late so I'm here to take you home."

"Gregory sent *you* to take me home?"

"Something like that. What's the matter, you don't wanna ride with me?"

Not really. "Gregory told me some pretty scary stories about your driving."

"Hey, that's the old Thomas." He placed his hand over his heart. "I done changed my evil ways."

Natalie side-glanced him. "What a difference a day makes."

"Ow! Dang Natalie that's cold."

Natalie lowered herself down onto the leather bucket seat.

"So what's the big emergency that Gregory had to send you to pick me up?"

"All I know is something, something, tax attorney, something, something pick Natalie up and take her straight home. Hey! I just hear and obey. I guess Cuz will catch up with you later. I'm sick of talking about him already. You hungry? I was thinkin' 'bout ridin' up to Top Hat's. I got a taste for a burger and a chocolate malt."

"No thanks, my mother has dinner waiting for me at home."

Thomas licked his lips. "Wow, a home-cooked meal. Must be nice. All I have waiting for me is some beer and an eviction notice."

Natalie faked empathy. "Aw, you poor thing."

"So what's Mama Jordan cooking tonight?"

"I think she said something about short ribs, rice and gravy."

Thomas patted his neglected stomach. "Mercy!"

Natalie couldn't help herself. "Thomas, do you want a plate to take home?"

"Hey girl, I don't turn down no meals. Y'all got any dessert to go with that?"

Natalie couldn't believe Thomas' total lack of pride. "Mama made some bread pudding Sunday. There's probably a corner left."

Gregory's one-night assignment turned into a week-long project. Then Albertina discovered several other projects that she had inadvertently overlooked. "It looks like your father brought you back into the business just in the nick of time."

"Mother, sometimes you have a tendency to really dramatize things. I think you're giving me these paltry projects just to make me think I'm important. I feel like I'm doing bell work back in elementary school."

"Son, someday when you decide to take the family's business seriously, you'll look back on these paltry projects as necessary exercises in your development as a businessman."

"I am taking the business seriously Mother, but some of this stuff is not as urgent as you make it out to be. I haven't seen Natalie in a week and she's not crazy about riding around with Thomas - I have to say that I share her sentiment."

"No one is putting a gun to Natalie's head to make her ride with Thomas."

"Well, I'm not letting my fiancée ride the bus. Anyway, how did Thomas end up driving Natalie home? You told me you were going to take her home."

"No, that's not what I said. I told you I'd see that Natalie got home safely and I've kept my word to the letter. Surely you didn't expect that I would actually drive her home myself.

You know I loathe driving around strange neighborhoods. Besides, Thomas is between jobs right now. He seems to have a lot of time on his hands these days. I thought this would be an excellent opportunity for the two of them to get to know each other better since he missed the get acquainted party. After all, he is going to be your Best Man – isn't he?"

Natalie's customers were shoulder to shoulder in her basement beauty shop on Saturday morning. The women exchanged recipes and caught up on the latest gossip, while they patiently waited their turns. For a nominal fee, Hattie provided them with piping hot fried chicken and fish sandwiches, generous wedges of pound cake and sweet potato pie.

Dallas had bought a used vending machine and filled it with bottles of Coca-Cola, NuGrape, Orange Crush and Hires Root Beer.

"Somebody got a package," Hattie sang down to Natalie as she carefully descended the stairs carrying a long white box.

"Looks like somebody's tryin' to make up for spending so much time away from their sweetheart."

"Ok, Mama. Just a minute." Natalie had a six-year-old patron sitting on a booster seat in her chair. She dipped a hot comb into a jar of pressing oil. Then she wiped the hot comb on a scorched white cloth and blew on it to cool it down. "Bow your head like you're saying your prayers baby." The little girl obeyed and twisted her face. Natalie placed a hard rubber comb against the nape of her hair. Gray smoke rose, and the grease sizzled as she pulled the hot comb through the little girl's hair.

She expertly pressed the little girl's hair close to the roots, set the pressing comb on the stove's rest and wiped the excess grease from her hands so she could inspect her surprise package.

Natalie's customers eagerly watched as she slid the large yellow ribbon off the box. She retrieved a bouquet of twelve perfect yellow long stemmed roses with white baby's breath. Hattie exclaimed, "Ain't they the most beautiful flowers you ever seen?"

Natalie held the flowers close to her heart and searched for the love note she knew Gregory would have enclosed. The envelope was simply addressed, "*To a Special Lady.*"

She inhaled the sweet fragrance of the roses. "My baby is so thoughtful. I could just eat him up." She stuck the card in the pocket of her smock, sniffed the roses again and cradled them for a moment.

Hattie reached for the flowers. "Give 'em here. I'll take 'em upstairs and put 'em in some fresh water. They'll be dead before night from them hot combs and curlin' irons down here."

Natalie handed the flowers back to Hattie then began forming vertical curls in her young customer's hair. When she was finished, she handed her the mirror. The cherub-faced girl grinned a missing-two-front-teeth smile that let Natalie know she was very pleased. "Mommy, I look just like Shirley Temple!"

The little girl's mother asked, "How do I keep those curls up for another two weeks Natalie?"

"That's easy. All you have to do is tear some strips from a brown paper bag and roll the curls around the strip – then you just tie the ends together."

As Natalie prepared for bed, she emptied the pockets of her smock and pulled out hands full of cash – tips her customers had given her. She smiled when she saw the florist's card mixed in with the coins and dollar bills. She looked forward to reading Gregory's love note. However, as she began to read, her smile turned into a confused frown. *Natalie, thanks for the good times - Tom.* "Tom?"

Chapter Nineteen

Flee fornication. Every sin that a man doeth is without the body; but he that committeth fornication sinneth against his own body.

1 Corinthians 6:18

"You know we have no business being here alone like this."

"I don't see why. We're betrothed now. Isn't that what they call it in the Bible?"

"Yeah, but you're taking it out of context. Betrothed means promise, and commitment, but that doesn't mean we can..."

He put his finger to her lips. "Shhh, let's just enjoy each other tonight. We hardly have time to see each other these days. I was beginning to worry that you might let some other guy move in on my territory. You're practically my wife now, remember?"

"God doesn't recognize practically honey. Spending time together doesn't mean we have to... You know what I mean. When it does happen – it needs to be at the right time and in the right place. I can't believe I let you talk me into coming up here alone with you. Anyway, who comes to Idlewild in the dead of winter?"

"We do. I can't think of a better way for us to ring in the New Year."

Natalie was nervous. "This was a bad idea. I should have gone to the watch night service. The only time I've ever missed being in church on New Year's eve was when I was twelve years old. I had the flu."

"Baby will you relax and let us enjoy this rare moment together? We may not have another chance to be together like this until we get married – that's months from now."

"Chance is right. We're taking a chance being here like this. I don't know what I was thinking coming up here with you." She lifted her head off his shoulder and scooted down to the opposite end of the couch. She forced herself to look away from his alluring gaze. "Sex is a holy expression of love, a gift from God to his *married* children. If we do anything before we're married, we'll be fornicating – that's a sin."

Gregory ignored what he called her religious rhetoric. He slid over to her and with a light touch of his finger, made her face him as he looked lovingly into her eyes. "Very soon we'll be husband and wife. Everybody knows we're getting married, including God. Let me ask you something Natalie. God made these urges we have for each other - am I right?" Natalie didn't respond. "I know I'm right. So tell me… why would He give us these urges *now* if He didn't want us to enjoy each other *now?*" Natalie couldn't help but laugh. "Gregory Baptiste, you're full of hot air."

He threw up his hands. He stood and stretched as he crossed the room to place a stack of 45s on the record player.

"Alright since you want to play hard ball, I'm going to have to pull out my secret weapon. Wait here. I'll be back in a few. No peeking!" He left Natalie alone for almost half an hour. While he was out of the room, she struggled to keep her own pangs of desire in check. She tried to maintain pure thoughts as she watched snowflakes gently fall and cling to the living room window – forming patterns of frost that looked like fine crystal. The room suddenly went dark, saving the light from two candlesticks Gregory was holding.

"Oh now you're pulling out all the stops. You're not playing fair Gregory."

He set the candlesticks on the mantle. "They say all is fair in love and war – and I'm a man who's head-over-heels in love."

Natalie's eyes traced the silhouette of his handsome physique as he moved through the warm glow of the candle-lit room. He sat close to her on the sofa and began kissing her. Johnny Mathis crooned softly in the background as she allowed Gregory to caress her body.

She squeezed his hand when he started to unbutton her blouse. She sternly said to him, "Not yet."

"Sweetheart, whether it happens on our wedding night or not, I will always know you were *my* virgin. I love you so much Natalie. My body is aching to prove to you how much I love you. There are so many things I want to teach you, so much I want us to experience and enjoy together."

"You say that now, but I know we both may regret it later."

Gregory stroked her face softly, and kissed her reassuringly.

She stood and tried to move away but he reached for her hand to lead her back to the couch. The atmosphere was charged with sexual electricity. Natalie's knees buckled underneath her as he tenderly pulled her into his arms. She was entangled in his hypnotic embrace.

The Holy Spirit warned her that she was in danger. This would be her last chance to remain pure. She knew she should run for her spiritual life, but she didn't move. His kisses, his scent, his touch were mesmerizing.

Gregory kissed and caressed her in places her body yearned for. He lifted her from the sofa and carried her into the next room - to the chamber of love he had created.

A dozen candles softly illuminated the room. Rose petals formed a fragrant trail from the doorway to the bed. Brooks Benton's satiny voice now serenaded them as he gently laid her down and presented her with a single long-stemmed rose.

"Natalie, I love you with all my heart. I'd never do anything to hurt you."

Natalie had said all the right words and quoted all the right scriptures but on this night, she did not bring her flesh under submission – and sin prevailed.

Chapter Twenty

If any man among you seemeth to be wise in this world,
let him become a fool, that he may be wise.

1Corinthians 3:18

"I'm late Gwen." She glanced at the clock radio on her nightstand. "Where are you supposed to be?"

"I mean, the rabbit died. I've got a bun in my oven, I'm pregnant Gwen! Don't you get it?"

"Oh my God girl, are you sure?"

"Yes I'm sure; this is the second month in a row I missed. I'm never late and I don't know what I'm gonna do." Natalie threw herself across her best friend's bed and cried. "I can't believe this is happening to me. It was only one time Gwen, just one time!"

"News flash honey child, it only takes one time."

Natalie buried her face in the hand-sewn quilt Gwen's grandmother made for her. "How am I going to tell my parents? My poor mother. She's always bragging about how I've been saving myself for marriage. Now this is gonna make her look like a fool. My daddy is gonna have a fit! I will probably have to quit ushering and I sure won't be able to teach Sunday school. Folks won't want an unmarried pregnant woman around their kids."

Gwen sucked her teeth. "Church folks! Whatever happened to do unto others...? Turn the other cheek... Suffer the little children and all that stuff?"

Natalie shook her head.

"So you think you're about what... seven, eight weeks?"

Natalie nodded sullenly.

Gwen snapped her fingers. "Hey! You'll just have to move the wedding date up sooner, much sooner."

"You know what? I know this sounds crazy, but I've been so uptight about being pregnant I forgot all about the wedding. Anyway, Gregory's always talking about how he can't wait. You're right, we can just move the wedding up like you said. If anybody wants to talk, let 'em."

"I hate to be the devil's advocate, but what if Gregory doesn't want kids right away?"

"Well it's a little late for that. He should have thought of that when he was acting like we were the last two people on earth. I tried my best to keep him off me that night, but he acted like he was gonna bust somethin' if he didn't have me right then and there. Of course I'm just as much to blame as he is. I knew I shouldn't have gone up to that cottage alone with him in the first place."

"Woulda, shoulda, coulda. That's all water under the bridge now. I'm sure you have nothing to worry about."

"Right. In fact, he'll probably be happy to know he's about to be a daddy. I'm not so sure about his folks though."

"Forget his folks! You're marrying him!"

Gregory entered his parent's bedroom glowing. They were propped up in bed reading. He hopped them. "Hey grandma and grandpa."

Albertina took off her reading glasses and allowed them to dangle by the beaded chain they were attached to. "I beg your pardon. Did you just call us grandma and grandpa?"

Astor folded his newspaper and listened.

"That's right Mother. Natalie is going to have a baby. I'm going to be a daddy!"

"You've got to be kidding. You mean to tell me that girl has gone and gotten herself pregnant?"

"Tina, it takes two to Tango."

"Shut up Astor. Listen to me son. Don't be so quick to claim that girl's baby. How do you know you're really the father?"

"Mother, I don't know how you can sit there and accuse her of such a thing. I'm Natalie's first – her only. We only did it…"

Albertina snatched Astor's newspaper and hit Gregory with it.

"Please spare me the sordid details of your irresponsible escapades. I refuse to listen to any more of this tonight. We'll talk more in the morning. You go to bed now. And you're delusional if you believe you're that long-legged tramp's first."

Gregory's shoulder slumped and he retreated to his bedroom like a ten-year-old.

Astor said, "I can't believe the words you allow to tumble out of your mouth sometimes Tina."

Gregory tossed and turned throughout the night. He felt guilty for even entertaining the doubts his mother had planted in his mind. It was almost 3:00 a.m. when he called Natalie to reassure himself. "Hey sweet thing."

Natalie peered at her alarm clock. "Hey yourself. Why in the world are you calling me at this hour?"

"I just needed to hear your voice."

"Why? Is anything wrong?" He hesitated. "What's wrong Sweetie? You didn't call me this time of the night for nothing, just tell me."

"Never mind. It's like I said, I just needed to hear your voice."

"Are you sure? How did it go with your parents?"

"So-so."

Natalie's heart sank. "Only so-so?"

"Yeah. We'll talk about it tomorrow. Good night baby."

It seemed that Gregory had just closed his eyes when the morning's light interrupted his restless slumber. Sheila's warning from months ago resounded in his mind. He looked himself in the mirror while shaving and vowed that he would stand his ground no matter what his mother said or did.

Astor and Albertina were in their usual spot at the breakfast table, doing what they usually did.

"Good morning Mother, Dad."

His parents answered in unison. "Morning Son."

He reached for his keys and to his surprise, they weren't hanging in their spot under his name on the key tree.

"I don't see my keys. I know I hung them here last night."

Astor moved the breakfast plates and napkin holder to look for the keys. "Son, you do the right thing by that girl. Your mother's all emotional because she thinks she's too young to be a grandmother just yet."

Astor hoped he could lighten Albertina's somber mood. "She still thinks she's a spring chicken." Astor chuckled lightly; Gregory forced a half-smile.

"Well I'm glad the two of you think this is a laughing matter. I, for one, think it's a travesty."

Sheila shuffled into the kitchen wearing her robe, slippers and a head full of curlers stuffed under a satin sleeping cap. "Did somebody say something about a baby?" She turned to Gregory who was feeling along the top of the refrigerator for his keys. "Ooo Greggy. Have you been a bad boy?"

He growled at her. "Shuddup stupid."

"You mark my words. That girl planned to set this trap for you right from the start. Why it wouldn't surprise me if all of those Jordans were in on the scheme."

He searched the counter tops for his keys. "What scheme Mother? We were already engaged long before this happened. Remember?"

"They plan to use that baby as insurance that they'll always have ties to this family."

"You've been reading too many novels Mother. We're not wealthy and the Jordans are doing just fine without the Baptiste *fortune!*"

"Don't take that tone with me young man; and I hope you don't think you're going through with this ridiculous farce of an engagement. You'll marry that girl when pigs fly!"

He stopped moving. "Mother you can't be serious. Of course I'm still going to marry Natalie. I want to marry her now more than ever." He yelled, "Has anybody seen my keys?"

Astor said, "Check your jacket pockets son."

"Gregory I'm warning you. Those people..."

Astor interrupted. "That's enough Tina!"

Sheila whispered in a sing-song tone, "Told you so."

Gregory felt nauseous. "I gotta split before I say something we'll all be sorry for. Forget the keys. I'll just walk to work." He glowered back at his mother and sister. "I'll see you later Dad."

He stormed out of the house; Astor followed him. "Look son. Give your mother some time. This is shocking news to her."

He watched the muscles in Gregory's jaw tighten. "But you do right by that girl no matter what. If I were you, I'd just take her downtown to city hall and make things legal right away. Why wait?"

"Maybe I will. But first I need to talk things over with Natalie and her parents. They're really looking forward to a church ceremony. So was I."

"Well, whatever you decide, I'm behind you. Your mother will come around – eventually."

Chapter Twenty-One

Proverbs 17:4

Gregory's habit of letting his mail pile up unattended for weeks at a time irritated his mother to no end. Sheila brought the most recent pile in to him directly. "Mother says your mail is becoming a nuisance. I think you'd better do something about it before she throws it and you out of the house."

He carelessly tossed the mail on his bed. "My God Gregory would it kill you to take five minutes of your precious time to read through your mail? It looks like most of it could be pitched."

"Alright! Get off my back. I have more important things to worry about than a bunch of stupid mail. Anyway, when did you start to you care so much about my mail?"

"I don't know. I don't know why I care anything about you at all. You're such a sniveling brat. I swear Gregory, sometimes you can be positively infantile!" Sheila stomped out of his bedroom, slammed the door and yelled through it. "Mama's boy!"

Being claustrophobic, he snatched the door open and yelled after her. "Oh that's mature Sheila. You're such a role model." No wonder they keep sending her to the nut house. He began sifting through the pile. Just as Sheila had said, most of it consisted of sales promotions and other junk mail.

The pink envelope heavily scented with Tigress cologne gave away its sender's identity. He ripped it into shreds and let the pieces flutter into his wastebasket. He couldn't believe he was still getting love letters from a girl he hadn't even seen in almost two years. *What a fruitcake.*

Another letter was from the Church of the Latter Day Saints inviting him to let Jesus into his heart today; and Xavier's alumni association sent him a reminder that his annual membership fee was past due. A yellow envelope containing an invoice from Schelberg's Stems and Blooms was conspicuously included in Gregory's mail.   The attention line was simply addressed to *Mr. Baptiste.* He was certain it belonged to his father – and it had already been opened. But out of curiosity, he decided to take a look at it. He was surprised when he read that one of the orders on the invoice was for a dozen long-stemmed yellow roses delivered to Natalie Jordan at her home address. He was even more surprised when he read the instructions for the enclosure card.

"Why in the world is *Thomas* sending flowers to Natalie? And what in the world does he mean by good times?"

"I asked myself those same questions when I saw the invoice son. I thought it was addressed to your father so naturally, I was curious to learn who he might have sent flowers to."

Albertina inserted a Salem into her tortoise shell cigarette holder and casually leaned against her son's doorway. "I knew those two were getting too chummy. To think Thomas had the gall to have the flowers billed to our corporate account.

You'd better have a serious chat with your cousin and get to the bottom of this right away son."

Chapter Twenty-Two

"Come on in Tom." Gregory's face was grim. Thomas wiped mud from his feet and hung his dripping wet umbrella out in the vestibule.

"Man, it's raining cats and dogs out there. So what's up partner?" The two headed for the rec-room and sat down on opposite ends of the couch as they had done hundreds of times since childhood.

Thomas lit a cigarette while he waited to hear what his cousin had to say.

For several minutes, Gregory paced the floor mumbling and shaking his head. "Tom, you and me gotta talk man." He struggled to form the questions his heart needed answers to, knowing that those answers might change his life forever.

Finally, Thomas broke the silence. "Cuz, you wearin' Aunt Tina's nice wood floor out. If you got something to say, spit it out. What's so important you had me come out the house this time of night, in this weather?"

Gregory drew a deep breath. "Man, I don't even know how to say this, but I'm just gonna ask you some things. Don't say a word 'til I'm finished. Then Tom, I need you to tell me everything you know about the situation. No half-steppin'. I need to hear the truth man."

Thomas listened without interrupting while his cousin told him about the baby, the invoice for the flowers, then summarized Albertina's take on the situation. When he was done, Gregory waited to hear what his cousin had to say.

"Man, you remember how Gran' Daddy used to tell us if you go looking for trouble, you'll find it?" Gregory's heart pounded as he nodded.

"Look. First I'll say this. What's done is done." He rubbed his forehead and groaned. "Here it is in a nutshell. Me and Natalie had us a few good times, a few laughs. Boom, it's over. Now y'all getting' ready to get married. Like Jimmy Stewart said, it's a wonderful life."

"Thomas, this is no time for one of your sick jokes. You're talking about my future wife and the mother of my child."

"I'm serious as a heart attack, man. We just had us a few good times. Just a little boot knocking, no emotions behind it, just a couple of good rolls in the hay. But truthfully, I guess what we should really be thinking about is that baby. For all we know, that little crumb snatcher she's carryin' might be mine."

"What are you talking about Tom?"

Thomas stood and began pacing. "Man, we wasn't gon' say nothin because what me and Natalie did didn't mean nothin' to either one of us. I guess for some reason it was meant for you to find out though. Now that I think about it, it was kinda stupid of me to send her those flowers. It's just that Aunt Tina had me messin' around in the office one day and I saw how easy it was to send flowers and have 'em billed to the company's account." He crushed his cigarette in the lumpy lime green ceramic ashtray Gregory made for his mother at summer camp years ago.

"Truth is, me and Natalie started hanging around each other a lot and I guess you could say, we got a little too friendly. I mean you were working all those long hours at the drug store."

Acid churned in Gregory's stomach as Thomas recited the sickening details. "Don't blame her though man; I guess the girl got lonely. She was really missin' you. She talked about you every time we got together."

"So you're saying Natalie went to bed with you – but talked about me, because she was missing me? Am I understanding you correctly Thomas?"

"I know. The whole thing is kinda sick now that I'm talkin' about it. Maybe Natalie just figured a Baptiste is a Baptiste - and I'm still the dog I've always been. Man, you remember how you and me used to do it in back at "the X". It's all in the family Cuz, no harm done..."

"Tom, we're not talking about those girls back at the X, we're talking about the woman I'm about to marry!"

"You're right. I apologize." An insolent grin crept across Thomas' face. "In case you ever had any doubt, I can assure you that she definitely was a virgin before I had her man. I tell you what though... she catches on quick. You gon' be a very happy man on your wedding night. Man I taught Natalie some moves that will..."

Before Thomas could finish his sentence, Gregory leaped at him and smashed his fist into the middle of his face. Then he snatched him by the collar and delivered another hard blow to his mouth, pulverizing his front teeth.

The fury behind the second blow sent Thomas crashing through Albertina's smoked glass cocktail table. He was dazed, but managed to scramble to his feet. Blood began to ooze from his mouth. Hundreds of glass splinters protruded from his face, neck and back.

Soon, Albertina's parquet wood floor was covered with shattered glass and Thomas' blood. His first reaction was to pounce on his cousin in retaliation. He knew he could have easily beaten Gregory like a prizefighter's sparring partner - yet he didn't raise a hand to him.

"I guess I deserved that. I'm really sorry man. We never meant for any of this to happen. Come on. Take another swing at me and get everything out your system so we can all move on."

He imitated nobility and stuck out his chin; bracing himself for another blow. "Come on, I can take it." Instead, Gregory bolted out of the house to confront Natalie.

The pouring rain made visibility almost impossible. The winds were so intense that hundred-year-old trees bowed and swayed like mere saplings. Nevertheless, Gregory pushed past the speed limit. His Chevy skid and hydroplaned over the slick pavement through puddles and potholes. All the while, he talked to the empty passenger seat. "I loved you more than life itself Natalie. How could you do this to me? Why did you do this?"

He swerved to avoid hitting a woman and child who were crossing the street. An angel of mercy gripped the steering wheel, preventing him from crashing into a bus filled with teenagers returning home from late night skating at the Arcadia roller rink.

He envisioned Thomas and Natalie together, inhaling each other's essences. He imagined Thomas kissing and caressing Natalie - the way he had that night in January. He imagined Natalie calling Thomas' name instead of his. His stomach convulsed as its contents mixed with the agony of his emotions. Grace allowed him to slow down and maneuver the car to the side of the road. He tumbled out of the car, doubled over and emptied his ailing bowels.

A Detroit police cruiser pulled behind him. An officer got out of the car and approached him. He wiped his mouth with the tail of his shirt and asked the policeman, "Is anything wrong sir?"

"I'd say so. We've been tailing you for about a mile. You were driving like a nut back there. You look pretty tipsy."

"I haven't been drinking sir."

"Uh huh. Put your right index finger on the tip of your nose and walk up on this curb. Let me see you walk down to that fire hydrant and back." Despite his sick stomach and a throbbing headache, Gregory passed the officer's crude sobriety test.

"What have you been drinking tonight?"

"I told you sir, nothing, not one drop. I'm just upset about something. Very upset and I need to get to my girl."

"Well son, you aren't going to make it to that girl if you keep driving like a bat outta you-know-where. Let me take a look at your driver's license."

Gregory retrieved his driver's license and handed it to the officer. He opened the back door. "Son, get in the backseat while we run your record." Gregory cooperated. The officer slid under the wheel and raised his eyebrows when he read the name on Gregory's license. "Mr. Baptiste, we're going to let you go with only a warning. But please, slow down and drive like you have a brain in your head, son. The weather is treacherous tonight."

Gregory eased back onto the street toward Natalie. In a matter of minutes, the course of both their lives would change forever.

Thomas was trying to pick glass particles out of his face when Albertina entered the rec-room. She gingerly picked up Gregory's ashtray from among the shattered glass and blood.

She spoke without emotion. "Looks like you took quite a beating. I would advise you to see a doctor." She surveyed the damage he and Gregory had done to the room.

"I'll have to clean this mess up in the morning. I'm going to bed now. I've had a rough day today. And from the looks of things Thomas... so have you. Be sure to shut the door on your way out."

Thomas nearly knocked Sheila down on the wet pavement as he rushed to his car. A bolt of lightning illuminated his anguished and tattered face. The weather, the darkness of night and Thomas' injuries looked like a scene from a horror movie.

When Sheila saw the cuts, bruises and torn clothing - she knew. Their eyes met, but no words were exchanged.

A searing wave of remorse swept over Thomas' soul as he drove into the stormy night. He sorely regretted the part he played in the betrayal. *All that's missing is my thirty pieces of silver.* "Nothing personal Cuz, strictly business. Sorry."

Chapter Twenty-Three

...Weeping may endure for a night,
but Joy cometh in the morning.

Psalm 30:5

Natalie's water broke on a crisp Saturday afternoon in September. Twenty-one hours later, the 6 lb., 7 oz. baby girl was born. With the agony of the long, painful labor behind her, she smiled and thanked God as she kissed ten perfect fingers and ten perfect toes. The baby was a beautiful child with bright auburn hair, eyes the color of newly minted pennies and a creamy complexion dotted with tiny red freckles across her nose. She was the spit and image of Albertina.

The 2 a.m. feedings and sleep deprivation began to take a toll on the new mother. The stitches from her episiotomy were painful and itchy; and no matter how often she fed the baby and pumped, her breasts were constantly engorged. Natalie's hormones were on the rampage and she was still an emotional wreck over the breakup with Gregory.

Hattie reassured her, "Sweetheart, you just got what they call the baby blues. You'll feel much better just as soon as your body gets back to normal."

"It's not just that, Mama. I miss Gregory too. I miss him so much my heart aches more than my body does."

Hattie took the baby and sat in Natalie's rocking chair as she listened to her daughter's heart.

"It's all my fault. I should have kept my distance from Thomas. I knew something wasn't right about him."

Hattie remained silent and continued listening and rocking.

"Then there's Gregory's witch of a mother. It might be far-fetched Mama, but I can't help but wonder if Albertina might have something to do with all of this."

Hattie stopped rocking. "You *think* so? If I was a gambling woman, I'd bet on it. Shame on Gregory for letting other people run his life like he some kinda puppet. He should know better. He claimed he loved you so much, but when the first wind of trouble come along, he turned on you like a cornered mama cat.

You better get down on your knees and thank your Maker you didn't marry that boy! He gon' come to his senses one day and when he do, he will be very sorry.

And as for his mama. Hmph! I just hope I don't see her out on the street anywhere 'cause I might just have to put my religion up on the shelf long 'nuff to bless her out! I been trying to keep out of your business baby, but I can't hold my peace watching you suffer like this another day.

God forgive me but that's just how I feels. Now you a woman in love with your baby's daddy and I know it ain't nothing anybody on earth can say or do to take away your pain. I also know this, when you decides you want to quit hurting like this, you'll give your pain to God. When you truly give it to Him, I promise you He'll take the pain away and you will never look back. Mark my words Natalie, all them thas' involved in this mess gon' reap bitterly for what they done sowed. I just hope I live to see that day."

Chapter Twenty-Four

I looked for the one my heart loves;
I looked for him but did not find him.

Song of Solomon 3:1

Natalie hadn't heard from Gregory for months – since that night. Finally, she summoned the courage to call him. She needed him, she hoped he still needed her. Most of all, he needed to meet and establish a relationship with his daughter, even if they weren't going to be together.

The baby was sleeping peacefully in her crib when she nervously dialed the number. She prayed that Gregory would answer. The phone rang four times. She was about to return the receiver to the cradle when a young woman answered.

"Hello, Baptiste residence." Sheila's voice sounded strange. Natalie wondered why she was being so formal.

She tried to sound cheerful. "Hey Sheila, long time no see."

"Sorry, this isn't Sheila, she isn't in. Who's calling please?"

"My name is Natalie, but... I actually called to speak with..."

Albertina whispered to the girl, "Who is that on the phone dear?"

"She said her name is Natalie. She wants to speak to Sheila."

Albertina smiled pleasantly. "I'll take it darling."

"Hold on please, Mrs. Baptiste wants to speak to you."

"No, I..."

Natalie heard the click-clack of high heels on linoleum grow louder as Albertina came closer to the phone.

"Hello, Natalie?"

She was sure Albertina could hear her heart pounding over the phone.

She hoped she wouldn't choke on her words. "Hi Mrs. Baptiste, how are you?"

Albertina cheerfully sang into the phone, "I'm fine thank you Natalie; I must say I'm surprised to hear from you. It's been quite a while. How have you been?"

"I'm fine Mrs. Baptiste and you're right, it's been a long time – too long. I've been so busy with the baby you know."

"Oh so you had your child already. You must be so excited. Boy or girl?"

Natalie leaned over the crib and kissed the baby's little nose.

"A girl, she was 6 pounds, 7 ounces..."

"Yes, yes dear, I'm sure he's adorable. I wish we could chat longer, but Beverly and I were just on our way to Orchestra Hall, this is the final night of Aida. We'll have to send you a little gift for your baby. Are you at the same address?"

Astor sat by the fireplace with his newspaper pretending not to listen.

"Mrs. Baptiste, the baby is a *girl*. And yes, we're still on Linwood."

"My mistake. I'm terribly sorry we have to cut this short Natalie, but I really have to run."

She took a deep breath and blurted out, "Mrs. Baptiste, I called to speak to my baby's father. Is Gregory there?"

Albertina felt her blood pressure rise. Nevertheless, she disguised her anger and sang pleasantly into the phone again.

"Natalie, may I ask you to hold on for just a minute dear?" Without waiting for Natalie's response, Albertina laid the receiver down and spoke to the young woman.

"Beverly sweetie, it'll be just a couple more minutes." She reached into her purse and produced her car keys.
"Be a dear. Would you please go out and start the engine for me? Wait there for me, I'll be right out."

The young woman obediently draped her silver fox stole around her shoulders and headed for the door with the keys to Albertina's Lincoln. Once Beverly was out of earshot, Albertina put the receiver close to her mouth and spoke firmly.

"Did I hear you correctly? Surely you're not referring to my son as the father of your baby. "

"Of course I am. Gregory *is* her father."

"Natalie, we are not going to start that again are we? We settled all that months ago. Your little scheme didn't work. Really, you are making yourself look very foolish. My son is not interested in you or your little baby."

Natalie choked back tears as Albertina threatened her.

"Listen to me carefully and consider this a fair warning young lady. Once-and-for-all... stop running around town slandering my family by spreading tales about my son and *that baby.*

You've some nerve even dialing our phone number – let alone expecting to have a conversation with my son." She rolled her eyes upward. "I can't imagine where you get your nerve after what you and Thomas put my son through. Perhaps Thomas is the one you should be calling!   If this continues, we'll have no choice but to take some sort of legal action. Now I really must end this ridiculous conversation before we miss the opening curtain!"

"Legal action? Thomas? Mrs. Baptiste, all you have to do is take one look at this baby and you could see for yourself that she *is* your granddaughter. She looks just like you. She even has your eyes."

Albertina scoffed, "Don't be absurd Natalie. No one in my family has any intention of ever laying eyes on that baby. My son has come to his senses and has moved on with his life. He is keeping company with the lovely young lady you just spoke to. Perhaps you've heard of her or read about her family in the newspaper. Beverly Ware, Dr. Ware's youngest daughter?"

"No, I never heard of her or her family."

Albertina's eyes locked with Astor's when he rustled his newspaper and cleared his throat. She ignored him and continued.

"Well, that doesn't surprise me Natalie. Now, back to the matter at hand. I have given you fair warning. Stop harassing my son!" Albertina hung up.

Harassing her son? Albertina's condescending words resounded in Natalie's ears. She released bitter tears that flowed until they met under her chin and formed a wet circle on her blouse. She quietly left the baby's room.

Astor mumbled from behind his newspaper.

"Will you ever get enough of meddling in those kids' lives Tina?"

"Quite the contrary, I'm seriously thinking about contacting a lawyer or the police. We know very powerful people. I've had enough of Natalie Jordan! That pickinniny doesn't realize she's crossed the wrong family!"

"Up to your old tricks again, huh Tina?"

"Oh this is anything but a trick - believe you me. You should be grateful that I am so relentless. Someone has to look after our interests. After all, it turned out that my suspicions about that Dennis Harvey character were legitimate. Who knows what might have happened had we not found out the truth about his criminal background; a string of aliases, a fugitive from the law..."

Astor added, "And, he also had a wife and two children tucked away in Chicago. I'll admit your suspicions were right on the money about that joker. But Sheila hasn't been the same since we got rid of him. It's been a couple of years ago now and she still acts a little... strange sometimes. Her moods are as extreme and unpredictable as this Michigan weather. I think we made a terrible mistake by not telling her what we found out about him."

"I think you're wrong Astor. I believe Sheila would be crushed to find out she fell so deeply for a con artist. That man made a complete fool of her. Finding that out is what would be damaging."

"As far as I'm concerned, a three-month stay in a psychiatric hospital followed by weekly visits to a shrink for the past two years is an indication that she was damaged by not knowing the truth."

"There's nothing wrong with Sheila, she's just spoiled."   "In my book, anyone who swallows half a bottle of pills is crying out for help."

"For goodness sake Astor, don't be so naïve. That was merely a stunt. She was crying for attention, not help. Sheila isn't crazy Astor; but she is cunning."

Chapter Twenty-Five

I have not seen the righteous forsaken,
nor his seed begging for bread.

Psalm 37:25

No one knew exactly how old she was, but she was rumored to be at least ninety. The old woman's eyesight was very keen and she still drove her own car. She dressed very stylishly and was known for her trademark triple strand of pearls.

With slow, determined steps, she climbed the sloped walkway leading to the Jordan family's home carrying the foil covered pound cake she made for them. The aroma of the freshly baked delicacy greeted Dallas as he met Mother Winston at the door.

"Praise the Lord, Mother! Come on in."

"Praise 'im, Deacon Jordan. I brought y'all a little package."

"Ooo, I hope it's what I think it is."

She winked and smiled as she handed him the cake. "It is."

Dallas took the cake and ushered her into the living room.

"Rest yourself Mother. I'll call Natalie."

The plastic on the sofa crunched underneath her when she seated herself.

"She'll be down in just a minute Mother. I think she was on the telephone. I'll let Hattie know you're here too."

Within a few moments, Natalie appeared with the baby cradled in her one arm. She had her dressed in a pink sleeping gown and had tried to tame her unruly ginger-colored curls with baby oil. She hadn't done anything to improve her own appearance. Her eyes were red and her hair was tousled.

Mother Winston pushed herself up from her seat and stretched sinewy arms toward Natalie.

"Well, my Lord. Look here at this fine little lady! Come here little mother and give me a hug." She encircled mother and child and squeezed them gently.

"God bless ya both."

Natalie sniffed. "Thank you Mother Winston. God bless you too."

The older woman stepped back at arm's length to inspect Natalie as well as the baby. She saw that Natalie had been upset by something very recently. She sank back onto the sofa and patted the space beside her, signaling Natalie to sit next to her.

"Can I hold the baby?"

"Yes Ma'am." Natalie gently handed the baby to Mother Winston.

"Oh what a fine baby. Look at those pretty brown eyes and all these red curls. Ooo-wee! Did you suffer with the heartburn when you was carryin' her?"

"No Ma'am."

"They say women gets heartburn when they baby got a head full o' hair like she do – 'specially them with red hair."

She cackled softly. "I wouldn't know because my boys was born slick-headed. All five of 'em's heads was clean as a cue ball til they's 'least about two years old."

Mother Winston was still snickering about her bald-headed babies when Hattie entered carrying a tea service and three slices of Mother Winston's pound cake topped with fresh strawberries and whipped cream. She sat the tray on the coffee table and kissed the church's matriarch on the cheek.

"Praise the Lord Mother. Thank you for that delicious pound cake. I snuck me a little tiny piece already."

"Grace and peace to you Sister Jordan. You're welcome. You know I always love for y'all to eat up my goodies."

Hattie distributed the tea cups and reverently sat across from Mother Winston. The precious little one in her arms grasped Mother's boney finger tightly.

"Ooo she got a strong grip too. That's a sign of good character. This child is a blessing. What's her name?"

"I haven't named her yet Mother. The baby nurse at the hospital told me I have until the end of the month to name her. I want her name to mean something special so I'm still praying about it."

"That's wise. Folks need to get back to naming their children with a purpose like they used to do back in the Bible days. God is gon' tell you what to name her - soon. I'll tell you one thing I know, this child is going to be a blessing to many, many people Natalie. Yes sir, she certainly got an anointed call and purpose for her life. Sho' as you're born. You'll see it someday."

Hattie added. "Yes Ma'am and she were born with a veil on her face."

"Do tell! Praise Jesus!" A chill rippled up and down Mother Winston's spine and she began to praise God in a heavenly language.

"Veil? What are y'all talking about?"

Hattie answered. "You was knocked out with the pain medicine they gave you. The nurse from the delivery room told me and your daddy about it. A baby born with a veil on his face is said to possess a God-given gift. Could be prophesying like Mother Winston."

Mother Winston patted her foot. "Uh uh. I already see it. This child was brought here to heal! Glory to our living Savior! Our Lord, Jehovah Rapha gon' use this child to heal!" Natalie's eyes misted. Mother Winston cuddled and cooed with the baby for a few minutes then gave her back to Natalie, who waited expectantly for Mother to give her *a word.*

Mother Winston squeezed her eyes together tightly and rocked from side to side. Then she sat still and breathed deeply.

"Baby I know how you must feel. A long time ago, my husband died suddenly and I was left to raise five boys all by myself. For years, I had to work two jobs to keep a roof over our heads and food on the table. Many days I'd be down on my knees scrubbin' white folks' floors and I'd let my tears drop right in my wash bucket. Sometimes tears of sorrow, sometimes tears of joy because I knew my Redeemer lived and deliverance was on the way."

Hattie agreed. "I know what you mean Mother. Say on!"

Mother Winston continued. "There was a-plenty days I didn't know how we was gonna make it. But the good Lord always stepped in and see'd us through right on time. Hallelujah!"

"Hallelujah." Hattie echoed.

"My boys all grown and now they even got gran' chirrin. Every one of them takes good care of me. My chirrens and grans see to it that I don't have to want for nothin'. She squeezed Natalie's hand and spoke in a whisper.

"Let God have your pain and heart ache baby."

Hattie chimed in. "Thas' right Mother, thas the same thing I told her." Mother continued. "Have yourself one more good cry, then leave your troubles with Jesus and don't you take 'em back. You hear me?"

Natalie nodded. "Yes Ma'am."

"Natalie, the Lord gave you a gift to use for His glory. If you tend to His business, I promise you, He'll tend to yours."

"But Mother, I don't know what my gift is."

Mother Winston cupped her hands around Natalie's.

"Oh sure you do. You just been taking your gift for granted because it's so easy for you. That's what most people do. You ministers to those women who comes in here to get they hair done and you don't even know it.   Think about it. They come draggin' in here looking bad and feeling worse. Then you get 'em in your chair and they start tellin' you all they business, knowing they can trust you not to spread it out in the streets. Then you prays with them, encourages them and offers them comfort.

On top of all that, they leave outta here with a healthy, beautiful head of hair and a little 'mo pep in they step. I watches you when I come here. Now if that ain't a gift, I don't know what is."

Natalie smiled slightly. "I guess I never thought of my business as a gift."

She squeezed Natalie's hands together. "Yes Ma'am little mother; there are thousands of blessings right here in these gifted hands. So many peoples' blessings end up in the grave because folks don't recognize them as gifts. I believe that most of the time a person's greatest gift is the thing they love or desire to do the most. Only they mistake it for a silly wish or some kinda a pipe dream."

Hattie added. "When people have a burning desire to paint pictures, play an instrument or start a business... that's the Lord trying to stir up their gifts."

"That's so true. A gift ain't always got to be preaching or prophesying. Sister Jordan, I don't know if you know it or not, but you have the gift of hospitality." She looked around the room. "Look at how you got everything laid out so comfortably and beautiful. When I sets foot on your sidewalk, it just seem like your whole house is giving me a great big hug. The only person who could ever come in here and not feel welcome is Satan himself."

Hattie beamed. "Amen, he is not welcome in here!"

"Now come on, let's pray with this precious young mother."

The threesome joined hands and Mother Winston led them in prayer.

Dallas had been kind of listening in the next room as he tinkered with a light fixture. He silently prayed along with the women. Afterward, Mother Winston sat down and draped her lap with Hattie's linen napkin as Natalie poured the tea.

"What would you like in your tea Mother?"

"Just one lump of sugar and a touch of cream please."

Mother stirred her tea, savored a deep sip then set the cup back onto its saucer.

"Hmmm, ladies that just hit the spot. Seem like that tea going down is soothing to these old bones."

"Thank you Mother. I love serving folks."

"That's that gift of hospitality Mother Winston talked about Mama."

Hattie smiled. "I guess you're right baby."

Mother turned to Natalie. "Baby, I been walking this earth for a long time. I can surely say I ain't never see'd the Lord forsake His chirren, neither have I see'd them begging for bread. God loves you and He loves your baby – no matter how she got here. You have to ask Him to forgive you, and then you got to forgive yourself. On top of that... and it might be a hard thing to do, but you also have to forgive those who hurt you so bad. I can guarantee when you do that, the healing will begin."

The women chatted about baby names and ideas for the future expansion of Natalie's beauty shop as they continued to enjoy the tea and each other's company.

Then suddenly without fanfare, Mother Winston rose from her seat and shuffled toward the door. "I'd better be getting home now. It's time for me to feed Miss Kitty."

As Mother placed her hand on the doorknob, she called back to Natalie. "Young lady, just being in that child's presence brings joy to my Christian soul!"

Natalie suddenly felt the stirring of the Holy Ghost as the Lord revealed her baby's name and the destined call upon her life.

Chapter Twenty-Six

...Being filled with all unrighteousness, fornication,
wickedness, covetousness, maliciousness;
full of envy, and murder...

Romans 1:29

James should have been home an hour ago. The sun was slowly lowering itself behind McCord's mountain. With their newborn on her shoulder, Bernadette paced the circled pattern of the giant latch hook rug in the front room.

Their old basset hound Sadie had been howling all day for no apparent reason. Sadie was long past her hunting days, but James had her since he was a boy of no more than 10 or 11 years old. Bernadette tried feeding her and rubbing her belly with her foot, which she loved, but the miserable dog couldn't be comforted.

Bernadette sensed that Sadie's yelps were lamentations. She began to pray for James. "Lord, please protect my husband wherever he is now..."

Just as she ended her prayer, she heard the distant sputter and roar of an old pickup truck speeding up the dirt road toward her home. She was relieved, thinking perhaps James had stopped at the juke joint in town to drink with some of the other men from the carpet mill.

She laid the baby in his crib. "I'm gonna skin your daddy alive for making us worry like this Jamie."

She ran to the window and peered through the curtains. Two white men jumped out and stood in the back of the pickup. Two other men climbed into the truck's bed and lifted what appeared to be a large sack.

The men on the ground pulled the sack from their end as the others pushed. In a concerted effort, the four men lifted the sack and dumped it on the ground a few yards away from the Mitchell's front door.

The foursome laughed and slapped each other's backs as they re-entered the truck and sped off. When the truck was out of sight, Bernadette and Sadie ran out of the house to investigate the mysterious sack. The dog ran past Bernadette and sniffed the sack. She started yelping and running in tight circles around the sack, which was actually a large sheet of burlap tied around a human being.

In the dim light of dusk, Bernadette could see a pair of unshod feet. She cautiously knelt and felt for bunions, corns and callused heels - confirming that they were the same feet she massaged nightly. James' precious feet.

Although a dark crimson pool had formed at the other end, she was relieved to see James' feet were moving, twitching. She whispered. "Thank God you're alive."

She struggled to untie the rope that bound the burlap around James. "Hold on baby, I'll get this mess off you." She ran back into the house and brought back a butcher's knife.

James murmured something as she fought with the double braided rope. Finally, she severed the rope and freed James from the intended grave cloth. He lay limp in her arms, barely conscious. His face was barely recognizable. His head was swollen to almost twice its normal size. His eyes, shut from swelling, bulged out of their sockets. There didn't seem to be a part of his body that hadn't been beaten or kicked.

Bernadette blotted the gashes in his head and face with her apron. He touched her hand and whispered to her. "I love you Bern. Make sure our baby knows his daddy loved him too."

Bernadette screamed. "James Mitchell. Don't you die on me. You hear me? I just gave birth to your son. I cain't raise that boy without you. Now you quit talking foolishness."

James struggled to speak.

"Hush talkin' James. Let me run up to the Coleman's house and get Bobby to carry Doc Chaney up here."

The only medical doctor who would treat colored folks was over a hundred miles away. "Doc" Chaney was the woman who used roots, herbs and other natural remedies to treat the ailments of the local residents. But even she was miles away from the Mitchell's isolated property.

"Sadie you stay here with James you hear girl?"

The dog obediently positioned herself beside her master and resumed her lamentations.

Bernadette removed her apron and placed it under James' head. As she rose to run for help, James weakly gripped the hem of her skirt, forcing her to kneel down.

He laboriously whispered, "Stay with me Bern. If you leave now, I'll be gone when you get back. I know I ain't gon' make it baby. I'm so sorry. I love you so much. Make sure my son knows his daddy loved him Bern."

A few scattered stars against the clear indigo sky cast just enough light for Bernadette to witness life slowly draining from her husband's body. She kissed his battered face. "I love you James Mitchell. I will always love you." She sat on the ground, cradling his head against her breast and waited for the angels to take James home to live with Jesus.

Chapter Twenty-Seven

And Laban said to him, Surely thou art my bone and my flesh.
And he abode with him the space of a month.

Genesis 29:14

"Lord Bernadette I cain't believe you finally made your way up here. I thought we was gon' have to come down there and bring you ourselves." Hattie sat a plate of grits, sausage, eggs and toast in front of her niece.

"I can hardly believe it either Aint Hattie." The two hadn't seen each other since Dallas moved his family to Detroit. "I guess Natalie'll be here soon. She took the baby to the schoolyard to play in the sandbox. She'll be tickled pink when she sees you and little Jamie."

"I can't wait to see her either. I know Jamie's gonna love meeting his little cousin.

"C.J. and Jamie ought to get along like two peas in a pod. Ain't that somethin'? Them two being born on the same day?"

"Yes Ma'am, that's really something."

Natalie entered the back door with C.J. on her hip.

"Hey girl!"

"I must be dreaming! Bernadette, why didn't you let me know you were coming?"

Bernadette jumped up from her seat to embrace her cousin.

"Put that grown woman down – she big as me." The cherub-faced girl giggled when Bernadette tickled her sides.

117

"Get down and let me look at you. Wow you're a big girl aren't you?"

The shy child hid behind her mother's legs. Bernadette turned to Natalie. "Looks like life is treating you just fine since you moved up here."

"You know I've had my ups and downs, but I can't complain. Now where is that big boy? I wanna see my Jamie."

Hattie answered. "He's in the den watching George Pierrot with your daddy. He act like he really inna-rested in it too. That's the first time I ever know'd a child to want to watch anything on TV but comics."

"Jamie loves anything he can learn from. He even tries to read the newspaper."

"What? That boy trying to read already? You better have that child tested. He must be some kinda genius."

Bernadette shrugged her shoulders. "No telling what he'll grow up to be."

Natalie pointed to C.J. "Someday this little girl is going to be a doctor. I'm claiming that."

Bernadette answered wistfully. "Jamie's daddy would rejoice from heaven if he grew up to be a doctor or something. James was smart. He coulda been a business man or something if we had come up here sooner. I just wish we had moved on up here like we said we was gon' do. But he wanted to work and save some more 'til after Jamie got a little older first."

She sniffed back a tear. "God I miss that man."

Hattie moved next to Bernadette and let her rest her head against her hip. "That's alright baby. You're here with us now. With the help of the good Lord, we'll take care of you and Jamie."

Natalie asked Bernadette, "Are you just here to visit or you finally gonna make good on your promise to move here?"

"Looks like we're here to stay. We're gonna try to make Detroit our home. I know that's what James would want us to do."

Natalie applauded. "Thank God! Who would have thought you'd end up married to the nappy-headed rascal who gave me so much trouble when we were kids?"

Hattie scolded. "Natalie! It's not right to speak ill of the dead."

"She right Aint Hattie, James was a terrible little boy. Time brings on a change though. He grew up to be the kindest, sweetest man this side of heaven."

Natalie said, "I'm just so glad you're here. It's time you left those back woods sticks. Where y'all gon' be staying?"

Hattie tapped her daughter on the hand. "Where you think? They gon' stay right here with us."

"Only until I get a job and find a place for me and Jamie. I didn't come up here to be a burden. Hopefully, no more than a month or so."

Dallas entered the kitchen. "My brother's child ain't no burden. Now hush talkin' foolishness. Let's get your stuff upstairs and get you settled in your new home."

Hattie said, "And you take your time getting settled in. Don't you rush nothin'. Let us take care of you for a while."

Natalie said, "I'm surprised Baby Sis didn't come up here with y'all."

"Naw, she said she doesn't even want to be in the same state as Daddy and *that woman*. But you know Mama, she'll be up here before you know it. She ain't gon' be away from Jamie for very long."

Natalie nodded in agreement. "Bern, after you get some rest, I want to introduce you to my best friend, Gwen. We'll show you around the city. You're going to love Detroit. One day soon, I want to take you and Jamie for a boat cruise. You ride up the Detroit River for about an hour on the Bob-Lo boat. While you're on the boat, you can play arcade games, eat a whole bunch of goodies or just sit quietly and watch the beautiful shorelines of Detroit and Canada."

Hattie added, "Then the boat drops you off at Bob-Lo Island. It's a big 'musement park with all kinds of carnival rides, cotton candy, hot dogs on a stick and stuff like that... oh Jamie will love it!"

"Sounds wonderful. I know Jamie will be thrilled."

Hattie added, "Now me, I can't swim that good and the Detroit River is too much water for me to try to drink. But I do like ridin' on the big Ferris wheel and drivin' them bump'a cars though.

Personally, I likes to go to the park we got right here in the city – Edgewater Park. It's just as good as Bob-Lo and you ain't gotta worry 'bout drownin'."

Chapter Twenty-Eight

To appoint unto them that mourn in Zion,
to give unto them beauty for ashes...

Isaiah 61:2-3

Bernadette squealed then quickly clamped her hands over her mouth. Gwen peered over her shoulder at the newspaper she was reading. Without thinking, she also shouted, "I don't believe it!"

Natalie was at the stove preparing a pot of sassafras tea with her back turned to them.

"What don't you believe?"

Gwen tried to turn the page before Natalie could see it. "Nothing."

Natalie snatched the paper from them. "Nothing huh?"

Gwen and Bernadette watched helplessly as sadness crept over Natalie's face. "Oh my God." Natalie slumped onto the nearest chair. "How could he? How *could* he?"

Hattie rushed into the kitchen. "What's all the commotion?"

Natalie handed her the paper. The caption read *Wedding Bells Will Ring on Valentine's Day.* The entire center section of the *Michigan Chronicle's* society page was filled with photographs and captions describing an elaborate engagement party with an A-list of local celebrities and dignitaries in attendance.

The honorees were A. Gregory Baptiste Jr., Pharmacist, and Beverly Elise Ware, daughter of Dr. and Mrs. Stephen H. Ware.

Natalie shed a single tear as she stared at the headshot of Gregory and Beverly.

There was another photo of Beverly flanked by Astor and Albertina. They were each kissing their future daughter-in-law on the cheek. The caption read *Sealed with a Kiss.*

A third picture was of Beverly's 12 bridesmaids, including Gregory's sister Sheila, admiring her engagement ring, described as a three-carat sapphire and diamond ring, the Baptiste family heirloom.

Natalie sobbed. "Mama, he gave her *my* ring."

"No he didn't Sweet Pea. You gave him that ring back when he cut the fool on you. That ring belongs to them people; let 'em have it. Ain't no need of you frettin' yourself about Gregory. He been out of your life for a long time now."

Natalie answered sullenly. "I know you're right Mama, but seeing those pictures and reading about the ring that I used to wear just opens old wounds."

"That's understandable baby. Believe me, one day when you least expect it, the Lord is going to give you beauty for your ashes."

Chapter Twenty-Nine

*Thou shalt not raise a false report: put not thine hand
with the wicked to be an unrighteous witness.*

Exodus 23:1

With its chandelier lighting, signature *Aisles of Beauty* and full service restaurant, J.L. Hudson's department store in the heart of downtown Detroit transformed an otherwise mundane shopping trip into an elegant retail excursion on any given day. However, the holiday decorations added an element of virtual magic.

The 12th floor was converted into a veritable winter wonderland - the highlight of which was a visit to Santa's workshop. Visitors young and old were delighted by robotic elves whose eyes winked and followed you, singing toys, a life-sized replica of a gingerbread house adorned with peppermint candy canes, colorful gum drops, and of course, a big fat Santa with rosy cheeks and a long white beard.

After taking the children to visit Santa, Natalie, Gwen and Bernadette boarded the elevator with the children and mouthed the floors along with the elevator operator as the car descended.

"Eee-leventh floooo-or Hudson's fine furniture; tee-nth floor, ladies' shoes, hats, hosiery and handbags... eighth flooo-or, gentleman's clothing... fourth flooo-or, children's clothing."

Natalie called out. "Fourth floor please." The pecan-colored attendant was clad in a crisp gray uniform, white gloves and shiny black sensible shoes. She cranked wheels, pulled knobs and a handle to bring the elevator car to a halt, opened the gate, then the polished brass doors. "Ladies, please watch your step as you exit the car."

The trio took the children to the Sugar and Spice department where they examined several ensembles for C.J.

Bernadette looked longingly in the direction of the Little Gentleman's department.

"Bern, go over there and pick out a couple of outfits for Jamie. I'll buy them."

Bernadette lowered her eyes and answered softly, "Maybe some other time. Jamie don't need nothing right now."

Natalie looked past Bernadette to Gwen. She understood.

"Well, help me pick some outfits for C.J." Bernadette was drawn to a pink crocheted dress trimmed with pink ribbons and lace with a matching bonnet. She handed it to Natalie for approval.

"That's cute, just what I had in mind." While Bernadette was preoccupied with shopping for C.J., Gwen ventured into the boy's section and purchased four outfits for Jamie. Meanwhile, Natalie noticed that the pink outfit didn't have a price tag.

The only sales clerk in the girl's department was chatting with an elderly Jewish woman. She made eye contact with Natalie, but continued her conversation with the old woman.

She took the ensemble and stood near the store clerk who in turn, screeched at Natalie.

"Please don't handle the merchandise."

"I beg your pardon?"

The sales clerk stringently repeated herself. "I said, please do not handle our merchandise."

Gwen joined the others with Jamie's gifts in hand.

"Suppose she wants to *buy* the merchandise?"

The elderly customer looked at Natalie and said,   "The items here might be a little out of your price range honey. You'd probably make out better at Robert Hall or Federal's. My girl tells me she gets nice things for her children there."

Gwen shouted, "You don't know what she can afford."

Both women were shocked by Gwen's *insolence*.

The clerk snapped at Natalie. "Well, are you going to buy that outfit or not?"

"I haven't decided. How much does it cost?"

The woman answered smugly. "This one costs $11.00. It's hand-made."

Shoot, that's one day's tips alone. Natalie deposited the outfit into the woman's hands and returned to the layettes.

"Hold on to this for me please, I want to look for a few more."

Gwen and Bernadette helped Natalie select four additional ensembles in peach, yellow, mint green and soft lavender, and then strolled to the counter.

The sales clerk lied, "We don't take lay-a-way."

Gwen snapped. "Nobody asked you about no lay-a-way."

The woman ignored them again. "So Mrs. Levinson, how is your sister? Did she ever have the surgery?"

"Oh, yes. And after the surgery, she and Maury sold their house in Oak Park and moved to Boca Raton." The elderly woman continued. "And your motha, is she well?"

Gwen was ready to snatch the clerk by her collar and drag her over to the counter, but Natalie waited patiently - visualizing how adorable C.J. would look in the outfits.

"Mrs. Levinson, it's almost time for my lunch break, would you like to join me?"

"I would love to dearie, but Sol is upstairs buying himself a new hat. I really must run now. Nice tawkin' to ya honey."

"Goodbye Mrs. Levinson, say hello to Dr. Levinson for me please." The older woman waved a liver spotted hand and shuffled toward the gilded doors of the elevator. She looked down at the children. "Cute little monkeys aren't they?"

The irritated clerk interrupted. "Well, are you going to buy any of these?"

"I'm going to buy all of them."

The store clerk's eyebrows formed two arches. "Do you know how much that would cost you?"

Gwen was hot and itching to slap somebody - anybody.

"Just do your job and ring that stuff up so we can get outta here."

A burley floorwalker stood over Gwen's shoulder. "Everything ok here Gertie?"

"I guess so Hank." She winked signifying that the man should stay nearby just in case, as she rang up Natalie's purchase.

Natalie pulled out her wallet and counted out the exact amount.

The clerk examined the currency as if she suspected it to be counterfeit. "Here." She dumped the items into a shopping bag and shoved it at Natalie.

The floorwalker said to the clerk, "Don't you hate it when their kind gets all uppity on you Gert?"

Gwen stopped in her tracks. "Hold up! Did that big greasy buffalo just say what I think he said?"

Bernadette tugged at Gwen's elbow. "Never mind that ignorant fool. I'm hungry. Let's go get something to eat."

Natalie agreed. "Good idea. I could use a good meal right about now."

This time they chose to ride the escalator upstairs to Hudson's restaurant. A line of mostly white shoppers with their little darlings snaked around from the restaurant's entrance well into the hallway.

Natalie said, "Gwen, you hold our places in line while we take the kids to the bathroom."

The line had barely advanced when they returned to their places.   A white woman and her drippy-nosed little boy had gotten in line behind Gwen. She made a fuss when Natalie and Bernadette returned with the children.

"Hey, you can't take cuts like that!"

Natalie started to explain. "We were already in line, but our kids needed to go to the bathroo..."

The woman ignored Natalie and abruptly left her place in line. Natalie saw her talking to a store employee and pointing at them.

The employee seemed to reassure the woman and stepped away briefly.

In the meantime, Natalie and the others continued to slowly inch forward as the line progressed. The children were hungry and grew agitated.

They were nearly at the front of the line when a man dressed in a gray flannel suit and wearing some sort of badge pushed his way through the crowd with the alleged line-jumping victim following closely behind him.

The woman pointed at them. "There they are." All eyes were on Natalie's entourage. Gwen sighed. Natalie and Bernadette hoped this wouldn't send Gwen into another one of her tirades.

The woman smirked at Gwen and said to the man. "They just marched right in front of us like me and my little boy weren't even standing here. I had just taken my baby to see Sanny Clause."

The man folded his arms across his chest and listened.

Natalie tried again to explain. "That isn't the way it happened sir..."

"Girl, are you calling this lady a liar?"

Gwen answered, "She's nothing but a liar!"

The man glared at them. "That does it! He pointed at Natalie's party. "You girls get out of line and leave this store before I call the cops." The other patrons watched as Natalie and Bernadette moved out of the line. He turned to the woman. "Ma'am I apologize on behalf of J.L. Hudson's. Please try to enjoy the rest of your day." He went inside the restaurant and returned with a small card embossed with the J.L. Hudson logo.

He handed the card to the woman. "Ma'am, please accept this as a token of our sincere regret for the inconvenience you endured." He tousled the boy's blond locks. "This entitles you and this fine young man to have your meal free today – order anything on the menu."

Gwen remained in place. "Oh, you just gon' take *her* word and not listen to *our* side of the story?"

The man spoke through his teeth. "Listen, I've had about enough of your smart mouth. Now you get out of this line and out of this store!"

Gwen positioned herself for a showdown. Instead of stepping out of line, she widened her stance and planted her feet firmly in place. Natalie simply didn't have the energy for a civil rights showdown.

Bernadette pulled on Gwen's coat sleeve. "Come on, we got the kids with us. Let's just go across the street to Woolworth's."

Gwen reluctantly conceded and followed them out of the restaurant. As they walked toward the bank of elevators, they heard cheers and applause.

Chapter Thirty

For unto us a child is born, unto us a son is given.

Isaiah 9:6

oodward Avenue was bustling with holiday activity. A popcorn vendor was posted on the corner in front of Hudson's. The aroma of fresh popcorn and roasted chestnuts permeated the air. The steam from the chestnut roaster warmed shoppers waiting to cross the street.

Husbands and wives huddled together at the crossing light to keep warm. Playful children tugged and swatted at each other. Strangers cheerfully greeted each other, "Merry Christmas." "Happy Holidays."

The street was gray and slushy. Natalie picked Christian Joy up and then cautiously stepped down off the curb. A faceless uniformed soldier gently took her by the elbow to steady her as she waded through the slushy street. She thanked the man and carefully entered the store. She and Gwen stomped the snow from their boots.

Gwen stomped harder than she needed to. She was still seething about the fiasco at Hudson's.

Jamie and Bernadette were shivering as they made their way to the counter. "I don't know if I'll ever get used to these Michigan winters."

Gwen plunked the packages that Bernadette still had not noticed on the seat next to her. Natalie pulled C.J.'s hood off, releasing a cascade of auburn curls.

A gum-cracking waitress brought menus. "What a cute kid. How old is she?"

"She's three."

"Aww, they're so cute at that age, ain't they? I bet her daddy is crazy about her."

Bernadette interrupted. "Can I see a menu please?"

Gwen had already decided on a toasted tuna salad sandwich, with French fries and a Coca-Cola. Bernadette ordered the same.

The waitress asked Natalie, "You ready to order?"

"Not yet, give me a couple of minutes ok?"

Gwen huffed. "Why do we have to go through this every time we're at a restaurant? You *know* you gon' order the same thing you always order."

"Hush Gwen, one day I'm going to surprise you and order something different."

"Well I'm hungry. Could you please make a decision – today?"

Bernadette looked apologetically at the waitress as they observed the two friends playfully arguing.

"Take all the time you need, I ain't going nowhere 'til five."

Gwen covered her face with her hands. "Oh God, please don't encourage her!"

After studying the menu for several minutes longer, Natalie ordered a cheeseburger with the works, hold the mayo, extra pickles, grilled onions, fries and a root beer float – her usual.

Gwen looked at Bernadette. "What did I tell you?"

Natalie stuck her tongue out at Gwen. "So what."

Every seat at the counter was full with the exception of the seat that held Gwen and Natalie's packages. The uniformed soldier approached Gwen and politely asked if the seat was taken. "Obviously it is, don't you see we've got our bags there? What would you like me to do, put them on the wet floor?"

Bernadette was embarrassed by Gwen's rudeness. She scowled at Gwen. "We can move the bags. Look, the couple sitting in that booth is about to leave. We can scoot over there." She motioned for the waitress. "Excuse me Miss, we'd like to move over to that booth please."

"Sure thing. I'll get it cleaned off for you in just a couple of minutes."

The man smiled at C.J. and Jamie.

"Cute kids. How old are they?"

Bernadette answered. "They're both three."

"Oh. Are they twins?"

Gwen blew hot air. "Do they *look* like twins to you?"

The soldier shrugged. "You never know. There is such a thing as fraternal twins."

"Hey little man. Gimme some skin." He extended his palm for Jamie to slap, but the boy shyly turned away.

Bernadette forced an embarrassed smile. "I taught him not to talk to strangers."

Gwen said, "Grown folks should learn to do that as well."

The waitress announced, "Ladies your booth is ready. Will the gentleman be joining you?"

Gwen answered quickly. "No"

"Nonsense. The gentleman is welcome to join us if he wants to." Natalie smiled.

The man answered. "I'd be honored if the ladies don't mind."

Natalie shot a look at Gwen – daring her to challenge her.

"Please excuse my friend. She's tired from shopping all day. Isn't that right Gwen?"

"If you say so." After nursing Natalie back from sanity's edge, Gwen had become very protective of Natalie. She whispered, "I have two words for you. Gregory Baptiste."

Natalie ignored her.

When everyone was done with their meals, Bernadette convinced Gwen to go with her to put Jamie on the mechanical rocket ship and let C.J. ride on the penny pony.

Natalie chatted with her new acquaintance and learned that Sergeant Curtis Harris, Jr. had recently returned from a two year post-war tour of duty in Korea. In a few weeks, he would receive an honorable discharge and planned to return to his hometown of Youngstown, Ohio. Curtis said he had a job waiting for him with a freight trucking company.

He told her that he would be in town until Monday afternoon and was looking for something to do and someone nice to spend time with in Detroit.

Natalie invited him to visit her church the next day. *How much harm could be done in the house of the Lord?* She gave him directions to the Little Rose of Sharon and the two agreed to meet there.

Chapter Thirty-One

I was glad when they said unto me,
let us go into the house of the LORD.

Psalm 122:1

Natalie was dutifully on her post ushering as Curtis' gleaming smile caught her eye when he entered the sanctuary. With a tattered Bible tucked under his arm, he was neatly packaged in his army dress uniform. Heads turned when Natalie proudly escorted him to the visitors' seating in the front pew.

A young girl entered the pulpit to address the congregation. The little girl's Dixie Peach pressed hair was slicked back into a curly ponytail with bangs. She wore a powder blue and white pinafore dress with a fluffy bow tied in the back. Legs glistening from Vaseline suspended from underneath the dress and down into lace-trimmed anklets in black patent leather shoes. Her face and arms glistened too. The little girl ruffled a sheet of loose-leaf paper then read an invitation for visitors to sit back, relax and make themselves at home.

"And be assured that after today, you will never again be a stranger at the Little Rose of Sharon Church. At this time, the Golden Jubilee choir will render an A and a B selection. Following that, the next voice heard will be that of our beloved pastor, Reverend C.W. Healy, Sr."

The young announcer curtsied then exited the pulpit. The choir led the congregation in praise with two melodious selections. Afterward, Pastor Healy flashed a warm smile at the congregation as he took his place behind the podium.

"Can we say praise the Lord for the choir?" He turned and faced the choir stand. "Y'all did good children. We also thank the Lord for our new assistant choir director, my son Timothy.

And we certainly can't forget our little announcer, my baby girl, little Miss Cathy Healy. First Lady and I are very proud to have all of our children working in the Lord's vineyard with us."

The pastor then looked over his left shoulder at his twenty-something-year-old son and namesake, who was seated next to the pastor's chair in the pulpit. "Someday, if the Lord says the same, Cedric Junior back there will pastor this church." The son proudly beamed back at his father.

"The word of God tells us to train up a child in the way he should go and when he is old, he shall not depart. Some folks think children ought to be seen and not heard in the church." He paused and scanned the congregation.

"I know none of y'all think like that."

Someone from the audience yelled. "No sir, that ain't right." "Well, 'nuff about all that for now. Saints, I don't want to take up much of your time today, but the Lord has sent us a message - as the prophet Jeremiah said... it's like fire shut up in my bones."

"Take yo time and preach Rev'en."

"Turn with me in your Bibles to Joshua 24:15. If you see someone who don't have a Bible, tell 'em shame on you."

A few shame on you's could be heard throughout the room, mostly from the section where the teenagers congregated. "Now share your Bible with them."

The preacher repeated the verse. "When you have it, say Amen." The head usher signaled the others to be seated. Sister Marcie Pope noted that a male usher placed a folding chair next to Curtis for Natalie.

Pastor Healy took little time to reach the pinnacle of the message that was burning in his spirit. He preached fervently about the need to choose holiness or hell.

"It ain't good e-nuff just to give the preacher your right hand in fellowship. It just ain't e-nuff. *Hah* to believe in your heart. *Hah* and confess with your mouth. *Hah* that Jesus Christ is Lord."

He pounded the pulpit desk and stomped with every whoop for emphasis. "The demons in hell believe and confess. *Hah.* You got to live holy! *Hah!* You cain't just talk the talk. *Hah!* You got to walk the walk. *Hah!* The straight and narrow way! *Hah!* Each and every day. *Hah!*"

Pastor Healy's nurse mopped perspiration from his forehead. His evangelical robe was drenched. Huge veins in his neck bulged. He preached as if this sermon would be the last before judgment day. The anointing of the Holy Ghost moved upon the church like a powerful tidal wave. Choruses of Amen sprang up from all over the room. Refrains of "Hallelujah," "Thank You Jesus" and "Glory to God" reverberated from one end of the church to the other.

The organist began to play in sync with Pastor Healy's sermon. A woman jumped up from her seat and began leaping. The drummer joined in and sped up the tempo. The choir stood on its collective feet and began clapping, shouting and passing tambourines. Hattie turned a rub board and a spoon into percussion instruments that declared God's awesome splendor.

Curtis rose from his seat with his arms stretched toward heaven, surrendering to God. Tears welled in the rims of his eyes. "Glory to God! Take me back Lord. Sweet Jesus, take me back."

Pastor Healy's message had penetrated his heart. Natalie's soul sang. Deacons leaped from their posts and danced in the spirit. Worshippers raised holy hands, rolled on the floor and praised God in heavenly languages.

Spry church Mothers waved their canes and forsook their walkers.

Others remained seated and rocked violently - shouting praise instructions to the able-bodied. "Go 'head, go 'head, praise 'im. Let Him bless ya. Let Him in."

Women held their hats and whirled in circles. The forgiving wooden floor creaked and shook under the weight of the worshippers. The sisters in the kitchen down below could hear Pastor Healy's powerful message through the aged floorboards.

Mother Wright turned the flame under the chicken she was frying down low and joined the others in a praise dance.

Sister Doss stopped stirring the potato salad, threw her spoon in the air and took off running into the dining hall.

The Holy Spirit tenderly rested upon the congregation as Pastor Healy led the transition of animated praise into gentle worship.

"Ummmm, Lord you are worthy... yes, yes, yes! Do the best you can children, yes Jesus is worthy... I dare not dismiss this great service without calling sinners to be saved and backsliders to be restored." He stretched out his arms. "Meet me here at the altar to be saved."

Members of the choir collected themselves and began to hum softly as Pastor Healy pleaded for sinners and backsliders to surrender their souls to Jesus.

The choir director mouthed the words *"Don't let it be said, too late, too late to enter that golden gate..."* One by one, souls seeking salvation and restoration made their way to the altar. Curtis was among them.

Pastor Healy declared, "Heaven is rejoicing over these souls."

Altar workers waited patiently with beckoning arms extended.

Pastor Healy asked one final time. "Is there another?"

After dismissal, Natalie introduced Sergeant Curtis Harris to Pastor Healy. "Fine message you preached today Reverend, set my soul on fire."

"Well brother you welcome to come here anytime, don't let yourself be a stranger ya hear?"

"No sir, I don't intend to be no stranger." He locked his arm into Natalie's and looked at her. "I intend to be spending a lot of time here if it's alright with this young lady."

Natalie's response was an ear-to-ear grin.

Chapter Thirty-Two

How beautiful you are, my darling! Oh, how beautiful!
Your eyes are doves.

Song of Solomon 1:15

During his next visit to the Little Rose of Sharon, Curtis was baptized in Jesus' name. Hattie and Mother Winston accompanied him to the tarrying room as he sought the in-filling of the Holy Ghost.

Natalie paced and prayed outside the tarrying room. The altar workers spread newspapers on the floor beneath the bench to catch saliva and foam that was sometimes discharged by candidates seeking the Holy Ghost. Mother Winston said that was called "purging."

Hattie and Mother Winston knelt beside Curtis and coached him. "Just open your mouth and praise Him son. Let Him in."

Hattie echoed Mother Winston's instructions. They clapped their hands and called upon the Lord to fill him with His spirit. Curtis' heart was ripe to receive God's blessings. Before long, he and the altar workers were praising the Lord in a language driven by the Holy Spirit. This was evidence that he had indeed received the precious gift of the Holy Ghost as described in Acts 2:38.

When Curtis emerged from the tarrying room, the Lord revealed to Natalie that he was the man she would marry.

First thing Monday morning, Curtis called his mother to tell her that he had gotten saved - and about the special lady he had met.

"Hallelujah! Thank you Jesus! My prayers finally been answered! Bring that young lady here so I can meet her. I got a good feeling about her. I had a dream 'bout a week or two back - no it was more like a vision because I was wide 'woke. Curt I saw you plain as day standin' at the altar in a church all dressed up. Your bride was standing next to you. Y'all was just smiling and everything was so beautiful…"

"Mama, ok, but I'm not sure about us getting married yet. That's why I wanted you to meet her. I've only been seeing Natalie for a few months, but I really think I want to marry her. First she's got to pass your inspection though."

"Well son, sounds to me like you already done made up your mind. Curtis, if you love her then so do I sweetheart.

Now when you gon' bring my future daughter-in-law here and make me 'quainted with her?"

"I was thinking of bringing her with me when I come to see you on your birthday. There's one ahh, catch. Something you should know about Natalie Mama. I want everything out in the open right from the start."

"Alright son, I'm listening."

"See Mama, Natalie has a child and she ain't never been married."

Mamie was silent.

"Mama, you still there?"

"Yeah son I'm still here. I'm waiting for you to tell me about the catch. So far all you told me is that I'm gon' be an instant granny. Is it a girl or a boy?"

"A gorgeous little girl."

Mamie clapped her hands. "Ooo-wee I finally got me a little girl. Are you bringing the baby too?"

Curtis exhaled a sigh of relief. "I don't know if Natalie will want to bring her yet, but you'll get to meet her soon."

"How old is the baby Curt?"

"She's three years old."

"What's her name?"

"Mama you won't believe it. Her name is Christian Joy. We call her C.J. most of the time. Natalie says she was born with a veil over her face, whatever that means."

"What you say! Born with a veil over her face! Christian Joy! That's a blessed child. Curt you hurry up and get her here to me!"

Curtis proudly continued to babble about C.J.

"Curt you sound like a proud papa already."

"I want to be Mama. If Natalie says yes to my proposal, I'm going to ask her if I can adopt C.J. too."

"Now hold on Curt, what about her *real* daddy?"

"He don't want nothin' to do with her – or Natalie. He ain't never even laid his sorry eyes on her."

"That's a cryin' shame. Well, it's his loss son."

"That's right. His loss and my gain. I can't wait for you to meet them Mama."

Mamie looked at the clock and saw that they needed to wrap the conversation up. "Me neither honey, give Natalie my love and kiss that baby for me too. Now Curt, Mama got to get off this phone so I can go watch the Secret Storm. We done already talked clean through the Edge of Night. Bye-bye sweetie."

Curtis sighed. "As long as I live, I'll never understand why you're so stuck on those corny soap operas. I love you Mama, see you soon."

Chapter Thirty-Three

*Is any one of you sick? He should call the elders of the church to pray
over him and anoint him with oil in the name of the Lord.*

James 5:14

Jamie was feverish and had been coughing all day.
Bernadette tore a brown paper bag into large pieces
and bathed him with tepid wintergreen alcohol water.
Then she rubbed his chest with goose grease and wrapped him in
flannel. She spoon fed him a concoction of lemon, rock candy
and whisky. Afterward, she got him settled into bed, then rocked
him in her arms until the two of them fell into an exhausted
slumber.

The morning's light hadn't brought any improvement to
Jamie's condition. Bernadette phoned Natalie, who in turn
dialed Robinson's Children's Clinic, but there was no answer.

"I'm coming right over Bern. Wrap him up and be ready to
jump in the car. Dr. Robinson will squeeze him in once we get
there."

They arrived at the clinic at exactly 9:30. The front desk was
deserted, but the waiting room was already filled with impatient
mothers and agitated children.

Bernadette found a handwritten sign taped next to a pad of
lined paper that greeted visitors: PLEASE SIGN IN - THE
DOCTOR WILL BE WITH YOU SOON. She thought, *He can't
be much of a doctor if he don't even have a secretary.* She wasn't
impressed with the clinic's décor either.

The walls were a pasty beige color. The room was littered with old magazines and tattered children's books.

A huge aquarium with more algae than fish stretched across the wall facing the entrance.

Jamie pointed at the aquarium. "Pish!"

"Right, that's a fish tank. Look Jamie, that's an angel fish, can you say angel fish?"

"Anga Pish" the boy repeated.

Bernadette continued the aquatic name game until Jamie got bored. It had been almost an hour when she finally heard Jamie's name called.

She was pleasantly surprised to learn that Dr. William Robinson was a handsome Negro doctor who looked to be just a few years her senior. She was mesmerized by his good looks. She quickly surveyed his hands; of course, no calluses and to her delight - no wedding ring!

"Hello, I'm Dr. Robinson. I apologize for the long wait. Monday is always my busiest day. Kids come in with a lot of cuts and bruises from weekend rough housing. What brings this little man in today?"

Bernadette absently released their handshake as she began to describe Jamie's malady.

"Well Jamie, let's see what's making you feel so bad."

He lifted Jamie up high in the air then zoom-landed him on the examination table. Then he gently tilted the boy's head back and instructed him to lift his tongue as he slid a thermometer under it. He frowned "Hmm, 103." He took out his stethoscope and held it in front of Jamie.

"I'm going to put this right here so I can listen to you breathe. Ok Jamie?"

"Ok." Jamie cooperated while Dr. Robinson listened to his chest and heart, looked in his nose, and even when he stuck the tongue depressor in his mouth and made him say "Ahh." But when he tried to look into his ears, Jamie let out a high-pitched wail!

"Oh oh, Mommy, you're going to have to hold him down. I have to look into his ears."

Both Jamie's ears were inflamed.   "It looks like he has an ear infection. Ok Jamie, it's all over. I think I have something that will make you feel better."

He reached for a tubular glass jar full of lollipops. "Here, choose one." Jamie plunged his miniature hand deep into the jar and plucked out a lemon-flavored one.

"Lello!"

"That's right honey, yellow."

Dr. Robinson turned to the table and began scratching some writing on a pad of paper. Then he wrote something on another pad of paper and tore off the three sheets he had written on.

"Here are some prescriptions for him. The last one is for nose drops; you don't need a prescription for the drops - this is just a reminder. He should start feeling better within the next couple of days. If it seems he's getting worse, bring him to me right away. How about his shots, is he up to date with his immunizations?"

"Well, I never let anybody give him no shots, he's just a baby and he don't understand. I was going to get all his shots when he got old enough to go to school."

"Mrs. Mitchell, you must understand that vaccinations are very important. Now Jamie is already behind. I strongly urge you to get him started as soon as his ear infection clears up."

"Alright Dr. Robinson. I'll get him started when he gets better."

"Great." He walked out to the waiting room with them.

"Now, little man, I think you better get your mother home and let her take a nap, she looks a little sleepy." He winked at Bernadette.

"Yeah, I am getting sleepy Jamie, let's go home now. Tell Dr. Robinson bye."

"Bye-bye Dat-tah Rob-a-son."

As he scanned the crowded waiting room, Dr. Robinson apologetically explained the chaos to Bernadette.

"My wife runs the office but she hasn't been feeling well lately – morning sickness. I guess I'm going to have to find someone to fill her position, she won't be coming back to work – we're expecting our first child in a few months."

Bernadette managed to hide her disappointment.

"Oh, your wife is having a baby? How nice." She almost choked on her words as her heart sank. "Thanks for everything Dr. Robinson; I hope you find a replacement for your wife soon. I mean, to fill in here at the office."

The handsome doctor chuckled at Bernadette's faux pas. "Yes, it had better be soon or I might lose all of my patients."

Natalie stayed in the car with Jamie while Bernadette went inside the Motor City Pharmacy to pick up Jamie's prescriptions. As the attractive auburn-haired man filled Jamie's prescriptions, a thought struck Bernadette like a bolt of lightning. *Dummy! Why didn't I offer to take the job at the clinic?*

When she returned to the car, she shared her idea with Natalie.

"Dr. Robinson needs a secretary and I need a job! I don't know why I didn't think to talk to him about it while I was there."

Kelly Girls had trained her to do office work. She could type 55 wpm, take Gregg shorthand at 120 wpm, operate an address-o-graph, a ten-key adding machine, and answer a switchboard. She was sure she could do the job at the clinic. She decided to check back with him in a few days.

Natalie later told her, "I've been thinking about what you said about that job at the clinic. Here's what you do honey. You give the good doctor a call first thing in the morning and tell him all about your qualifications. He'll probably ask you to start right away."

"That's a good idea. If Jamie feels better tomorrow, I'll ask Gwen if I can come over and use her typewriter. I want to have a resume ready when I apply for the job. They taught us that at Kelly Girls."

Natalie pulled in front of Bernadette's apartment. "A resume will make a really good impression."

"I have to stand out. I really need this job."

Natalie turned off the car's engine. "Something's going to break for you soon Bern. With all you and Jamie have been through, you deserve it. You want me to help you get Jamie settled in? I still have a little time before I have to get back home."

"No, girl. You better get on back home to C.J. Me and Jamie can handle things from here. I'm so glad you introduced me to Dr. Robinson. Jamie really likes him too." She leaned over and kissed her cousin's cheek. "Thanks for everything girl. Now you get on outta here."

As she approached her first floor apartment, Bernadette saw a note tacked to the door. *Oh shoot! I bet that's from Mr. Russell.* She snatched the note down. Sure enough, her landlord had placed a past due notice in plain view. MRS. MITCHELL, YOUR RENT IS 45 DAYS PAST DUE. BRING THIS UP TO DATE BY THE END OF THE WEEK OR YOU WILL BE EVICTED. She mumbled to the sleeping three-year-old on her shoulder. "Jamie baby, it looks like Mommy had better get in touch with Dr. Robinson right away."

Chapter Thirty-Four

*Thou wilt keep him in perfect peace, whose mind is stayed on thee:
because he trusteth in thee.*

Isaiah 26:3

Natalie nervously drummed her fingers along the open window of the truck during the ride to Curtis' childhood home. Silently, she practiced what she would say when she met Mrs. Harris. She hoped the long ride wouldn't make C.J. fussy.

Curtis sensed her anxiety. "You don't have to worry about meeting my mother sweetie, she already loves you. She just wants to love you and our little angel in person."

Natalie tilted her head.

"*Our* little angel?"

"Am I moving too fast?"

"I think I could get used to sharing her with you – under the right circumstances."

"Really? And what would those circumstances be?"

"Never mind."

He pulled her hand to his lips and kissed it lightly.

"Guess what else?"

"What?"

"I have a little surprise for you when we get there."

"A surprise? What is it?"

"If I tell you it won't be a surprise, now will it?"

"Well then why did you say anything about it at all? You're a tease, you know that Curtis?"

"Yeah, I know it and you love me for it don't you?"

Natalie stuck her tongue out at him and he pretended to try to grab for it. The truck swerved a bit.

"You'd better keep your eyes on the road and quit worrying 'bout my tongue."

She stuck her tongue out at him again.

"You keep fooling with me and I will pull this rig over."

"I dare you."

"Oh, now you did it. I don't take no dares from nobody."

"Yeah, well I dare you. Now what you gon' do?"

Curtis began clutching and shifting gears to slow the truck down then commandeered the vehicle to the shoulder of the road.

C.J. was asleep on Natalie's lap. "You are a nut Curtis Harris."

"I'll show you who's a nut, now bring your little sassy self over here to me." He motioned for her to lean over to kiss him.

"Curtis, we're in the middle of the highway. What if somebody passes by and sees us?"

"Then that's just what they need to do – see us and pass on by.   Now come here woman."

She eased C.J. off her lap and slid as close to Curtis as the truck's interior would allow. He pecked Natalie's lips lightly, then the kiss became intense and passionate. The thought of possibly getting caught was exhilarating to both of them. Curtis knew his surprise wouldn't come a moment too soon.

Natalie pulled away, sliding C.J. back onto her lap. "Ok Mr. Harris, we'd better quit while we're ahead." She scooted back over to her side of the truck.

"You're right. We'd better get back on the road. We've got about an hour to go. We'll be at my mama's house in no time."

Natalie laid her head against the seat and slowly closed her eyes.

"I love you Curtis Harris."

"I love you too Natalie Jordan."

Three hundred of the Baptiste and Ware's closest friends cooed as C.J. tossed yellow rose petals onto the aisle runner. A broad smile stretched across Albertina's fuchsia painted lips when the organist began to play the Wedding March, signaling that the bride was about to enter the cathedral. She breathed a sigh of relief when Beverly reached the altar and joined hands with Gregory.

Natalie was the only one who heard Albertina's voice as the priest administered the wedding vows. "Perfect, now everything is perfect."

Little C.J. broke the wedding formation and began to pull at the tail of Gregory's tuxedo coat. "Daddy, Daddy!" Gregory ignored the child and continued to stare into Beverly's hazel eyes. C.J. tugged Gregory's coat tail harder.

Finally, Albertina bolted from her seat and snatched the child by the arm, dragging her away from the altar. C.J. wailed until Albertina pulled a handkerchief from her purse and stuffed it into her mouth, ordering the child to sit beside her in the pew. "Sit here and behave you little brat."

From the back of the cathedral, Natalie was frozen with horror, unable to move or speak. Astor Baptiste sucked his teeth and watched when Albertina pinched the child for squirming in her seat. She was relieved that the wedding guests ignored the child as they focused on the ceremony. Natalie desperately wanted to rescue her child but she was paralyzed by an evil force. She opened her mouth to cry out. Finally, the scream that was trapped in her throat escaped. "Stop that! Take your hands off my baby!"

Beverly turned to Gregory, her eyes pleaded with him to do something. He angrily ran to the back of the cathedral toward Natalie and grabbed her throat, the way he had done on her parents' porch that night. A crowd of her parents' neighbors gathered and watched.

Hattie burst through the crowd waving a butcher's knife and Dallas brandished his shotgun. Natalie watched helplessly as two police officers led her parents away in handcuffs.

Astor read a newspaper while Albertina, who now joined the growing crowd of spectators, laughed and blew rings of smoke.

Well-wishers threw rice as the gleeful newlyweds skipped down the cathedral stairs.

Dressed in a chauffeur's uniform, Thomas stood by waiting to whisk the newlyweds away. The cobalt blue limousine was decorated with yellow and white puffs of tissue and a "Just Married" sign.

Chapter Thirty-Five

Whoso findeth a wife findeth a good thing,
and obtaineth favour of the Lord.

Proverbs 18:22

The brakes from Curtis' truck noisily blasted air as he pulled to a stop in front of his mother's house. He gently stroked Natalie's grimaced face. "Natalie, sweetheart, we're here." She awakened from the horrible dream and looked over at C.J. Curtis told her, "She just fell asleep about fifteen minutes ago. She's been keeping me company - not like *some people* I know."

"Sorry about that. I guess I didn't realize how tired I was."

"Aw, don't take me so seriously, I was just teasing you baby. Come on, let's go meet my mother."

Before they could exit the truck, Mamie Harris emerged from the house wearing slippers and a frilly apron over the clothes she had worn to morning worship service. Her dentured smile stretched across her whole face.

"Well, my Lord looka here! Curtis hurry up and get in here so I can visit with my soon-to-be daughter-in-law."

"Mama!" Curtis gave his mother a harsh look. Mamie clamped her hand over her mouth then reached out to hug Natalie and C.J.

She mocked Curtis. "Is it alright if I hug 'em?"

"Mama, would you behave?" Mamie gave Natalie another squeeze and played with C.J.'s rust-colored braids.

"Girl, don't pay me no mind. I'm just messing with my son."

She grinned at C.J. "Oh, what a precious little baby doll."

Natalie answered timidly. "Thank you. It's very nice to meet you Mrs. Harris."

Mamie winked at Curtis and he winked back. Natalie pretended not to notice the exchange as she followed Mamie onto the front porch. "Y'all come on in and rest yourselves some."

Once inside, Curtis and his mother stood in the living room whispering, hugging and grinning at each other with suspicious-looking expressions on their faces. Natalie sensed some sort of conspiracy.

"Mama, let's sit down in the living room. I want to give you your gift right away." He handed her his customary gift - a heart-shaped box of assorted chocolates.

"Happy Birthday Mama. Now don't try to eat these all at once. Remember your sugar."

"Hush, Curt. Whatcha give 'em to me for if you don't want me to eat 'em?" Mamie opened the box immediately and plucked out a cluster of chocolate covered cashews. "Yummy, my favorite!"

"I have a little present for you too Mrs. Harris. Just a little token. Happy Birthday."

"Oh y'all spoilin' me. I could get used to this."
Natalie presented Mamie with a small flat gift box and an even smaller one tied to it with a shiny red ribbon.

Mamie perched herself on the edge of the sofa and carefully untied Natalie's homemade bow. The smaller box contained a heart-shaped brooch. The larger box housed two white handkerchiefs trimmed with lace and another one that was printed with yellow and purple pansies.

"Oh, these are simply gorgeous. Thank you sweetheart. I am truly a blessed woman on my 67th birthday." She took the handkerchiefs to her bedroom and put them in her dresser drawer.

"Y'all must be tired from the long ride. What time did you leave De-troit?"

"The ride from Detroit to Youngstown isn't that long Mama. We left right after Sunday School, around 11 o'clock this morning."

"Ooo and here it is not quite 2:30 yet. You made good time. Curt, you must have had your foot in that gas tank the whole time. You better be careful speeding up and down the road. Johnny Nab'll get you. You know these po-leeses here in Ohio don't play no games."

"I wasn't speeding up and down the road Mama."

"Not much." Natalie added.

Mamie chuckled. "Soon as the rolls brown, we can eat."

"Well, let's cool our heels for a few minutes. Ok mama?"

"That's fine with me. Y'all get comfortable."

"Yes Ma'am, as a matter of fact, I would like to freshen up a bit. C.J. looks like she could use a quick nap before we eat. Is there some place I can lay her?"

"Wait, let me get something to put under her then you can lay her down on the sofa." Mamie disappeared then quickly reappeared with a floral printed sheet and a pillow.

"I just love these new no-iron sheets, don't you Natalie?"

"I know what you mean. How did we ever get along without them?"

Curtis helped his mother spread the sheet over the plastic covered couch then took C.J. out of Natalie's arms and gently laid her down.

"Look at him, don't he act just like a daddy?"

"Mamaaa!" Curtis pleaded.

Natalie blushed. "I need to go to the little girls' room, which direction is it in?"

Mamie pointed, "Go down this hallway. It's the second door on the right. Ok darlin' me and Curt'll be out on the sun porch when you get back. The baby will be fine." Curtis gave his mother a light pinch as he held the door open for her.

He whispered, "Mama, you 'bout to blow my surprise with all that daughter-in-law and daddy talk!"

"I'm sorry baby, you know your mama can't hold water when I'm excited. I'll try to keep quiet. Now when you gon' pop the big question?"

He pulled a tiny velvet-covered box from his pocket and handed it to Mamie. She took the ring out of the box and placed it on her pinkie. "Good job Curt! This is a beautiful ring, I know she'll love it."

"Hold on to it for me until later Mama. I was planning on asking her after dinner. I wanted you and her to spend some time together first so I can be absolutely sure y'all would hit it off."

Mamie reached for another bon bon. "I'll take care of the ring Curtis, but I already done told you, I appreciate you wanting to get my approval, but you done already made up your mind you gone marry. Now it's between you and the Lord. And once you say those wedding vows, the Bible says a man should leave his father and his mother, and cleave to his wife. That's what Mama wants you to do. Now Curtis, the question is do you love Natalie with all your heart?"

"Yes Ma'am. With all of my heart."

"And did you ask the Lord if she's the one?"

"Yes Ma'am."

"What did He say?"

"He said she's the one Mama."

"You sure?"

"Yes Mama, I'm sure."

"Alright then. It's settled. Now when you feel the time is right, you go on and ask that girl to be your wife and marry her. And don't be draggin' it out with no long engagement."

"Ok Mama. But first we gotta see if she accepts my proposal."

"Oh, she'll accept."

Chapter Thirty-Six

Behold, how good and how pleasant [it is]
for brethren to dwell together in unity!

Psalm 133:1

The walls in the house where Curtis grew up were littered with photographs. There were several pictures of Mrs. Harris and a handsome brown-skinned man who looked a lot like Curtis, except he had a mustache. Natalie scanned the walls and mantle over the fireplace. Right in the center was a sepia toned wedding photograph of Curtis' parents in a freshly polished silver frame.

A younger, much slimmer Mamie Harris was linked arm in arm with Curtis Harris, Sr. The photographer had arranged Mamie's long train to swirl around in front of her. She held a bouquet of lilies. Curtis' dad sported a military dress blue uniform.

Natalie studied the contents of a curio cabinet filled with Lieutenant Harris' military memorabilia. A United States flag folded into the shape of a triangle, along with an encased Purple Heart medal and a framed letter signed by President Franklin D. Roosevelt was placed on the top shelf.

Curtis called inside. "Natalie, you ok?"

"Shhh. You'll wake C.J. I'm on my way out."

Natalie joined Curtis and Mamie on the sun porch. Curtis slid over to make room for her on the porch swing.

"Mrs. Harris you have a very nice home. I was admiring all the pictures. Curtis you were a cute little boy – except for those ears."

"Oh, I know you not talking miss-thumb-in-your-mouth-til-you-turned-twenty." She poked him in the side and he tickled her. Mamie enjoyed watching their playful banter.

C.J. toddled up to the screen door rubbing her eyes, "I want you Mommy."

Mamie reached for the doorknob. "That's my cue. I'll have the food on the table in a jiffy."

"I thought she'd sleep at least another half hour." Natalie reached for C.J.'s hand. "I need to get this little one washed up. Then I can help you Mrs. Harris."

Mamie shoo'ed Natalie. "No need, I got it all under control."

She was adding a crystal water pitcher to the elaborate table setting when Natalie and C.J. joined them.

"Sit here babe." Curtis stacked two telephone books in a chair for C.J. then pulled out seats for Natalie and his mother.

"Mama, you sit next to me ok?"

Mamie had pulled out all the stops. She was delighted to have an opportunity to use her Wedgewood China, Irish linen tablecloth and matching napkins, her crystal drinking glasses and pitcher; and her sterling silverware. The table was elegant, but the food was deliciously down home.

Mamie served smothered chicken, candied yams, fried corn, collard greens, rolls and spicy Chow Chow to complement the greens.

Natalie inhaled. "Everything smells delicious Mrs. Harris – and your table is beautiful!"

Curtis boasted. "Believe me it tastes even better than it smells."

"Aw Curt, you should quit, I'll get the big head with all that talk."

"Mrs. Harris, I don't know where to begin. There isn't anything here that I don't like."

"Let's quit talking and start eating, I'll bless the food Mama."

Natalie and Mamie chatted pleasantly through dinner. Curtis' face was practically buried in his plate while the ladies talked.

"Y'all save room for dessert. I got a peach cobbler and some homemade vanilla ice cream."

Natalie groaned. "After the meal I just ate, I don't think I have room for dessert." She jabbed her stomach pretending to look for empty spaces.

"Well, if I have to poke a hole somewhere, I'm gonna make room. I ain't missing Mama's ice cream and peach cobbler for nothing."

"Maybe you can eat some a little later Natalie, after your dinner goes down."

"Don't count on it Mama. She eats like a bird."

"Well I ate like a vulture today. Mrs. Harris everything was delicious."

"Yeah Mama, you put your foot in them greens."

"Y'all can take some home. I cooked plenty."

"Mama you cooked enough for the whole block."

"I wanted to make sho' y'all had enough so you could take some home."

"No, really I couldn't."

"You ain't gotta beg me Mama. Load up them Tuppa-ware dishes."

"Well, I guess I could take home some of that peach cobbler."

"Too bad they don't make Tuppa-ware that'll keep ice cream from here to Detroit. Natalie, you gotta get some of Mama's ice cream before we leave. You ain't had no ice cream 'til you taste Mamie Harris' ice cream."

"Ok, you convinced me. I'll make sure to get some before we head back home. Now Mrs. Harris, if you could loan me one of your aprons, I'll help you get the table cleared and clean up the kitchen."

"Oh no you don't. You and Curt take y'all's hips out to that sun porch and court for a while. Me and C.J. will take care of the dishes. You wanna help Granny clean up baby?"

C.J. nodded.

"Good, then when we're through cleanin' up, Granny Mamie has a surprise for you." Mamie retrieved a bottle of soap bubbles from the kitchen cabinet. "After we clean up, we going out back and blow the biggest bubbles anybody ever did see. Ain't that right baby?"

C.J. jumped up and down, clapping her little hands. "Yeaaa!"

Chapter Thirty-Seven

Let him kiss me with the kisses of his mouth:
for thy love is better than wine.

Song of Solomon 1:2

The young lovers sat together closely on the porch swing and relished the sights and sounds of Youngstown at sunset. The evening skyline was as colorful as an artist's palette. The enormous cherry tree in Mamie's front yard flaunted bursts of fragrant magenta-colored blossoms against the deep amethyst sky and the descending tangerine sun.

Clusters of children raced to their homes as the streetlights began to flicker. Mothers called into the twilight, bidding stray offspring to come home.

A few tardy sparrows seemed to be in dispute as they navigated their way back to their nests and tree branches. Curtis searched for the words to phrase his proposal to Natalie. He wondered if he should do it on one knee, or simply present her with the ring.

Sensing his intentions, Natalie was every bit as anxious as Curtis. She pretended to listen as he babbled about various adventures he had experienced during his travels across the country.

She sat quietly, interjecting an occasional "You're kidding" or "Oh my God." She wondered when he was going to get to the "surprise."

"I'll be right back, Natalie." He went out back to Mamie.

"Mama I'm gonna pop the question now – let me get the ring!"

"The ring? Lord have mercy, what did I do with the ring?"

"Mama, are you for real? You lost Natalie's ring?"

"It ain't lost Curt. I guess I put it up somewhere so nothing would happen to it. I just can't remember where. Give me a few minutes. You go on back out there with Natalie. I'll let you know when I find it."

Mamie took C.J. inside with her to search for the ring. She retraced her every step. From the front door, to the living room, dining room, kitchen – even the bathroom. No ring. She went to the front door and whispered. "Curt, can I see you for just a minute?"

"Sure Mama. I'll be right back Sweetheart."

"Curt, Mama, looked everywhere. I'm so sorry son, I can't find it. You know how I hides things from myself sometimes."

"I can't believe this is happening. Surely this must be a sign."

"Yeah, it's a sign that your mama is gettin' old and forgetful. Now you better go back out there and take care of your business. You can give her the ring later."

"No I can't. I can't go to Natalie empty handed and ask her to marry me. She'll think I'm a cheapskate."

"Not if you explain what happened. Just tell her what I done."

"Nope. No ring – no proposal. I'll just wait until you find the ring."

"You not giving that girl much credit. I believe she'll be more interested in the proposal than the ring, don't you?"

"Maybe the timing ain't right for me to get married."

"Maybe so son. If you willin' to give up this quick, then maybe you ain't ready to settle down yet. Natalie don't deserve to be strung along though. I got a feeling she been expecting you to propose soon."

"I don't want to make a mistake Mama. I don't want to mess up my life – or hers."

C.J. tugged on Mamie's apron. "Can we go back out to the bubbles now Granny Mamie?"

"Curt, Mama's really sorry about losing the ring. Let's all try to enjoy the rest of the evening. One thing we know – that ring is somewhere in this house. She smiled down at the child and calmly walked through the back door. "C.J. come on let's go make us some more bubbles." Curtis rejoined Natalie who was anxiously awaiting his return.

"Everything ok? You took off like something was after you."

"Yeah Sweetheart, everything is ok."

Curtis and Natalie continued to make idle chatter for another hour or so. With each passing moment, Natalie's expectation for a proposal waned. Maybe she had misread his intentions.

"Listen Honey, I guess we've been having so much fun, I lost all track of time. I think we'd better get back home before Deacon Jordan sends out a search party."

She couldn't hide her disappointment. "But... yeah, I guess you're right. I'll go get C.J." Natalie was on the verge of tears as she watched Mamie and C.J. joyfully catching fire flies in a glass jar.

"I'm sorry to break this up, but I'm afraid it's time for us to head back to Detroit."

"Natalie I'm so glad I got a chance to spend some time with you and C.J. Y'all come back real soon. Ya hear?"

"Thank you Mrs. Harris. It's been nice meeting you too. I hope we'll see each other again soon."

Mamie's heart sank as she watched the threesome drive off into the Youngstown darkness. "Lord, I don't understand it, but I know You know what's best."

Curtis sensed that Natalie was upset with him for dragging her all the way to Ohio, then coming up short.

Natalie replayed every move she made and every word she spoke. She wondered what she had done to make Curtis leave his mother's house so abruptly.

Heavy silence loomed between them during the entire ride back to Detroit.

Dallas pulled C.J. out of Natalie's arms and hoisted her up on his shoulders. "Did you have a good time in Youngstown baby?"

The girl giggled. "Yup! I played with Grandma Mamie's bubbles and I caught some fi-flies."

"Oh you played with Grandma Mamie? Well, sounds like we got some talking to do C.J. I want to hear all about it."

Curtis looked at the ground. His plans were to formally ask Dallas' permission to marry Natalie tonight.

Dallas spoke into the night air. "Anybody have something they need to talk to me and Mama about?"

Curtis avoided Natalie's eyes as she answered, "Not tonight Daddy."

"Well, I guess I'd better let y'all get inside. Thanks for riding with me Natalie."

He pecked her on the cheek and tickled C.J. "Don't forget to brush your teeth and say your prayers young lady."

"Good night everyone."

Chapter Thirty-Eight

God is able to make all grace abound toward you; that ye,
always having all sufficiency in all things,
may abound to every good work.

2 Corinthians 9:8

Bernadette tried reaching Dr. Robinson all afternoon, but the phone just rang and rang. *He needs me as much as I need him.* Finally, at five minutes to five, she gave it one last try. "Hello, this is Dr. Robinson."

Her heart pounded. "Yes, uh Dr. Robinson this is Bernadette Mitchell, Jamie Mitchell's mother, you know, the little boy with the ear infection and the bad cough?"

He frowned. "Yes, Mrs. Mitchell, what can I do for you? Is Jamie alright?"

She nodded into the phone. "Yes, he's fine. Umm, the reason I'm calling is, um, well... do you still have that job opening in your office?"

"Why yes I do. Do you know someone?"

She allowed herself to relax slightly. "Yes, me! I have training from Kelly Girl and I..."

"How soon can you start?"

"Start? Really? Shoot! I can start tomorrow!"

"Really? I hate to sound desperate Mrs. Mitchell, but I am!"

"To tell you the truth Dr. Robinson, so am I. And yes I really can start tomorrow."

"Well that's wonderful, I guess we're just two desperate people then, aren't we? We'll work out the details of your salary and all that tomorrow if that's ok with you?"

"That's fine with me." She paused. "Dr. Robinson, after tomorrow neither one of us will ever be desperate again. What time do you want me to come in?"

"Can you be here at 8:30?"

"Yes, sir, 8:30 sharp! Thanks again Dr. Robinson." Then she took a deep breath. "Ah, Dr. Robinson, there is one little favor I'd like to ask you. I know it's not a good way to start off but..."

"Yes, go on Mrs. Mitchell."

"Is it possible that you can pay me in advance?" Whew! She let it out then braced herself for his response.

"Well, that is a bit unusual, but I'm sure it's for a good cause, right?"

"Yes sir, I promise you I wouldn't ask if it wasn't absolutely necessary. I'd say it's an emergency."

"I have a good feeling about you, Mrs. Mitchell. We'll talk about it more tomorrow. I don't have any patients coming in until 10 o'clock. That should give us time to get the ball rolling."

Their first staff meeting only took about 30 minutes. They discussed Bernadette's general duties, her schedule and of course, her salary. Then he wrote her a check for two full weeks' salary.

Dr. Robinson told Bernadette that the office and waiting room were her territory and she was to run it as she saw fit. His immediate concerns were his accounts receivable and the patients' records. Bernadette eagerly went right to work. She began by reviewing the appointment schedule, which was currently scribbled on little pieces of paper and thumb tacked to a cork bulletin board, this was Cynthia Robinson's brainchild.

She noticed that Dr. Robinson generally had patients booked from 9 o'clock straight through until 4 o'clock.

"Dr. Robinson, don't you take a lunch break?"

"Not ordinarily Mrs. Mitchell, why?"

"Well, I know it's none of my business, but I just thought it would be a good idea to block off an hour for you to rest or eat or something."

"You know Mrs. Mitchell, you're right, but let's make it 30 minutes. I don't eat much. Thank you for thinking of me."

Bernadette's next order of business was to give the clinic a face lift. Dr. Robinson gave her permission to replace all the old office equipment and furniture. He gave Bernadette carte blanche with the project. She hired the Stevens brothers from the church to paint the entire suite. She also ordered a new aquarium – including new tropical fish. She ordered a subscription to *Highlights* magazine and purchased an assortment of books for the children. She also ordered subscriptions to *Look*, *Ebony* and *Jet* magazines for the parents.

Dr. Robinson liked Bernadette's idea to have an Open House after the renovations were complete; then to make it an annual event and call it Patient Appreciation Day. This would be a wonderful opportunity to attract new patients and to introduce his new office manager.

On the day of the Open House, Hattie catered hot dogs, cookies, popcorn and sodas for the children. She served Watermelon Lemonade and trays of hors d'oeuvres for the adults. Cynthia Robinson hired the clown her sister used at her niece's birthday party earlier in the year.

There were balloons, door prizes and games. Everyone seemed to enjoy the clinic's festivities and cheery new décor.

Cynthia and her twin sister Celeste drank frosty glasses of Watermelon Lemonade while they scrutinized Bernadette's every move. She fluttered about the room, cheerfully greeting and mingling with the guests. The sisters paid close attention to the cozy way she and Dr. Robinson interacted.

"It looks like your replacement breathed life into this dreary old place. You'd better watch out Cindy, she might try to replace more than your job."   Cynthia snarled. "She may assist me, but she'll never replace me."

Celeste raised her eyebrows. "You're awfully sure of yourself. She's a pretty little chunk of chocolate - and apparently very smart. You'd better hope *your job* is all she's replacing."

"Are you kidding me? Bill has his precious appearances to keep up you know. He'd never replace me with a... chunk of chocolate, especially not a fat chunk. Bernice must wear a size 14 or 16 dress! But, to tell you the truth Sis, if Bill is that attracted to her, this could work out in my favor.

Bernice might be just the distraction needed to supplement Bill's insatiable appetite...in exchange for a few crumbs falling from the Robinson's table."

Chapter Thirty-Nine

Whoever has haughty eyes and a proud heart,
him will I not endure.

Psalm 101:5

"Dr. Robinson's office. Oh hello Mrs. Robinson, Dr. Robinson is in with a patient right now."

"Actually I was hoping to speak to my sister. My niece has an appointment today, have you seen them?"

"Let me check the sign in sheet, what is your sister's name?" Cynthia was incensed that Bernadette didn't know who her sister was. "Mrs. Patterson, Celeste Patterson. Stephanie is my niece. She said they were coming in this afternoon for Stephanie's check-up before going back to school. She'll be going to Saint..."

Bernadette interrupted. "Yes, they checked in. I see her name here. Hold on for just a moment and I'll get her." Bernadette was not interested in hearing Cynthia Robinson's ramblings about her niece's private school or her ballet and piano lessons. For months, it seemed that Cynthia Robinson used every possible opportunity to remind Bernadette how well off the Robinsons were and how poor she was.

She called into the waiting room. "Excuse me. Is there a Mrs. Patterson in the room, Mrs. Celeste Patterson?"

"Here we are. Come along, Stephanie"

"Oh no Mrs. Patterson, the doctor isn't ready for Stephanie. There is a phone call for you." She pointed the telephone receiver in Celeste Patterson's direction.

"Is there someplace I can take this privately?"

Bernadette responded dryly. "Sorry." *Where does she think she is –
the Ritz?*

Celeste flipped her hair behind her ear and snapped off her
earring. "This is Celeste Patterson. Oh, hi Sissy. Well I had plans
to do a little more school shopping for Steffie after we leave here.
Sorry Sweetie, it's just impossible. I have so much to do to
prepare. Steffie starts school in just a few days. Can't you get
someone else? Alright then, next week after I get Steffi settled in
at school, I can come and visit with you and my little nephew
Cindy, I promise. How did Billie like the birthday present? I
know a train set is a bit premature for a one-year-old, but I just
couldn't help myself. He'll be big enough to play with it in no
time – you'll see. Alright then. Ciao Bella." *Chow bella, who talks
like that?*

Celeste handed the receiver back to Bernadette.

"Here you go Bernice, Mrs. Robinson would like to speak
back to you."

Bernadette retrieved the receiver. "Hello?"

"Yes, Bernice?"

Bernadette was livid. *You would think that after a year she'd at
least know my first name!* "This is Bernadette speaking. What can I
do for you Mrs. Robinson?"

Cynthia ignored the edginess she detected in Bernadette's
tone. "Oh, dear, I really feel awkward asking you, but I'm in a
terrible jam."

When Celeste walked away, Bernadette held the receiver at
arm's length and let out an exasperated breath.

"What's wrong Mrs. Robinson?"

"I had some alterations done to some dresses I bought from
the Ruth Joyce Originals boutique on the Avenue of Fashion. I
need to wear one of them to a dinner party tonight and I'd been
so busy making preparations for little Billie's first birthday party,
that I completely neglected myself. I was wondering if you would
be a dear and pick them up for me. Of course my husband will
pay you extra for your trouble. Can you bail me out?"

"Umm, I'm sorry Mrs. Robinson, I would like to help you out, but I have to pick my son up from the babysitter right after work. Mrs. Harper is very strict about having him picked up on time."

"Well she must be somewhat flexible with the irregular hours you and my husband have been keeping lately. Say, I have an idea, perhaps your husband could pick your little boy up from the sitter."

"That's not possible. I have to go now Mrs. Robinson. We have a lot of patients today." Having said that, Bernadette hung up. The dial tone stung Cynthia's ears. She was offended by what she later described to her husband as Bernadette's blatant insolence.

When she escorted Jessica Norwood and her mother to the examination room, she whispered to Dr. Robinson that she needed to speak with him briefly.

Bernadette realized she was taking a risk, but it had to be done. She recounted the conversation she had with Dr. Robinson's wife earlier that day. He didn't seem at all surprised. He apologized and assured Bernadette she would never be inconvenienced by his wife again.

Chapter Forty

"The poison of vipers is on their lips."

Romans 3:13

After the last patient of the day was seen, Bernadette closed the blinds and watered the Philodendrons, Mother-in-Law's Tongue, the African Violets and the Wandering Jew.

"Are you going home or do you plan to stay here the entire weekend?"

"Oh! You scared me."

"I'm sorry, I didn't mean to startle you." Dr. Robinson teased.

"I feel I owe you for that nasty little encounter you had with my wife. How about I try to make it up to you by treating you to dinner tonight?"

"Tonight? I thought you had a party or something to go to tonight?"

"No. She's going out of town for the weekend. Her sorority is having its annual convention." He grinned. "That's too much estrogen under one roof for me."

"Who's taking care of the baby?" She asked more out of curiosity than concern.

"Cynthia's parents are taking care of Billy for the weekend."

"Oh, I see. Well I can't possibly go tonight. There's no way I can get a sitter on such short notice."

Dr. Robinson put on his most pitiful face. "That's too bad. I guess it'll just be me, the dog and some Chicken Delight tonight." He shrugged. For a moment, Bernadette felt responsible for his being alone for the weekend. *Snap out of it girl. This man has a wife.*

Bernadette was relieved when she learned that Natalie didn't have any appointments until three o'clock. The two women were on the telephone cackling like a couple of hens at 7:30 Saturday morning. Natalie started off by telling her about her trip to Youngstown.

"None of what you're telling me makes sense Nat. Something must have happened when Curtis went back in that house."

"I know Bern. Everything had gone great all day. His mother seemed to like me, the food was wonderful and I even offered to help clean up."

"Maybe that's it. Maybe Mrs. Harris got offended when you offered to clean up. You know some women are funny about those things."

"That doesn't make sense either. She would have thought I didn't have any manners if I hadn't offered. I haven't heard a word from Curtis since then and here it's almost Sunday again."

"Well don't panic. I'm sure it'll all blow over soon. In the meantime girl, let me tell you what happened to me on the job yesterday..."

Bernadette described the bizarre conversations she had with Cynthia Robinson and her twin sister.

"Girl, you are lying. She did what? She really thinks she's Miss It-On-A Stick huh?"

"Yeah girl, I couldn't believe what I was hearing. She just don't know how close she came to getting her feelings hurt."

"You're a good one cause I woulda told her off and Dr. Robinson would have to give me a raise for my trouble."

Jamie entered the room whining and rubbing sleep from his eyes. "Mommy, I'm hungry."

"Let me call you back Natalie, I gotta give my little man his breakfast."

"Say, I've got an idea, let's take the kids to Belle Isle later today. We can let 'em play on the swings while we get some fresh air and sunshine. Then you can fill me in on all the juicy gossip about your new lover and your wife-in-law."

They laughed. "Natalie Jordan, you need to repent."

Natalie held up her right hand. "Forgive me Lord. I was just kidding."

"Anyway, I like your idea about Belle Isle... let's make a day of it. We can bring some food and some blankets."

Bernadette said. "I'll fry some chicken and make some potato salad. Do you feel like baking some cookies?"

"Yeah, I guess I could whip up a couple dozen right quick. I'll make us some iced tea too. Hey, you wanna call Gwen and see if she wants to come too?"

"I'll call her, but you know she probably isn't up yet."

"Yeah, knowing Gwen she probably just crawled into bed. But she'll have a fit if we take *her* kids someplace without inviting her."

"Ok, I'll call her."

"Tell her to bring her radio."

"What time? Around 11, 11:30?"

"Eleven thirty sounds good. Now let me feed Jamie and get started on this picnic feast. See you when you get here."

"Me and C.J. will be there at 11:30 to help you get everything out to the car then we'll swing by and pick Gwen up."

Bernadette got Jamie washed up and dressed. Then she seated him at the table in her tiny kitchenette to eat his breakfast.

"Now, bless your food like I taught you." Jamie bowed his head and interlaced his chunky little fingers in preparation to say his grace.

"Come Lord Jesus, be our guest and let this food to us be blessed, in Jesus' name, Amen."

"Amen. Good Jamie. Now eat your cornflakes then you can watch TV."

After breakfast, Jamie stretched out on the floor of the cramped living room to watch his favorite cartoon shows.

The horizontal hold on the television was rolling. "Mommy, the TV is messed up again."

Bernadette wiped her hands on her apron and came to Jamie's rescue. She moved the rabbit ears antennae and fiddled with some knobs beneath the screen. The rolling stopped, but the picture was fuzzy.

"Aww." Jamie whined.

"I think I can fix it but you have to stop acting like a baby." She went back to the kitchen and returned with a piece of tin foil, which she molded around the rabbit ears.

"There! Good as new."

A crystal clear picture of Rocky the Flying Squirrel outwitting Boris Badinoff and Natasha appeared on the screen.

"Yeaaaa! Thank you Mommy."

"You're welcome baby. Now mommy has to do some cooking. We're going on a picnic later today."

Bernadette started preparing food for the impromptu picnic. The phone rang while she was wrist deep in potato peels.

"Jamie Honey, can you answer the phone like mommy showed you? Jamie?" Jamie was so engrossed with Rocky and Bullwinkle that he didn't hear the telephone. By the time she got to the phone, it had stopped ringing.

She dialed Natalie, but didn't get an answer and she knew Gwen wasn't calling before 10 o'clock. She started back toward the kitchen then the phone rang again. "Hello?"

"Bernadette, did I wake you"

"Um no. Who is this? Dr. Robinson?"

"Yes, it's me Bernadette. I'm sorry for calling so early, but I thought I'd try to catch you before you started doing whatever you do on Saturday morning."

"That's ok Dr. Robinson, I've been up for quite a while. When you have a little one, there is no such thing as sleeping late on Saturdays, you'll see pretty soon."

"Yes I guess I will. So, you're probably really busy today - huh?"

Bernadette hoped he wasn't calling to ask her to come into the clinic. "Well, me and my cousin Natalie are taking our kids to spend the afternoon on Belle Isle."

"Oh that sounds nice, lucky kids. It's been a while since I've been to Belle Isle."

"Looks like we're going to have some really nice weather today."

"Yeah we're just going to take in the scenery and let the kids play, maybe let them collect some seashells and watch the sailboats and ships on the river."

"That sounds like heaven to me."

Bernadette was more than a little curious about why Dr. Robinson was calling her early on a Saturday morning. *Ok, what is he up to?* "So, what can I do for you on this bright Saturday morning Doc?"

"Well, I was hoping we could pick up where we left off yesterday evening. Since you turned me down for dinner last night, I thought maybe we could get together this evening. I really need to talk to you."

He sounded serious. She wondered if his urgent need to speak with her had anything to do with Cynthia.

"Well, there's still the issue of a babysitter. Mrs. Harper is busy on Saturdays and I don't have anybody else to look after Jamie for me."

"Is there any chance that one of your girlfriends could look after Jamie for you?"

"I don't want to bother them. Gwen only gets every other Saturday off and Natalie has customers this afternoon."

"Come on, just this once."

"I don't know Dr. Robinson, can I think about it while we're out this afternoon? I can let you know later, around 4 o'clock. Is that alright?"

He sounded disappointed. "Ah, sure. I'll call you then. I hope you'll say yes." Bernadette didn't know how to respond - so she didn't. She heard herself say goodbye.

Chapter Forty-One

And when she finds it, she calls her friends and neighbors together and says, Rejoice with me; I have found my lost coin.

Luke 15:9

Mamie couldn't make her fingers dial fast enough. "Curt! You won't believe it son. I was 'bout to eat some mo' of them bon bons you bought me while I watched my stories. You ain't gon' never guess what I found when I opened the box!"

"Let me guess Mama. You found a million dollars."

"Nope. Better than that smarty britches. I was sifting through the chocolates for a melt-away when I saw it sitting like it belonged there."

Curtis was sarcastic. "What was sitting there like it belonged Mama?"

"Natalie's engagement ring! It was just a-shinin' and a-sparklin' wedged between a caramel nougat and a chocolate covered cherry."

The mystery of the missing ring would be one of the stories Curtis planned to tell C.J. and the other children he hoped he and Natalie would have together someday.

"Natalieeeee. Curtis is on the phone wantin' to speak to you." Natalie was in C.J.'s room tying red ribbons on the two fat ponytails that bounced against her ears. She called down to her father. "Tell him I'll be right there Daddy." C.J. followed as she hurried to her bedroom to grab the extension. "Hello Sergeant

Harris. I was beginning to think some Martians had carried you off in a spaceship or something."

"I know, I know. I've been missing in action. I just had some stuff I needed to sort out before I..."

"Before you what Curtis?"

"I don't want to put the cart before the horse. Can we have dinner tonight? I have something important to talk to you about."

"Oh, you're in town?" Natalie's heart leaped, but she kept her excitement in check. "Well, I'm not sure. I need to check my social calendar. I'm a very popular girl you know?"

Curtis played along. "I'll hold while you consult with your social secretary."

"Thank you. Hold on please Sergeant Harris."
She looked at C.J. and said, "Miss C.J., do you think it would be alright for me to have dinner with Sergeant Harris this evening?" C.J. nodded eagerly. "And me too?"

"No baby, but I'll bet Nana and Papa will let you stay up late to watch T.V. with them." C.J. pouted, but agreed.

"Hello, Sergeant Harris? My social secretary says that I'm free this evening at 8:00 p.m. She wants to know where you're taking me so she can note it on the books."

"Tell her to just write fancy restaurant."

"Ooo that means I'll need to get all dolled up doesn't it?"

"You're always dolled up, even in your dungarees, but you'll want to wear one of your party dresses tonight. We're going to paint the town red."

"I can't wait. See you tonight my love."

"I can't wait either. I love you Natalie."

Chapter Forty-Two

And a little child shall lead them.

Isaiah 11:6

Surrounded by the Detroit River, the park also known as the "Jewel of Detroit" boasted over 700 acres of land. In addition to ample picnic grounds, the island had a children's zoo, an aquarium, a marine museum and a spectacular fountain which displayed colored lights at night. It also featured exquisite floral gardens outside a horticultural conservatory. Each year, hundreds of weddings were performed in the floral gardens. A giant floral clock greets visitors as they cross the Belle Isle bridge at the mouth of the bridge to the island.

Natalie picked Gwen up on the way to Bernadette's apartment building. It was a gorgeous late summer day in September. It had been unseasonably warm all week – typical of the unpredictable Michigan weather. The sky was a pale blue canvas dotted with scattered white clouds. A flock of Canadian geese and a few scavenger seagulls pierced the otherwise serene sky. The river was calm and clear.

As they crossed the bridge, Bernadette looked across the Detroit River and marveled at the Canadian shoreline.

Jamie yelled excitedly. "There's some swings! Can we get out now Mama?"

"Bern, what you think about that spot over there?"

"Looks good to me. I wanted to be near the water so the kids could pick up some seashells later."

"What do you think Gwen?"

"I don't care. Just try not to get around nobody drinking and cuttin' the fool."

Natalie maneuvered her Bonneville into a parking space close to the water's edge.

"Good. There's a picnic table under that weeping willow. Hurry up before somebody else gets it."

A couple with two little boys pulled alongside Natalie and backed into a parallel parking space behind her. "I can't park this big land yacht. Gwen do me a favor, get out and help me navigate. Bern, you and the kids get out and put something on the table before they get to it first."

Bernadette grabbed Natalie's radio as the kids tumbled out of the car. They raced to the picnic table. "I beat you," Jamie declared.

"No you didn't. I beat you."

"No you di-ent."

"Yes I diiiid."

"Uh uhhhh."

"Uh huhhh."

"Ok, ok you two, how 'bout we call it a tie?" Bernadette planted Natalie's radio on the picnic table. She and the kids spread the blanket under the tree then she had them bring over some rocks to anchor the corners.

"Y'all two stay here and guard the table while I help Cousin Natalie unload the car."

"We'll guard it with our lives," C.J. declared dramatically.

When the car was finally unloaded, Gwen looked at the bare picnic table.

"Dang, we shoulda brought a tablecloth."

"I brought one, look in bottom of the picnic basket."

"I shoulda known. What else you got in here, the kitchen sink?"

"Oh girl hush!" Bernadette set out the fried chicken, potato salad, and some deviled eggs. Gwen was delighted to see the feast

Bernadette had prepared. "Girl, you 'bout to make me marry you."

The kids looked at each other and giggled. "Ladies can't marry other ladies."

Jamie asked. "Yes they caaaan, can't they Mama?"

"No baby. Auntie Gwen was just joking when she said that."

Gwen teased, "Who's joking?"

Natalie jumped in. "Quit messin' with that boy's head. Jamie, ladies only marry men and men only marry ladies."

Bernadette told her, "Yeah Gwen, this is Detroit, not Sodom and Gomorrah."

The women continued setting out the picnic feast as the kids explored the shoreline for seashells.

"Don't y'all go too far, we'll be eating lunch in just a few minutes. And don't get in that water!"

As soon as the children were out of earshot, Gwen started in on Bernadette. "Ok missy. Spill it. What's this about you going out on a *date* with Dr. Bill?"

"Dang Natalie, you like an old refrigerator. You can't keep nothin'!"

"Oh so now you got secrets? Sounds shady to me."

"First of all Gwen, I'm not going *out* with Dr. Robinson. He just wants to talk to me about something over dinner. And if ace reporter Brenda Starr over there hasn't already told you, he wants to take me to dinner to make up for his rude wife."

Gwen was blunt. "Yeah, I heard about that. You just be careful that's all I have to say. I don't see why y'all couldn't have this little business meeting at the clinic."

"Gwen, you're suspicious of every man on earth."

"No I'm not. I think the world of your daddy. I believe Papa Jordan could walk on water if he wanted to."

Natalie laughed. "I'm not sure my mama would agree with you on that."

"Seriously though Bern. Something about this don't sound kosher. You better watch yourself girl."

"Dr. Robinson loves his family. Even that witch he's married to. He wouldn't do anything like what you're suggesting. Now that I've talked it out with y'all, I've made my decision. I'm going to prove to everybody that I have nothing to worry about. I'm going to that meeting tonight. Can Jamie stay at your house tonight Natalie?"

"Nope."

"What? Why not?"

"Because I got a date. Curtis called a while ago and said he wants to take me out on a very special date." She couldn't contain her excitement. "I think he's going to ask me to marry him tonight!"

"Don't blow it trying to play all coy and stuff. Just say yes for God's sake."

"I agree with Gwen, don't be acting all stuck up. You know you love that man to pieces so just say yes so we can start making *real* wedding plans."

Bernadette packed Jamie's overnight case and sent him home with Gwen. She searched her closet for something suitable to wear to her dinner meeting with Dr. Robinson. It dawned on her that she didn't know where they would be "meeting." She decided to wear her red geisha girl dress with pearl tear drop earrings and high heels.

She was almost relieved when she hadn't heard from Dr. Robinson by 4:20. She was beginning to lose her nerve about meeting him. Then at precisely 4:30, he called her.

"Hello lovely lady, do you have some good news for me?"

"Well, I guess you could call it that."

He was always amused by Bernadette's very southern drawl.

"You are quite the southern belle aren't you?"

"What do you mean? Are you making fun of me Dr. Robinson?"

He tried not to let her hear him chuckling. "No, no I think your southern accent is charming. Did I understand you to say you'll have dinner with me this evening?"

"Yes under one condition."

"And what might that be?"

"You have to promise not to make fun of the way I talk for the rest of the evening."

"Bernadette, I'd never make fun of you. I really mean it. I am very fond of your southern mannerisms, especially your accent. I promise not to make fun of your accent." He held up three fingers. "Scout's honor."

"Well, alright then. May I ask where we're going?"

"I guess I should have asked you where you'd like to go. Do you like Chinese food?"

"I can't say whether I like it or not. I have never had Chinese food before. Do they really cook dogs and cats?"

The doctor laughed aloud. "Well I have to admit, I've never seen a dog or a cat anywhere near a Chinese restaurant."

"Eeeyuk! In that case, I think I'll pass on the Chinese food."

"I'm kidding Bernadette. I'm certain we will not be served any canines or felines."

"Are you sure?"

He laughed again. "Bernadette, you're such a treasure. Now for the last time, there are no dogs and cats on the menu. So will you just trust me?"

"Well, ok but if I hear one "woof" or "meow" coming from the kitchen, I'm high-tailin' it out of there!"

"Alright then, how about going to Yee's?"

"Oh! I've heard about Yee's but I've never been there. Where is it? Do you have to dress up?"

"Well you don't have to wear a ball gown, but it's a pretty nice place."

"That sounds great."

"Then Yee's it is. May I pick you up at around 7 o'clock?"

"I'll be ready."

"Great. I'll see you then."

Chapter Forty-Three

Whosoever looketh on a woman to lust after her
hath committed adultery with her already in his heart.
Matthew 5:28

ernadette decided that the outfit she chose would be perfect for the evening Dr. Robinson described. The crimson fabric of her oriental-style dress complimented her almond shaped eyes and made her look like a chocolate China doll. The dress hugged in her slightly-plump-but-curvaceous figure. She gave herself a final inspection and smiled back at the woman in the mirror. The doorbell startled her. She talked through the intercom. "Is that you Dr. Robinson?"

"Yes Ma'am. In the flesh." He had arrived at exactly 7 o'clock.

She buzzed him into the building and met him at the door of her apartment.

"Wow Bernadette. You look like a million bucks!"

She fluttered her eyelashes and with an exaggerated southern drawl, said, "Why thank ya suh."

Dr. Robinson took her arm and escorted her outside.

As soon as they stepped onto the sidewalk, an eleven- year-old on a pair of metal roller skates wheeled up to them. "Dr. Robinson, Miss Bernadette is that ch'all?"

Dr. Robinson answered in his usual mellow tone. "Who's that, Caroline Benson?"

"Yup. Sure is. Where y'all going?"

He ignored her question. "Hey little girl, where are you off to in such a hurry?"

"I had to go to the sto' to get my gram' mother's cigarettes."

"Well you better hurry home before something jumps out the bushes and grabs you."

The girl flashed a dimpled smile. "Ok, see you Miss Bernadette. Bye Dr. Robinson."

Bernadette was nervous about running into Caroline. Her grandmother was the biggest gossip in the neighborhood. Surely the old woman would misconstrue their intentions and have a scandal spread all over the neighborhood by morning.

Dr. Robinson opened the door to his steel gray Lincoln Continental for Bernadette. Cynthia Robinson's presence loomed from the moment she slid into the passenger seat. Her signature fragrance, Chanel No. 9, hung heavily in the air.

Dr. Robinson hadn't even shifted the car out of park when a feeling of guilt began to envelope her. She started to rethink this dinner that wasn't a date. An imp whispered in her ear.

Anything that happens between you and Dr. Robinson is his wife's own fault. She's the one who left him at home alone to eat Chicken Delight while she's out doing who-knows-what-with-who-knows-who. A good man like Dr. Robinson don't just grow on trees.

The blare of another car's horn snapped her back to reality.

"I was expecting you to be driving your station wagon."

"Cynthia usually drives this car. The station wagon is my work car, I call it my mule. I bought it from a friend of mine. I don't require a fancy car to get to work and from work." He added half-jokingly, "On the other hand, my wife has to keep up appearances."

Look at how he sacrifices for that woman! Look at how she rewards him. Leaving him alone for a whole weekend to fend for himself – and sending his son off so she can hang around a bunch of her snooty sorority girlfriends...

Dr. Robinson was surprisingly relaxed and upbeat. Maybe she had read more into this than she needed to.

He maneuvered the car into a tight parking space in front of Yee's restaurant. He hopped out and trotted over to open Bernadette's door. *I could get used to this.*

'The maitre d' flashed a warm smile when he recognized Dr. Robinson. "Good evening Dr. Robinson. Your usual table?"

"Yes please, Sammy, same table."

Sammy smiled politely at Bernadette as he escorted them to their table. Bernadette thought it was unusual that he didn't seem the least bit surprised that Dr. Robinson was with someone other than his wife. Nevertheless, she allowed herself to shrug off her suspicions.

Dr. Robinson's usual table turned out to be a booth that was located in an isolated section of the restaurant. A small Cantonese lantern on the table illuminated their faces but barely provided enough light for Bernadette to read the menu.

She was relieved when Dr. Robinson asked permission to order for her. Even if she could see the menu better, she still wouldn't have known what to order.

While waiting for the food to arrive, Bernadette nervously chattered about the picnic on Belle Isle, about Jamie, her family, and her southern upbringing.

Finally, Dr. Robinson interrupted Bernadette's seemingly endless recounts of her days in Sweet Water by bringing up a subject she wasn't prepared to discuss - with anyone.

"Bernadette, I don't mean to pry, but I have to confess I'm more than a little curious. Where is Jamie's father, your husband?"

"She responded stiffly. He's no longer with us."

"Ok, I know I seem nosey, but I want to make sure I understand. When you say he's no longer with us, do you mean that you and he simply live in different places or..."

"He died."

"Oh. I'm sorry to hear that. How long has it been, if you don't mind my asking."

She couldn't believe she was finally able to push the words out of the depths of her soul. "Jamie was only a month old."

"Really? That's unfortunate." He delved deeper. "What happened to him?"

She felt her stomach churning and her mouth became dry, but now it was out there. She continued. "They killed him, back home. Some white men killed him." The light from the lantern reflected off pools of tears that were forming in Bernadette's eyes.

"Who? You mean the KKK?"

"They didn't call themselves by no particular name. Even long after James was gone, they kept after me and Jamie too." She stopped talking. "My family wanted me to move back home, but I tried to stick it out on my own. My brother gave me some guns and taught me how to shoot. He said he's gon' come up here and teach Jamie how to use the shotgun he gave me when he gets a little bigger. Every time Ray Jay talks to him on the phone, he makes him promise to take care of me." She smiled. "Jamie takes his job of taking care of me seriously. He really thinks he's the man of the house."

Doctor Robinson moved to the seat next to her and put his arm around her shoulder. "Sounds like you have a very loving family. Bernadette, I'm sorry about your husband; I had no idea. Oh you poor girl."

She allowed the tears to spill onto her face. It felt good to release the agony she'd hidden for so long.

"I been carrying this burden inside me for years. Nobody really knows all I been through. Nobody."

"Well, it looks like it was time for you to let it all out Bernadette. You haven't had it very easy have you?"

"No, Dr. Robinson it's been rough, but thank the Lord, things are looking up for me and Jamie.

I have a place to stay, good friends and family, a place to worship..." She turned to him. "And I work for the best doctor in the world. I absolutely love my job."

"I'm glad to hear you say that. And I might add; it's not hard to be a great doctor when you don't have to worry about your office being run well. So I guess that means you'll stay with me." He pointed to himself. "I'm the one who should be thanking you."

She touched her runny nose with a handkerchief. "I should go powder my nose, I must look a mess." She excused herself from the table and looked around to locate the ladies room.

The wait staff and a couple sitting at an adjacent table avoided making eye contact when she passed them. It was obvious though that they had witnessed the whole scene. Bernadette's imagination – and a sense of guilt were working at full throttle. She almost had herself convinced that the whole restaurant knew the Robinsons and suspected that Bernadette was Dr. Robinson's mistress.

The restroom attendant looked to be about the same age as Bernadette. *She knows I'm with Dr. Robinson too.* Bernadette acknowledged her and proceeded to examine her face in the ladies' room mirror. Her eyes and nose were red and puffy. She was glad she had decided not to wear eye makeup otherwise she was sure she'd have been looking like a raccoon by now. She made a cold compress out of toilet paper then sat down at the vanity. She tilted her head back and laid the compress across her face until she felt more composed. She removed the compress and washed her hands. The attendant handed her a finger towel then dutifully offered to pour lotion into her hands.

She was about to exit the restroom when the attendant cleared her throat and touched the corner of her mouth, indicating that Bernadette's lipstick was smudged.

She used her handkerchief to wipe off the smudges then reapplied the Ruby Rumors lipstick.

"That's better". The attendant croaked. Bernadette thanked the woman and handed her a dollar.

"Thank you... Ma'am."

They exchanged smiles.

"You're welcome... Ma'am."

When Bernadette returned, she was surprised to see Natalie and Curtis sitting with Doctor Robinson.

"What in the world? Did you all plan for us to meet up?"

Curtis answered. "Don't worry. Our table isn't ready yet. We want privacy tonight. I have a very important question to ask this lady and I don't need an audience."

Dr. Robinson extended his hand. "At the risk of being premature, let me be the first to congratulate you two."

Sammy notified Curtis he was ready to seat them.

"Bern, I'll call you later girl."

She kissed Curtis and Natalie. "Bye y'all. Congratulations."

Bernadette watched with just a hint of envy as Curtis lovingly helped Natalie into her seat.

Dr. Robinson turned to Bernadette. "Now, where were we?"

"I think I was bawling all over you."

Releasing years of pent up anguish and rage made Bernadette feel stronger. Dr. Robinson's inquiries had triggered Bernadette's healing process. Until now, she had been merely functioning for Jamie's sake, but not living.

She hadn't shed a single tear since the day James died. She couldn't feel anything. The tears she finally shed were emancipating. What she felt now was reminiscent of how she felt back home after attending the annual tent revivals. Bernadette's tears had baptized her spirit with renewed hope and a determination to live well, not just exist. The tears washed away the stifling fear and counterfeit courage.

"Dr. Robinson, I'm so sorry. You brought me here to talk about something important and I've been just runnin' off at the mouth."

"Please don't apologize. I'm glad we were able to talk about this, you needed this. And young lady... from this day forward you're to drop that doctor stuff. We've been working together long enough for you to call me Bill."

"That might take me a while. How about I call you Dr. Bill like the kids do?"

"Well, I guess that's alright for starters but eventually I expect you to call me Bill. I know I'm a few years older than you but we're both adults. Now do we have a deal?"

"It's a deal."

"Great. Now let's eat. I'm famished."

He motioned for the waiter to bring their food. Bernadette didn't realize it but while she was having her moment, Bill had directed the wait staff to hold off on serving the food. He had ordered a smorgasbord of Moo Goo Gai Pan, Sesame Chicken and Sweet and Sour Shrimp, Won Ton Soup and Chinese vegetables.

Bernadette faked enthusiasm about the peculiar meal. "Everything smells delicious."

The waiter offered tea. Bernadette nodded for the waiter to pour the tea. She awkwardly grasped the Chinese handle-less teacup.

"No tea for you?"

"Nah, I despise tea. I'm a staunch java man myself."
Bernadette picked through the strange-looking food while listening to Bill randomly jabber about his college days, his patients, and about his childhood.

She learned that Bill came from a family of high achievers. He had lived in Michigan all of his life and his knowledge of the south was limited to his days in Georgia when he attended Morehouse College.

His mother, who had left his father when Bill was still in college, was a pediatric nurse. His father founded their pediatric clinic, his uncle was an accountant in Benton Harbor; and his older sister was a social worker in Grand Rapids.

Bill was a junior at Morehouse when he met Cynthia and her sister Celeste, who were sophomores at Spelman.

"Oddly enough, I dated Celeste first." He playfully rubbed his chin. "I don't know *how* I ended up with Cynthia. I must have been under some kind of voodoo spell or something. Anyway, we got married soon after I graduated from med school. Maybe too soon."

Chapter Forty-Four

Beware of dogs, beware of evil workers,
beware of the concision.

Philippians 3:2

ernadette realized they'd talked through the whole meal when the waiter arrived to recite the dessert menu. Neither of them was up for dessert, besides they still hadn't had their *business meeting.*

When they stepped outside the restaurant, a crisp breeze off the Detroit River made Bernadette shiver.

"You chilly? Here, take my jacket." He valiantly draped her shoulders with his dinner jacket. She felt treasured and cared for, if only for one night. She hadn't felt that way since James died. Bill had awakened her desire for courtship and romance.

They were halfway across the Belle Isle bridge before she realized where they were.

"Oh, I didn't know we were going for a ride."

"Well, we hadn't gotten around to the talk we were supposed to have. I decided the restaurant was inappropriate for what I have to say to you after all. I hope you don't mind my being so presumptuous."

She lied. "No, I don't mind."

He drove past the floral clock, past the island's casino and pulled between the aquarium and the horticultural conservatory. He rolled down his window. "Let me know if you get cold."

Bernadette rolled down her window slightly to enjoy aroma of roses, honeysuckle, iris and hyacinth. She shivered slightly again.

"Are you still cold? I can turn the heater on."

"No, I'm fine, your jacket is keeping me warm."

"Let me know now." They sat silently and for a few moments, Bernadette indulged herself further in fantasy. As she inhaled nature's perfumed night air, she imaged how different her life could be if *she* was Mrs. Bernadette Robinson - doctor's wife, mother, and socialite.

She would continue to work by Bill's side, maintaining the office. She would convince her mother to move in with them - knowing full well that Baby Sis would be thrilled to help look after Jamie and the other children she and Bill would have.

"A penny for your thoughts."

"Oh, I wasn't thinking about anything in particular, just missing my baby."

"I'm sure Jamie is in lullaby land right about now, dreaming about Popeye and Superman."

She strained to see her watch under the dim lights. "My goodness. It's after 11:00 o'clock. I had no idea it was this late."

"Well at any rate, Jamie's in good hands and his mother is having a good time. No harm done right?"

"I guess you're right, Doc."

Awkward silence hung between them. Until he spoke at last.

"Bernadette, I don't know any other way to say what I've been thinking than to come right out and tell you. I know I'm taking a risk here but I have to be honest with you. I think, no I *know*, I've fallen in love with you."

"Say what?"

He reached for her hand but she stiffened and clutched her purse. "I said I'm in love with you Bernadette, I mean it."

She turned away from his intense gaze. Her pulse raced. She looked out at the silhouette of the hydrangea shrubs in the garden outside the conservatory. The shadows of the night made them look like a huddled cluster of children whispering secrets.

Bernadette was stunned. "Dr. Robinson, you're a married man. What about your wife?"

"Cynthia is the mother of my son, and in my own way, I love her. But I'm not *in* love with her."

"Look Dr. Robinson, I..."

He continued. "I think we got married for all the wrong reasons, or maybe we should never have gotten married at all. I'm not asking you to do anything about it Bernadette, but I just couldn't continue to hide my feelings for you. I'm not the kind of man who keeps my feelings bottled up inside."

Although this was what Bernadette had been fantasizing about, Bill's confession was overwhelming.

"Well Dr. Robinson... *Bill*, as flattering as this is, I have to tell you that I'm not the kind of girl who goes with a married man." *No matter how much I love him.*

"As I said before Bernadette, I'm not asking you for anything." He placed his hand over his heart and rolled his eyes heavenward as if he were taking an oath.

"I just want you to know how I feel. I want to take care of you and your son. Even more so now that I know what you've been going through all this time. You've been such a little soldier through this ordeal with your husband's death and moving up here, trying to raise Jamie all alone. You deserve to be taken care of."

Had he been reading her mind? Had he overheard her conversations with Natalie?

"But Dr. Robinson..."

"Bernadette, you have got to drop that Dr. Robinson routine and start calling me Bill."

"Ok, Bill. I've had a lovely evening but it's getting late. I have to be in the choir stand at 7:30 tomorrow morning."

"See, that's what I mean Bernadette. You're such a caring, responsible woman. You deserve to be taken care of. I have the resources and I intend to do just that if you'll only allow me."

She turned and looked at him pointedly. "If I were your wife, I wouldn't appreciate you taking care of some other woman and her child."

"Bernadette, I know you can't relate to what I'm about to say but some wives actually appreciate their husbands having a distraction. Now you could greatly benefit from what I have to offer - starting with a decent place for you and Jamie to live. Think about it. Wouldn't it be great if you lived in a house where Jamie could have his own bedroom and a fenced-in backyard where he could play safely? I own a house in a nice, safe neighborhood that is not far from the clinic. You could walk to work from there if you wanted to. I can make it available to you within 30 days.

Think Bernadette, winter will be here before you know it. Wouldn't it be nice if you and Jamie could get around in the warmth and comfort of your own car, instead of catching buses and hailing cabs in Michigan's snow and cold?"

In the wee hours of the morning, Bernadette lay in bed thinking long and hard about Bill's offer. She stared at the cracks in the ceiling and the broken light fixture that the landlord had been promising to repair since the day she signed her lease. She listened to the whistling wind that forced its way through the rags that were stuffed in the sill in an attempt to keep Detroit's cold air outside her apartment. In a few weeks when winter set in, the rags wouldn't help. Then she would have to keep the oven door open to counter the cold air in her one-bedroom apartment.

For the first few hours, she tossed and turned; and thought and prayed. As sleep continued to elude her, she continued to toss, turn, but stopped praying. Then she fantasized and rationalized - until she decided. Baby Sis and God would just have to understand. She had to do what was best for Jamie.

They say God works in mysterious ways. Surely this is God making a way out of no way for me and Jamie.

Dr. Robinson said he loved me. He has enough money to take care of me and Jamie without taking anything away from that ungrateful, spoiled wench he's married to.

Who knows? Maybe someday he'll finally get tired of Cynthia, give her a fat check and get rid of her for good. I wouldn't even mind raising

Billy as my own. Cynthia doesn't seem to have a motherly bone in her stuck up little body. I'll have at least one baby with Bill, hopefully a girl – for insurance. That's what those rich white women I used to work for did. They'd have a bunch of babies to make sure if the man ever left them, they'd always have money coming in for those babies… 18 years apiece. Yup. I'll love Bill so good he'll be wantin' to throw that snot-rag Cynthia out on her ear and marry me before the ink on the divorce papers dries.

Chapter Forty-Five

But a certain Samaritan, as he journeyed, came where he was: and when he saw him, he had compassion on him.

Luke 10:33

Curtis pulled into a rest stop at the Kentucky/Cincinnati border. This last run had been grueling and he was anxious to get to his room at Howard Johnson's in Detroit for a hot shower. He was ready for a home cooked meal and to spend some quality time with Natalie. They were scheduled to meet with Pastor Healy to discuss wedding plans.

He considered pushing straight through but knew of too many truckers who had been in terrible accidents as a result of pushing themselves too hard.

On the way inside the rest stop's snack bar, he spotted a young blond woman who looked like she had been on the wrong end of somebody's fist. She stared out into the highway looking lost and bewildered. When he came out a half hour later, the girl was standing outside Curtis' rig with that same look of helplessness.

She approached him. "Hey Mister, can you help me?"

"What kind of help do you need?"

"I'm lost, well. I'm stranded."

"Stranded?"

"Yeah, my husband left me here."

"Husband? You don't look old enough to have a husband."

195

"Everybody says that, but believe me I'm married." She stuck out her hand to display a plain, gold wedding band. Curtis nodded and the girl moved closer.

"We was driving up to Michigan from Kentucky and we got into a little scrap. I told him to let me out at the next stop - and he did just that."

"Tough break. How can *I* help you?"

"I'm trying to make my way to Michigan. You going anywhere near Monroe?"

He shook his head. "Sorry, my company has rules against picking up hitchhikers."

"Please Mister. It's getting late and I don't want to be out here after dark by myself."

"Lady, I don't mean to be rude but you should have thought of that before telling your husband to let you out of the car."

The woman lifted her shirt and showed Curtis bruises on her torso.

"I had my reasons."

Curtis' kind nature overpowered his common sense.

"Ok, I guess it will be alright. Are you hungry?"

"Yes, I'm starvin' but I don't have no money on me right now. I got outta the car so fast I brought my bag but I left my purse."

"I'll get you something to eat. Go ahead and hop in." *Lord help me.*

The girl carefully placed her duffel bag in the truck's cab and climbed in. Curtis went back into the restaurant and duplicated the order he had bought for himself. When he returned, Curtis noticed that the young woman was rambling for something in her duffle bag. She quickly pulled zippers and fastened snaps when he got in.

He handed her a greasy sack. "Here you go... what's your name?"

"Amy."

"Here you go Amy."

"My name is Curtis Harris." Amy nodded and continued chewing like she hadn't eaten in days. She ripped open a bag of potato chips.

"You got a last name Amy?"

"As of today, I'm just Amy." She spit bits of hamburger as she spoke.

"Pleased to meet you *Just Amy*." Curtis started the truck's engine then eased onto the highway.

He hoped nothing would happen to make him regret his humanitarian deed. The sooner he could get *Just Amy* to Monroe, the better.

Several miles down the road he heard a siren blaring. Curtis checked the side view mirror. Red and white lights were flashing - sure enough, the Ohio State Police were signaling him to pull over.

"Shoot! Johnny Nab." *And me with this little white girl in my truck.*

The tall, husky officer didn't look too pleased when he discovered Amy riding in Curtis' truck. Judging from her swollen lip and bruised face, his first assessment of the situation was that Curtis had probably kidnapped somebody's child. He and his partner would be hailed heroes for rescuing her.

The second trooper was a rotund fellow with stubby arms and legs. His belly rested on his thighs and you could see his chest rise and fall with each labored breath.

"Well sir! What in the world do we have here? Where you going in such a hurry?"

Curtis read the name on the trooper's badge, Lieutenant James E. Bixby. "Sorry, I guess I didn't realize I was speeding."

"I'd estimate you were derned near 15 miles over the speed limit son."

Lieutenant Bixby asked, "Who's this you got in here with you junior?"

"This is Amy. I'm taking her to meet her husband in Michigan."

"Is that a fact now? You telling me this here little girl got a husband?" The officer eyed Amy. "That true what he says little lady?"

Amy nodded robotically and showed him her wedding band.

"Tell you what, why don't you and Amy step out of the vee-hickle." Curtis and Amy stood on the shoulder of the road while the state troopers inspected the truck.

"You got proper papers to operate this vee-hickle son?" Curtis was eager to cooperate with the officers. "Yes sir I do. They're underneath the sun visor. I'll get 'em." He reached for the door handle.

"Step back son. Elroy, look in there and see what you can come up with." Officer Elroy McAllister retrieved the paperwork and verified its contents.

"Umm hmm." Bixby said. "I 'spect we need to get some more de-tails bout this here situation, don't you?"

McAllister nodded in agreement. "You gon' have to come with us."

Curtis asked, "What for? Can't you just write me a speeding ticket and let us go?"

Bixby slid his cap up and down on his brow. "We could do that but now tell me why in God's name would we want to let you go with this little girl here. For all I know you could be holding this itty bitty lady against her will."

Curtis cooperated and Amy seemed indifferent. She didn't offer any information that would assist Curtis. McAllister and Bixby handcuffed him and directed him to get into the back seat of the patrol car. They assisted Amy into the patrol car as well – without handcuffs.

Bixby searched the cab of the truck while McAllister made radio contact with the station. He returned to the patrol car with Amy's duffel bag. Upon inspection he sang out the inventory.

"Women's underwear, socks, two shirts, one pair of ladies' dungarees, a pack of Juicy Fruit gum, a hair brush; and wait a minute... ooooo looky here." He thumbed through a wad of currency. "Six, seven, eight... we got near 'bout a thousand dollars in cash, and my God a sawed off shotgun. Where'd y'all get all this money from?" Curtis was astonished.

"Sir, I don't know nothin' about that money or that shotgun.

I was just giving the young lady a ride because she said she was stranded." He glared at her. "In fact, I bought her some food because she told me she didn't have any money."

McAllister asked, "What you got to say about all this missy?" Amy nonchalantly shrugged. The troopers took them to the station where another set of officers questioned them separately.

Curtis had no criminal record. However a review of Amy's record revealed that she had been arrested up along I-280 for solicitation several times before and that she and a male accomplice were wanted in Kentucky and Ohio for armed robbery.

The pair was wanted for robbery of three truck stops along that stretch of highway over the past six months. Curtis was repaid for his act of kindness by being arrested and charged with kidnapping and rape.

"Mama, it's me. I'm in trouble and I need your help."

"What is it Curtis?"

"I don't have long to talk Mama so I need you to listen to me carefully." Curtis briefed his mother on the details which led up to his arrest.

"I need you to tell Natalie for me. Make sure she knows I didn't do nothing but try to help that girl Mama. I shoulda left her tail out there. This is what I get for trying to be a good Christian."

Mamie patted her lap as if her son's head was lying on it.

"Don't you worry son, the Lord will straighten out this lie."

Chapter Forty-Six

Deliver us, and purge away our sins, for thy name's sake.
Psalm 79:9

Natalie stood in the doorway waiting for her father and uncle to exit the U-Haul truck Bill had rented for Bernadette's move.

"Bernadette, are you sure you know what you're doing? If your daddy knew how you got this house he'd…"

"My daddy is the last person on earth who can pass judgment on me. He never did nothin' for us – or Mama. I'm doing this for my son and hopefully for my Mama too. Maybe now that I have a nice house I can convince her to move up here with me and Jamie."

"Two wrongs don't make a right Bern. Eventually, Baby Sis will find out who really owns this house and it will break her heart."

"Natalie, if you came here to preach hellfire and damnation, you gave up your Saturday customers for nothing and you can leave now!"

Gwen wedged herself between them. "Don't waste your breath Nat, we been tryin' to talk sense into her head for weeks. You might as well be talkin' to a brick wall." She turned to Bernadette. "One day this is going to come back and bite you in the butt."

Bernadette answered. "I'll take my chances."

Chapter Forty-Seven

If God be for us, who can be against us?

Romans 8:31

Curtis met with his court appointed attorney in the visitor's room of the jail. He studied the man's features. His clothes hung loosely on his slack frame, his mud-colored hair was wispy, his cheeks were sunken in and his complexion was ghostly.

The unorganized attorney riffled through his disheveled briefcase in search of Curtis' file among fifty or so other files.

"Ah! Here we go." He flashed a broad smile and extended his hand to Curtis. "Mr. Harris, I'm Simeon Arrington, I will be representing you."

He scrunched his face and scratched notes on a long yellow pad. After glancing at Curtis' file he looked up to meet Curtis' concerned eyes. "Well Mr. Harris, based on the information I've been able to ascertain, and the evidence gathered at the rest stop, I recommend that you plead guilty and throw yourself on the mercy of the court in hopes of the minimum sentence, which is 15 years."

Curtis was stunned. Had he heard right? Did this lawyer who looked like he just graduated high school have him mixed up with another one of his clients? "Sir, I can't plead guilty to a crime I didn't even commit."

Arrington leaned close to Curtis and whispered. "Listen Curtis. I'm not even supposed to know what I'm about to tell you, but the prosecutor is a good friend of mine so mum's the word. My friend the prosecutor has informed me that you could also be linked to a series of armed robberies along I-280. They're sure Miss Whitcomb, and a male accomplice are the perpetrators."

Curtis held up his hand. "Whoa! Come on now! How could anybody possibly think that me and some white girl been running up and down the 280 robbing people? That don't even add up. Them people woulda hung me on the spot the first time around.

I'm being railroaded. I didn't rob nobody, I didn't kidnap nobody and I sho' didn't rape nobody! I picked that girl up at that rest stop 'cause she said she needed help and…"

Arrington interrupted. "I understand all of that Curtis. However, in light of the circumstances, it would be in your best interest to follow my advice. The prosecutor assured me that because you have no priors, with good behavior you could actually be released in as little as six or seven years."

"Six or seven years of my life for something I didn't do – you call that little?" Curtis shook his head violently. "No sir. I ain't going to plead guilty to something I didn't do. Even if I did what you want me to, who's to say I wouldn't end up in prison for the rest of my life anyway?"

"The way I see it, you have no choice, my hands are tied Curtis."

"Look man, I've got principles, I have a family and my good name to protect."

"Curtis, if you don't follow my advice you won't even have a name anymore – just a number. But if you will just play along, everything will be alright, I can guarantee you that."

"I don't mean you any disrespect Mr. Arrington, but I don't believe you giving me good advice. No sir, no deals. I'm innocent and I'm going to trust in the Lord to make the truth come to light."

The legs of Curtis' aluminum chair made a loud screeching sound as he pushed back from the table. He slowly positioned his hands on the table and stood. "I'm sorry you wasted your time coming here today Mr. Arrington, but our business is over now."

"Curtis, are you telling me you don't want me to represent you any longer?"

"The way I see it, you weren't going to represent me in the first place. Good bye sir."

Arrington yelled for the guard to let him out. "You're a darned fool Harris. You're throwing your life away."

"God is on my side Mr. Arrington. He'll fight my battle for me."

Chapter Forty-Eight

*For out of the heart proceed evil thoughts, murders, adulteries,
fornications, thefts, false witness, blasphemies...*

Matthew 15:19

Curtis sat in jail for months after he was arrested in Cincinnati. Thanks to his new lawyer, he would finally have his day in court. Administrative red tape and indifference had robbed him of his constitutional right to a speedy trial. Mamie hired David Epps to defend her son. Epps was a confident, handsome defense lawyer with clout in the community as well as a very impressive track record. Curtis' boss and several of his fellow truckers, along with Pastor Healy, and a busload of members from the church had made the trip to Cincinnati. They were all prepared to testify as character witnesses on Curtis' behalf.

Several of the women squirmed in their seats and hunched each other when the caramel-colored attorney entered the courtroom. He was dressed in a tailored gray suit with a paisley printed tie in complementary tones.

"He's kinda flashy." Natalie noted.

Mamie whispered to Natalie. "They say he's the best colored lawyer in Ohio."

Everyone rose when Judge Rupert Dill entered the courtroom. Although the prosecutor rejected all six of the black prospective jurors, Epps was still confident that he would win his case.

He said to Curtis. "We'll be fine. Judge Dill is a fair man."

After opening statements were made, the judge instructed the jury and told the prosecutor to call his first witness.

It was obvious that the prosecution was trying to capitalize on Amy's youthful appearance. Her hair was styled in a pony-tail and she wore a tortoise shell headband. She was dressed in a modest A-line skirt, a cardigan sweater, bobby socks and Saddle Oxfords.

The ridiculous costume along with her tiny frame, made Amy look like a 13-year-old. She placed her left hand on a Bible, raised her right and swore to tell the truth, the whole truth and nothing but the truth – so help her God.

The prosecutor began to question her. "Please state your full name Ma'am."

"Amanda Lynette Whitcomb."

"Miss Whitcomb, how old were you on the day you and the defendant were stopped by the Ohio State Police?"

Epps interrupted. "Objection Your Honor. The witness is married and should be referred to as *Mrs.* Whitcomb."

The judge rolled his eyes. "Counselor, we are not going to turn this into a chess match. Overruled. Proceed please."

"Miss Whitcomb, how old were you at the time of the incident."

"My eighteenth birthday was last Wednesday. I was only seventeen when it happened."

"Only seventeen. The prosecutor repeated Amy's statement with emphasis. And will you tell the court how you came in contact with the defendant?"

"I was stranded in Ohio. I was tryin' to get to Monroe, Michigan. He saw me at a truck stop and he asked if I needed a ride. I told him where I was going and he said he was headed my way. Then he offered me a lift."

Curtis yelled out. "That's not true, that's not how it happened it all!"

The judge pounded his gavel. "Mr. Epps, control your client. He'll have his turn to testify."

The prosecutor continued. "Miss Whitcomb, did you offer to pay the defendant to take you to Monroe?"

"I told him I didn't have no money on me. I told him I'd be glad to mail him some money later. But he said not to worry about it 'cause he had to go through Monroe to get to De-troit anyways."

"Did he suggest any other methods of payment?"

Epps stood. "Objection Your Honor, the prosecution is clearly leading the witness."

"I'll allow it but you're close to the edge Counselor. The witness will answer the question."

"Miss Whitcomb, you told the police that the defendant asked you for favors in exchange for the ride to Michigan. What exactly did he say?"

"Well, when he first got me in the truck he was talking real nice. We got to talking about our families and stuff. He told me he was getting ready to marry this real nice lady from De-troit and talked a lot about her little girl..."

The prosecutor interrupted. "Yes Ma'am, now at what point did things begin to turn sour?"

"Well after we was riding for about thirty minutes, he got quiet on me. I thought maybe he was just tired of talking by then 'cause he had said he'd been drivin' all night." Amy's eyes widened. "Then all of a sudden he said... well it's kind of delicate word'n."

The prosecutor looked at her sympathetically and spoke softly.

"I know this is difficult for you but please try to go on Miss Whitcomb."

"Well he said he wanted to *do it* to me. Said that was how I could pay him back for the ride."

The people in the courtroom gasped collectively.

"What was your response Miss Whitcomb?"

"I said no and promised to mail him some money for the ride but he wouldn't take no for an answer. Then I begged him to pull over and let me out."

Amy looked at the prosecutor, then at Curtis. "He said I wudden't going nowhere 'til he got what he wanted."

"What happened next Miss Whitcomb?"

"Then he pulled off the highway into a clearing, right at the mouth of some woods. There wuddn't nobody else around from what I could see." Amy began talking faster. "Then for no good reason he smacked the daylights outta me! Clean upside my face. Then he told me to strip down naked real slow while he watched. I was scared of him so I done what he told me to do."

"Did he threaten to harm you?"

"He did more than threaten me. He beat me so bad I thought for sure he was gon' kill me."

"At this time Your Honor, I'd like to enter the People's Exhibits A through F." The judge nodded.

The prosecutor handed the judge a stack of photographs depicting Amy's face, arms and torso - covered with bruises and lacerations. He examined the photos then instructed the bailiff to give them to the jury.

"These photographs show the brute force the defendant used to assault the victim."

Amy conjured tears and blew her nose into a prissy handkerchief as the jury perused the pictures.

"Miss Whitcomb, please try to go on." Amy prolifically described the alleged beating and sexual assault. The occupants of the courtroom clung to her every word as she fabricated a series of lewd sexual acts that Curtis allegedly coerced her to perform. Natalie felt sick to her stomach. The courtroom was buzzing with comments of shock and disgust.

The judge slammed his gavel. "The court will come to order."

Curtis looked over his shoulder searching for Natalie. The look in her eyes assured him that she believed in him. He lowered his head and muttered to himself. "I don't know why that girl is lying on me like that."

"Please continue Miss Whitcomb."

"Well, after he done his business on me, he made me get dressed and get back in the truck with him. He told me I'd better straighten up and look like nothing ever happened if I knew what was good for me. It wudden't hardly ten minutes 'fore the cops pulled him over. That's when I got my break. Hadn't been for them, I'd probably be dead now."

"Objection!"

"Thank you Miss Whitcomb. That's all for now. Your witness, counselor."

Chapter Forty-Nine

*And Jonathan made a covenant with David
because he loved him as himself.*

1 Samuel 18:3

After two days of Amy Whitcomb's damaging testimony, Epps had been merely tap dancing in the courtroom. He had no solid evidence that could refute Amy's lies. He examined reams of records and transcripts looking for something he could use. Nothing.

The law says a man is innocent until proven guilty. Epps believed his client wholeheartedly, but it all came down to a colored man's word against the word of a young white girl, two white highway patrolmen and a lily-white jury – not to mention the judge.

Epps was startled when his secretary, Bonita entered his office with the mail and his morning cup of coffee. "You ok today Boss-man?"

"Yeah, I'm ok. I have to admit that I'm concerned about Curtis Harris though. It'll take a miracle to get him acquitted."

"You doubting your abilities Boss-man?"

"So far I'm just shooting blanks. There's got to be something we can use, I know this man is innocent. I can feel it in my bones."

"Well, keep your chin up. I'm sure something will break the case. I'll say an extra good prayer for you."

Epps sifted through the mail and came across a letter with child-like handwriting marked "Open Immediately".

He struggled to read the scribbled text. The letter was from a woman who said she used to date a state trooper in Cincinnati. She said she had information that would break the Harris case wide open. If proven true, this would be the miracle Curtis needed. He hoped it wasn't just a cruel hoax by some sick-minded person.

Epps contacted his former partner, Jonathan Echols. The two had been great friends since they were undergrads at Michigan State University. After graduating from law school and both passing the Michigan Bar on the first try, Echols and Epps, P.C. seemed inevitable.

However, in 1949 most folks weren't ready for an integrated law firm where the attorneys were equal partners. After four years of gallant efforts, they were forced to dissolve the partnership.

Echols used his legal background and inquisitive nature to transition into the field of private investigation. Epps returned to Ohio and established a private law practice. He had called upon Echols in an emergency – as he put it, every time he heard from Epps it was an emergency.

Echols tracked McAllister's ex-girlfriend and after meeting with her, was able to substantiate her incredible account of what really happened when Curtis and Amy were brought in. At the time, she worked as a dispatcher at the same station as her former boyfriend. She told Echols she was on duty when Amy and Curtis were brought in for questioning.

She provided complete details of the arrest, described both Amy Whitcomb and Curtis, and was even able to substantiate the contents of Amy's bag when they brought them in. She said that only a third of the cash from Amy's duffel bag was recorded in the "official" records.

She also said that they discovered that Amy and her husband were wanted for a string of armed robberies in Louisiana, Kentucky and Ohio. Their hot sheets nicknamed them Bonnie and Clyde. Oddly enough, the woman said that the men at her station were really ticked off at Amy for willfully riding with that colored man. She said they didn't even seem to care that they had apprehended a wanted criminal. The woman said she overheard the captain telling Amy he should let her rot in jail, but he needed to send a message that 'them colored truckers' would never forget.

She told Epps that the Cincinnati station had concocted a story to pin a crime on Curtis. She said there is an "understanding" between several police agencies in that area.

"They can just make "things happen" and everyone involved cooperates – no questions asked."   The woman also said she overheard them tell Amy they'd make her problems go away if she cooperated with them and promised to stay out of trouble from now on. Then she handed Echols an envelope that contained copies of two sets of documents pertaining to Curtis' arrest. The factual police record completed by McAllister, and the sanitized version.

She told Echols he could do whatever he wanted with the information, but she warned him to be very careful if he chose to follow up on the information she provided him.

"That bunch is just plain crazy. They'll kill a man as quick as they'd squash a bug."

She also warned that if anyone ever tried to implicate her as the person who provided this information, she'd deny it 'til Jesus comes.

"Just out of curiosity Ma'am, may I ask why you're blowing the whistle on your boyfriend?"

"*Ex* – boyfriend thank you." She paused and sighed. "If that man gets convicted of raping that girl, I don't even want to imagine what would happen to him in that prison. I've looked the other way for as long as my conscience could stand it. I believe in the hereafter. I've got to look out for my soul."

Chapter Fifty

Greater love hath no man than this,
that a man lay down his life for his friends.

John 15:13

Echols' Doberman, Sonya, barked furiously from behind the front door of his Grosse Pointe home. Sherry, Echols' girlfriend/secretary pounded on the door. It was almost 10 o'clock in the morning and she hadn't seen, nor heard from him since last night.

He was always in the office no later than 8:30. After her sixth unsuccessful attempt to reach him by telephone, she sensed something was very wrong.

She peered through the bay window from the front porch but couldn't see inside. She let herself in with the emergency key Echols had given her. Sonya nuzzled at her skirt tail as she called out to Echols room by room. There was no sign of him.

After she had searched the interior of the house, she called Sonya and exited through the back door. The dog rooted around the backyard as Sherry headed for the garage.

Echols' two-car garage door was open and both his cars were still inside. The motor of his '59 Deuce-And-A-Quarter was running and Jonathan was behind the wheel. He appeared to be reading or looking at something in his lap.

Sherry breathed a sigh of relief and was poised to give him a piece of her mind. She wedged herself into the narrow space between the Deuce and Echols' two-seat convertible roadster. She hoped Echols would be startled out of his skin when he saw her. *Serves him right for not calling.*

When she reached for the handle, she saw that Echols wasn't reading – he was slumped over. She snatched the door open and dove into the passenger seat. Echols was still wearing the clothing from the day before.

There was a huge bump just above his left temple and his breathing was shallow. Sherry used all the strength she could muster to pull him over to the passenger's side. She then slid into the driver's seat and drove furiously to Cottage Hospital.

Bonita buzzed Epps saying that Sherry was on the phone.

"Hey Sherry baby. What's up?"

Sherry was hysterical. She screamed a string of unintelligible words. The only thing he could make out was, "it's all your fault."

"Sherry, slow down. What's my fault? I can't understand you."

Sherry slammed the receiver down. Epps pressed the switch hook to dial the number at Echols' office, but before he could begin dialing his second line was ringing. This time Sherry was just calm enough to tell him that she had found Echols in his car unconscious – and that David and his client were to blame.

Epps practically broke the sound barrier making his way to Detroit. At the hospital, the emergency room physician looked past Epps to Sherry. "Family of Jonathan Echols?"

Both Epps and Sherry stood. "I'm his fiancée and this is his best friend." The doctor continued to ignore Epps and spoke to Sherry. "I'm doctor Hanley Ma'am. Mr. Echols' doesn't have any life threatening injuries although it appears that he'll be pretty sore for a while." He described Echols' condition in further detail. "His collar bone and left femur are fractured..."

The laundry list of his injuries and prognosis made Sherry feel lightheaded. Epps helped her sit down as the doctor continued.

"The good news is that the wound to his head is somewhat superficial. He has a concussion but we fully expect that he will heal very nicely overall.

Epps joked. "In other words, he has a hard head."

Sherry wasn't laughing. She looked sternly at Epps. "This is no time for sarcasm. They could have killed Johnny."

Echols had been able to substantiate McAllister's ex-girlfriend's claims. Unfortunately her ominous warning had been on the money as well.

Thankfully, this was the break Epps needed to exonerate Curtis. But the price Jonathan paid for his friend David had nearly cost him his life.

Chapter Fifty-One

*For God hath not given us the spirit of fear; but of power,
and of love, and of a sound mind.*

2 Timothy 1:7

Bill rested his hand on Angela Casey's shoulder a little bit too long. She had lingered in the clinic nearly an hour after her four-year-old son's appointment ended. She smiled at Bill too much. Bill smiled back at her too much. She stood too close to him, he didn't seem to mind.

This had become a familiar scene. It had played out with Danielle Schaefer's mother, Gerald Parker's mother, Desmond Nance's mother and Gail Sweeney's babysitter. Come to think of it, it wasn't long ago that the same scenario had played out between Bernadette and Bill.

Natalie grew impatient as she and Gwen waited for Bernadette to arrive at Mario's for their monthly Thursday night dinner-and-a-movie. "I wonder what's keeping that girl."

"Nat, it's not a matter of what's keeping her, it's *who's* keeping her. I'm pretty sure we both know *who* the who is."

"I hate to admit it but you're probably right."

Twenty minutes later, Bernadette breezed in and plopped beside them at the table. It was obvious that she was deeply disturbed about something.

Gwen was the first to speak. "Well hello to you too Mrs. Mitchell."

"Don't start with me Gwen. I'm not in the mood."

215

"Well shoot, don't bite my head off 'cause you had it out with your fake husband again – or was it your wife-in-law this time?"

Bernadette shot her a look. "I'm not playing with you Gwen, one more word and I'm going to slap the taste out of your mouth!"

"Both of y'all hush before you break out in a cat fight." She turned to Bernadette.   "We can see something is wrong though girl, we're here to listen if you want to talk about it."

They sat in silence for several minutes waiting for her to respond, but Bernadette didn't say a word.

Gwen grabbed her menu. "Forget this, let's order."

When their orders came, Bernadette pushed the food on her plate around with her fork while Natalie and Gwen discussed Curtis' trial.

"I'm breaking up with Bill. This time I'm really going to do it."

Gwen and Natalie exchanged looks.

"I know y'all don't believe me but I'm serious. He ain't never gon' leave Cynthia and Jamie is getting too old to be exposed to all this."

Gwen asked. "What happened this time?"

"A lot. A whole lot. I think he's messing around with one of his patient's mothers. Nat you know her, Angela Casey. She used to go to our church."

"I don't know what to tell you girl. That's the nature of the beast."

Bernadette ignored her. "On top of that, Cynthia called my house looking for Bill last night after midnight. She said he never came home and she knew he was with me. Only he wasn't! I hadn't seen Bill since I left work."

Gwen was sarcastic. "So the cheater is cheating on you *and* his wife."

"Funny Gwen. I know I deserve that. I guess I just got all caught up in having things. But the truth is I can't even enjoy them. I spend all my weekends and holidays either with y'all - or

216

it's just me, Jamie and my mama when I can get her to come over. She says she feels condemned whenever she comes to my house, or as Mama puts it, that den of iniquity."

"That's the price you pay when you're the "other" woman. There's never a happy ending. I hope you stick to your decision this time."

"I *am* serious, but I need a plan of action. Bill won't let me walk away just like that. Then, there's the house, my car – not to mention my job! Even if I could find another job, who's going to pay me as much as Bill does?" She covered her face with her hands. "I just feel like a caged animal. I don't know how to get out of this. And I can't even begin to tell you how guilty I feel whenever I see Cynthia and little Billy."

Gwen looked at her with cynicism. "This is us you're talking to Bern. We've heard it all before. So what happened to make you say you want to quit Bill this time?"

Bernadette's demeanor suddenly transformed from contrite to rage.

"That lying, cheating rascal! All this time he's been telling me that he wasn't sleeping with Cynthia – and I believed him."

"Bern, come on now, you don't really expect a young, healthy, married couple to live in the same house and not be sleeping together do you? Not even you could be that gullible."

Bernadette scowled. "Alright. I need to get something else off my chest before I lose my mind. Cynthia's pregnant."

Natalie said. "And that surprises you?"

"And she's going to have the baby."

Gwen sneered. "Why wouldn't she have her baby? You're not making sense. There's something you're still not telling us. What's the real deal Bern?"

"Ok. You're right. I'm ticked off because I was pregnant just a few months ago. I let Bill convince me to get rid of the baby. He sent me to some sleazy woman who butchered me with a coat hanger in her basement. I bled so much afterward, I just knew I was going to die."

Gwen asked. "Wait, was that when you were supposed to have had pneumonia?"

Bernadette nodded.

"Well I'll be darned."

"Bill said the timing wasn't right for us to have a child together. He told me that would complicate the divorce proceedings. He promised me that we would have lots of kids together after we got married. But the way that woman scraped and juked at my insides, I seriously doubt I'll be able to have any more kids. God I hate him for doing that to me!"

"You did this to yourself Bernadette. You should have known what you were getting into from the jumpstart. You play, you pay."

Natalie was too stunned to speak. Bernadette overlooked Gwen's scolding and purged her soul further. "I'm constantly having nightmares and all sorts of bad feelings. Especially when I'm around babies. Working in that clinic don't help. I know God is punishing me for murdering my baby."

Natalie stroked Bernadette's hand. "We all make mistakes honey. Really bad mistakes, but God said he'd forgive all of our sins if we truly repent and give our burdens to Him."

Gwen added. "Just remember that abortion ain't a form of birth control Bern. Don't you do this mess no more. You need to just keep your legs crossed from now on."

"Gwen Brewster I *know* you ain't judgin' me. Don't forget you told me you got quite a history yourself."

Gwen was reminded that her own past was anything but pristine.

"Yeah, you're right girl. So do us all a favor. Learn from my mistakes – don't repeat them."

Natalie refereed again. "Alright y'all. Let's focus on getting Bernadette and Jamie out of this mess. There's only one person who can do anything about this. Let's pray."

The trio hugged, cried and prayed together over dinner. Then they mapped out a plan for freeing Bernadette from Bill Robinson once and for all.

Chapter Fifty-Two

Have not I commanded thee? Be strong and of a good courage; be not afraid, neither be thou dismayed: for the LORD thy God is with thee whithersoever thou goest.

Joshua 9:1

Bernadette sat Bill's *World's Greatest Dad* mug filled with his usual black-coffee-with-two-sugars in front of him. Instead of heading for her work station, she planted herself in one of his visitor's chairs.

"Something you need Sweetheart?"

"Bill, I need to talk to you. I need you to hear my heart and take what I'm about to say to you seriously."

He cleared his throat gruffly. "I hope you're not going to start in on me about leaving Cynthia again. You know I can't do that while she's in the family way. I'll have my lawyer draw up the divorce papers as soon as..."

She interrupted and spoke to him unequivocally. "I'm not going to ask you to leave your wife and children. I'm the one who is leaving Bill."

She handed him a typewritten letter of resignation addressed to both he and Cynthia. The contents of the letter were quite generic. Basically she thanked the Robinsons for the wonderful opportunity to work at their clinic for the past five years; and wished their family a happy future.

"I start my new job in two weeks. That should give you enough time to hire someone else. I bet Angela Casey would love to take my place." Bill choked on his coffee and began coughing uncontrollably.   "Are you ok Bill?" He nodded his head as the cough finally subsided.

"Anyway Bill, the files and records are all in order so it will be very easy for the new girl to jump right in."

A wicked expression etched across Bill's face. He balled up the letter and threw it in the wastepaper basket. "Bern, we both know I'll never let that happen. Since we've been together, I've given you more than most women receive in an entire lifetime. What else do you want from me?"

"I don't want anything from you Bill. Let's be clear - I'm not walking out on you, I'm walking out on this sinful, adulterous affair."

"Affair? Is that what this is to you? We belong together. You're mine! I bought you. I own you! Everything you have belongs to me. I hold the deed to that house you and Jamie live in. I paid for every stick of furniture in that house. Do you honestly think I'm going to let you leave me after all I've invested in you?"

Bernadette remained calm while Bill ranted. "Have you forgotten the deplorable conditions you and Jamie were living in before I came along? How do you expect to maintain the kind of lifestyle you've become accustomed to? What are you going to say to your son when you tell him you have to move back to the slums and start riding the DSR again?"

Then he reached what he thought was an epiphany. He snapped his fingers and smiled empathetically. "Ohhhh I get it. Mother Nature is beating up on you again, isn't she? That's what has you talking out of your head. You'd better take an aspirin. Why don't you make yourself a pot of that ginger tea you usually drink when this business is going on? Better yet, why don't you just take the rest of the day off? I can manage. Maybe I'll see if Angela, Mrs. Casey can fill in for you. Would you like that Sweetheart?"

She stared at the portrait of Bill's wife hanging on the wall behind his desk. Cynthia's confident smile taunted her.   "I'm fine Bill."

"Well, you're not acting fine but suit yourself." He looked at the clock. "Listen Love, Kenny Gray was admitted to Children's Hospital last night. I have to check on him." He reached for his jacket. "I'll see you when I get back. What time is my first appointment again?"

She answered without taking her eyes off Cynthia's portrait. "Eleven o'clock."

He tapped the face of his watch. "Eleven o'clock. Alright, I should be back around 10:30, quarter 'til at the latest."

She felt stupid when he kissed her brow, then left her sitting in his office... still staring at Cynthia's picture.

When Bernadette returned from lunch, Bill had placed a whimsical-looking stuffed panda bear in her chair. The bear was holding a bouquet of pink carnations and a greeting card. The cover of the card had an illustration of a sad-faced puppy sitting inside a dog house holding a sign that said *I'm Sorry*.

She tossed both the card and the stuffed panda bear into the trash. She hesitated before dumping the flowers. *The wife gets roses. The concubine only gets carnations.*

For the rest of the afternoon, she and Bill went about their regular activities as if nothing happened earlier. Bill didn't bring up Bernadette's threat to break up with him - and she didn't acknowledge his gifts. Nothing unusual. That was their customary break-up-and-make-up routine.

It was almost 5 o'clock, just before dusk, when Bill walked little Darlene Davis and her mother to the reception area. He noticed that Bernadette wasn't at her desk. Her work space, which was always tidy, looked like it had just been sanitized. He saw what she had done with the apology gifts he left for her. A set of keys lay conspicuously in the center of the desk blotter. Jamie's drawings and the photos of Bernadette's family were missing.

He left the building and walked into the parking lot. He was surprised when he saw Bernadette's car - parked in its usual space next to his. He stood beside the car, denying the inevitable.

He returned to the office and dialed Bernadette's home phone number. Jamie answered.

"Hey Jamie. How's my boy?"

"I'm alright Dr. Bill. Mommy said to tell you she's not here."

He frowned at the receiver. "Boy put your mother on the phone!"

Jamie obeyed his mother's previous instructions and hung up. Bill called again - this time he got a busy signal. *Oh she's playing games. She must really be ticked off this time.*

Bill arrived at the two-bedroom bungalow where Bernadette and Jamie lived. Lights were on in every room. He parked across the street and watched the activity in the house through the translucent window shades. He could easily see Bernadette's silhouette moving quickly throughout the house. She and little Jamie were arduously wrapping items, packing them away and stacking the boxes. Houston would bring her a U-Haul in the morning before dawn.

As Bill spied on them from his car, disbelief turned into anger – and anger mounted to rage. He continued to sit and watch, watch and plot what he would do to stop her. "Nobody walks out on Bill Robinson!"

As his surveillance continued, he chewed on his manicured fingernails until they bled. Then he began to beat the steering wheel, repeatedly, rhythmically, like a drum.

His pulse raced, the cadence of his breathing increased rapidly. He watched Bernadette press toward freedom for nearly an hour. Finally, his volcanic emotions erupted. He rushed out of the car and burst through the front door using his own key.

Anger boiled in his chest when he saw that the living room was filled with stacks of boxes, crates and the furniture was covered with sheets.

In his haste, he tripped over the open box filled with Jamie's toys. He swore loudly.

Bernadette heard the clamor from the back of the house where she was wrapping dishes in newspaper.

She turned and scanned the room for a quick escape route - if necessary. Three large boxes filled with her pots, cast iron skillets, and small kitchen appliances were stacked against the back door. She tried to estimate how feasible it would be to un-stack the boxes. *Where is Jamie?*

"Do you really think I'm going to let you go through with this Bernadette?"

She whipped around and saw Bill standing there - staring down at her. His sudden appearance made her soil her underwear. Pretending to be unaffected, she turned her back and kept working. "This is the last night Jamie and I spend in your house. I take it you saw that I left your car parked in the clinic's lot?"

"Bernadette, if this is some elaborate ploy to rush me into leaving Cynthia and Billy..."

"You really think this is all about you don't you? Well it's not Bill. I've been telling you for months that I want out and you have never taken me seriously. Maybe it's because I never took myself seriously either. But this time I really mean it and there isn't anything you can say - or do to change my mind. It's over between us." She exhaled. "Thank God it's finally over."

A wooden crate on the floor put just enough distance between them to make his first swing fall short; however, the second one landed squarely on the left side of her face. She fell backward into a pile of newspapers and scurried to her feet. She grabbed the handle of her heavy wooden chopping board - and cold cocked him with all the strength and fury she could muster.

Bill lay in the middle of the kitchen floor dazed. She hoped she had killed him. She leaped over him and ran through the house looking for Jamie. She tried to sound calm. "Jamie? Where are you baby?" She peered over her shoulder, realizing it might be only a matter of moments before Bill would catch up to her.

She hurried to her bedroom and ran her hand under her pillow looking for it... it wasn't there. She snatched the top middle drawer of her dresser open and rummaged through its contents. She didn't find it there either. She was crouched down looking through the drawer of her nightstand... "Where is it?"

"Is this what you're looking for?" Bill stood at the door holding Bernadette's .38 snub-nose revolver. Her older brother Ray Jay had given her a sawed off shotgun and the revolver right after James was murdered.

"How? Where did you get that?"

"I found it months ago." He lied. "I took it away because I was afraid Jamie might get hold of it. You shouldn't keep loaded guns where children can get to them. I would think you'd know better than that Bern."

She responded placidly. "You're right Bill. I'll keep it in a safer place from now on."

She reached for the gun and he fired at her. The bullet lodged in the wall, only inches away from her head.

Bernadette knew that Bill's anger was at the point of no return. She realized that it was either kill or be killed. She had to protect Jamie. She had to survive. Jamie had already lost one parent; she wasn't going to let him become an orphan. She grabbed the lead crystal lamp from the nightstand and threw it at him. It connected with Bill's shoulder – forcing him to drop the gun. She tried to run past him. He grabbed her by her hair. *Where is Jamie?*

Chapter Fifty-Three

Shall not the Judge of all the earth do right?

Genesis 18:25

Friday morning before the day's court proceedings began Epps made the sign of the cross and said a quick prayer. "Ok God, we need that miracle Curtis has been talking about - today! Amen."

The prosecutor's so-called eyewitness took the stand. Frank Lattimore was the clerk on duty at the rest stop where Curtis met Amy. After the clerk was sworn in, he stared at the prosecutor's mouth then recited a sterile, obviously rehearsed account of how he alleged to have seen Curtis coerce Amy into his truck.

The prosecutor nodded his approval of Lattimore's testimony, silently encouraging him to continue as they had practiced. Suddenly, Lattimore's attention was drawn away from the prosecutor. The Holy Spirit compelled him to look directly at Curtis.

The prosecutor sensed that the next words to proceed from the mouth of his star witness would not be what he had instructed him to say. Lattimore made futile attempts to look away from Curtis. Finally he spoke. "The girl and a blond haired man were outside really going at each other so I called the cops. She put up a good fight but the guy beat the crap out of her then took off in a beat up old clunker."

The prosecutor attempted to steer the clerk back to their rehearsed script but the dazed man continued.

"That colored trucker came in and bought her some food. The same order he had just ordered for himself. By the time the cops showed up she had already left with the colored trucker. By then, the guy that beat her up was long gone.

I tried to give them a description of the guy, but seems like they quit listening to what I had to say about him soon as they heard the girl was in the truck with that colored feller."

The dumbfounded prosecutor's face turned beet red. He was thrown so far off base that he wanted to object to his own witness' testimony. He fumbled to regain control. Finally, he interrupted.   "Thank you Mr. Lattimore..."

The clerk couldn't stop talking. "When I told the police that girl left with the colored guy, they high tailed it outta there like something was afire!"

"Thank you Mr. Lattimore. You can step down now." The prosecutor looked helplessly at Judge Dill. "Your Honor, may I approach?"

The judge nodded. Epps joined him in front of the judge's bench.

Dill spoke. "Let me save you the trouble. You don't have a case."   He looked sternly at the prosecutor. "The whole country's like a pressure cooker because of that Medgar Evers *situation* last week. Everybody's on edge. The governor says he doesn't want to risk a riot breaking out in *his* state."

Epps was amused as he watched Judge Dill's nostrils flare and retract as he spoke. "Look Joe, you need to make this thing go away. And do it today – I want to get a head start on the weekend. I've got a lake full of largemouth bass waiting for me."

For the first time in his 27-year career as a prosecutor, he surrendered. He threw up his hands. "Mr. Lattimore, you may step down." With a defeated look on his face he said to the judge, "Your Honor, in light of circumstances which have just come to our attention, the People wish to drop the charges against Mr. Harris and dismiss this case."

The judge banged his gavel. "This case is dismissed.

Mr. Harris is to be released immediately with the Court's sincere apology for any inconvenience you and your family may have experienced."

The courtroom erupted in thunderous applause, shouts of victory and praises to God. Curtis thanked and embraced David Epps then waded through the crowd of his supporters. Natalie threw herself into his arms and they kissed for what seemed like an eternity. He asked her, "You still want to marry me?"

"More than ever."

C.J. chimed in, "Me too?"

Curtis picked her up and swung her around. "Yes, baby. You too."

C.J. yelled, "Thank-ya-lujah!"

Curtis' mind was racing. His body was charged with adrenaline.

"Baby, I know this sounds crazy but since we're in Ohio, let's get married. We can stop over in Toledo and do it on the way back to Detroit. Get my mama and your parents.   And,   oh catch Reverend Healy and the people from the church." Curtis was so elated he was talking a mile a minute. "While we're at it, we should invite Attorney Epps too."

Natalie looked apprehensive.

Curtis pleaded. "Baby we need to do this right now, before anything else gets in our way."

Natalie pressed her finger to his lips. "Ok sweetheart. We'll do it. And don't worry - starting today, the best is yet to come."

Chapter Fifty-Four

For the wages of sin [is] death; but the gift of God [is]eternal life through Jesus Christ our Lord.

Romans 6:23

After lying in a comatose state for five days, Bernadette regained consciousness. She had a sketchy recollection of seeing Jamie standing behind Bill outside her bedroom door, but she couldn't see the object he was holding. Images of Bill trying to wrestle the gun from her flickered in her mind. She remembered Bill knocking the gun out of her hand, then seeing it spin across the polished wood floor. She remembered that she had miraculously managed to retrieve the revolver. Then she remembered seeing Bill's fingers gripped tightly around the base of the broken lamp as it came crashing into her face.

She remembered the deafening silence after hearing the explosive blast. Her mind dredged up the disgusting sight of blood and flesh splattered all over the curtains, walls, the furniture – and all over her. She recalled the combined stench of torn flesh and post gun fire smoke.

She felt sick as she visualized the gaping through and through wound in Bill's torso as he lay on the floor in a literal puddle of his own flesh and blood. She recalled the look of astonishment on Bill's face, then the brief look of agonizing pain... then the look of imminent death. She remembered the ruckus of emergency medical personnel, police, newspaper reporters and photographers as they scurried about the house.

Finally, Bernadette remembered the horrified expression on Jamie's face as the police, a social worker and both her parents tried to coax the shotgun out of her little boy's hands.

Her senses slowly awakened. The voices of hospital personnel sounded muffled through the closed door of her private hospital room.   She thought she smelled fresh cut flowers along with another familiar scent that mingled with the hospital's hodgepodge of odors. *That's odd.* She was certain she smelled the sultry base notes of Chanel No. 9.

Through blurred vision she saw a large painted ceramic vase filled with a fragrant bouquet of pink and white carnations. Not unlike those Bill would have sent after the many times she'd threatened to break off their affair. She was relieved. She guessed he hadn't been hurt as badly as she thought. Evidently this was all just a very bad dream. She must have been in some sort of accident and was awakening from a drug-induced nightmare. A greeting card had been placed against the vase. *Classic Bill Robinson.*

She pressed the button that summoned a nurse to her room.

"Mrs. Mitchell, thank goodness you're finally awake. I'll get a doctor right away."

"Wait, before you get the doctor, could you please hand me the card next to those flowers?"

"Sure." The nurse waved the card under her nose. "Wow, someone likes Chanel."

Bernadette squinted to read the handwriting on the card but her vision was severely distorted from her injuries. She handed it back to the nurse. "I can't see very well, do you mind reading it to me?"

"I'd be happy to Mrs. Mitchell." But the nurse frowned when she read the message on the outside. "It says... *Sorry for your loss.* Do you want me to read from the inside as well?"

Bernadette's heart sank. She answered dryly. "Yes."

The nurse began to read then stopped. "Mrs. Mitchell, this might be too personal for me to read. I don't think..."

"Read it!"

The nurse continued. "It says *Bernice; I know you were hoping that someday you would be in my shoes. Sorry to disappoint you. Here's a little something for your trouble, and to tide you over until you get your hooks into someone else's husband.*

"There's something else inside the card Mrs. Mitchell."

"Find out what it is please."

The nurse tore open the envelope.

"It's a check Mrs. Mitchell. A check and a note."

"How much is the check for and what does the note say?"

"It says, *Here is the return on your investment.* Mrs. Mitchell, the check is for $5.00."

Chapter Fifty-Five

*When I call to remembrance the unfeigned faith that is in thee, which
dwelt first in thy grandmother Lois, and thy mother Eunice;
and I am persuaded that in thee so.*

2 Timothy 1:5

Natalie drained her tea cup then rose from Gwen's kitchen table. "Well Bern, it's getting late. We better get outta here."

Gwen asked, "You and Curtis have big plans for tonight?"

"No, actually I'm going to spend some time with my mama."

"You haven't gone over there for a long time, have you?"

Natalie shrugged. "Something strange is going on with Mama. Every time I call to tell her I'm coming over, she says she's not up to it. She doesn't even want me to bring C.J. Mama just hasn't been the same since Daddy died. I'm just going to show up without even calling."

Bernadette recalled, "Mama said she went over to see Aint Hattie last week but she didn't come to the door. Not even when she told her she brought some of her homemade peanut brittle."

Gwen said. "That's really unusual. That woman loves your mama's peanut brittle. Make sure you tell Mama Hattie I said 'hi' and that I'd like to come see her too."

Natalie gathered her sweater and purse. "Alright Bern, let's hit the road. I have to pick up a few things at Wrigley's before I go to Mama's. I'm going to cook her some neck bones and Hoppin' John."

Bernadette followed. "Yeah, we'd better get back.

Those kids probably have Curtis climbing the walls by now. Besides, you never know when or where those people from Social Services might pop up. If they find out I left Jamie with Curtis, they'll cut my visits with him."

"I can't believe the State is trying to terminate your parental rights. That mess with Dr. Robinson just won't go away will it Bern?"

"I know Gwen, it's been over a year since all that stuff happened and Bill is still running my life – even from the grave."

"Well Bern, you know you don't have to worry about Curtis. He loves hanging out with the kids. He's just a big kid himself. Right about now, Curt probably got James Brown on my record player hollerin' bout breakin' out in a Cold Sweat and got those kids trying to teach him how to do the Boogaloo. I can see it now, Jiffy Pop pans and pop bottles scattered all over my house."

"It's a blessing that Jamie can spend time with his uncle Curtis. He needs a good man in his life. I don't think he likes the foster family he's living with right now. He doesn't talk much about them. I guess he wants to keep his mind off his troubles."

Gwen tsked. "I don't know how in the world that judge figures it's better for Jamie to be in foster care, than with you – or least your parents. Shoot, I would have taken him if they'd let me."

"Or me and Curt. We would have taken him if they would have let us. Speaking of keeping your mind off your troubles, the kids have been giving C.J. a hard time at that new school."

"You can't be serious Nat. They calling her white girl and stuff like before? That was your main reason for moving her."

"Can you believe it? Now it's even worse. She overheard two *teachers* talking. One said she doesn't look anything like me and Curtis so she must be adopted and at least one of her real parents must be white. On top of that, the kids tease her because she's not black enough. She gets left out when they're choosing teams for games and group activities."

Gwen said, "It's no wonder she just keeps her nose buried in her books. That girl is going to grow up to be something great someday."

"Kids can be so cruel, but at least they have their innocence to blame. There's no excuse for the adults though."

"Tell me about it. Remember when we were kids back home Bern? People always gave me a hard time about being so dark, now C.J. ain't dark enough."

"People in this country are just too hung up on looks. If it ain't the color of your skin, it's your weight... if it's not your weight, it's your height... or your eye color... or the texture of your hair. It just never ends. It's like we're telling God he messed up when He made all of us to look different. But the bible says we're all made in His image and after His likeness. Somehow, that message isn't getting through."

"You're right Gwen. Anyway, Curtis is doing everything he can to cheer her up."

"Well Nat, we better get out of here like you said. And you're sure it'll be ok for Jamie to spend the night?"

"Positive. We love having Jamie with us. And don't worry about those Social Services people. It's the weekend."

It was dusk when WCHB's Butterball Jr. announced on Natalie's car radio that it was nine o'clock. The streetlights that lined Linwood Avenue summoned the neighborhood kids home.

Natalie pulled into the driveway of the house she'd practically grown up in. Manicured lawns and shrubbery, carefully planned flowerbeds and an array of lawn ornaments that ranged from tasteful to tacky were evidence that the residents still took pride in the neighborhood. She was surprised that her mother didn't meet her at the door when she tooted the horn. Perhaps Hattie hadn't heard her.

She started hauling grocery bags up to the porch and rang the doorbell but got no response.

She guessed her mother might be in the basement with the washer going so she decided to pull the car into the backyard. She let herself in with her own key and searched for her mother throughout the darkened house.

"Hey Mama, woo-ooo, it's me."

She heard movement in the front of the house. There was a foul stench in the air.

She spoke into the darkness. "Good Lord Mama, when was the last time you took out the garbage?"

Hattie moaned.

Natalie groped familiar surfaces as she made her way to the reading lamp next to Hattie's rocking chair and was horrified by what the lamp illuminated.

Hattie was lying on the sofa with a blanket pulled up to her chin. The telephone, a dirty jelly glass and a pitcher of cloudy water sat on the cocktail table amidst a barrage of spent tissues that were saturated with blood and pus.

A wastebasket next to the sofa with more of the same spilled over onto the floor. Hattie's eyes were sunken and dark, her face was emaciated.

"Mama!" Hattie wanted to sit up but was too weak. Natalie rushed to her mother's side. As she came closer to Hattie, the stench was overwhelming.

"Mama what in the world is wrong with you?"

Hattie tried to keep the blanket pulled underneath her chin. Natalie wondered why she would be cold in July. She tried to gently pull her mother to an upright position but Hattie howled in anguish.

"What did I do?" She accidentally yanked the blanket from beneath Hattie's chin. Dried blood and pus had glued Hattie's filthy nightgown to her chest.

"Mama for God's sake, what happened to you?" Hattie was in so much torment she couldn't even speak. Her eyes pleaded for Natalie to help her.

"I'll get you some help." Natalie couldn't connect the surreal image before her with reality. Her mind raced back to recent conversations with her mother. *Mama sounded weak the last few times I talked to her – but I never imagined she was sick!* She rushed to telephone an ambulance.

The ambulance arrived almost an hour after she called. One of the white-uniformed men asked Natalie a series of questions that seemed irrelevant to her. They were wasting precious time. The men exchanged grave looks which Natalie interpreted as their way of telling each other that Hattie's condition was critical.

"Can we please get my mother to the hospital now?"

Concerned neighbors began to huddle near Hattie's front door. Natalie heard whispered questions and prayers as the men wheeled Hattie to the ambulance.

The next-door neighbor, Mrs. Jenkins, pushed through the crowd. "Don't you worry baby, God gon' see that your mama pulls through this. You need me to call your auntie for you?"

"Yes Ma'am. Tell her to meet us at Crittenton Hospital."

Natalie could barely see through her tears as she drove behind the ambulance to the hospital. "Lord I don't know what I would do without my mama. Please have mercy on her Lord, and on me."

Hours had passed since the ambulance brought Hattie to the hospital - still no update on her condition. Nurses promised to let Natalie know something as soon as information became available. "Family member for Hattie Jordan?"

A man with a heavy Austrian accent extended his hand to shake Natalie's. "I am Dr. Kleinhauer; I've been working with Mrs. Jordan this evening. May I ask what your relationship is to her?"

"I'm her daughter, Natalie Harris."

The doctor lowered his voice. "I see. May we speak privately?"

The doctor's tone concerned Natalie. "What's wrong with my mother?"

"Well, unfortunately I must say that a lot has happened to her. May I ask if your mother has been under a doctor's care lately?"

"Not that I know of."

"I suspect not."

"Why do you say that?"

"From all appearances, it is evident that your mother has an advanced stage of breast cancer. It is apparent that she has not received any treatment."

Natalie's knees buckled as the doctor continued. "I'm afraid that both breasts have been affected by this. A double mastectomy might buy her some time but..."

Natalie struggled to understand the profusion of information she was receiving. The shock of Hattie's condition, the doctor's foreign accent, and his use of medical jargon made it difficult for her to comprehend what he was trying to tell her.

She swallowed hard. "Alright, then will the cancer be all gone once she has the surgery?"

"I'm afraid it's not that simple." He guided her to a chair.

"Please, let's sit down. Cancer is a very serious and complicated illness. We are not done assessing your mother's condition yet; however, to be frank with you the preliminary prognosis does not offer very much hope. We might have been able to do more for Mrs. Jordan had she sought treatment earlier."

Natalie couldn't believe what she was hearing. The doctor continued explaining. "Unfortunately, I suspect that all we can do is to try to keep her comfortable. She must have been experiencing a lot pain and discomfort for some time now."

The room spun around Natalie. "Doctor, are you saying that my mother is dying?"

He frowned. "I don't want to speculate without having documented proof of the extent of Mrs. Jordan's illness;

however, I would venture to say that her condition is certainly very grave."

He rose from his seat. "I will check back with you as soon as we receive the test results I am waiting for."

Natalie demanded. "I want to see my mother now!"

"Please be patient with us Mrs. Harris. We are not finished evaluating her. Due to the medication we gave her, she is quite drowsy right now anyway. You can visit with her in a short while, ok?" The doctor saw that Natalie was distraught. "Is someone here with you?"

"No. I'm here by myself but my aunt should be here any minute."

"Very good then." He patted her shoulder. "I feel very sorry Mrs. Harris."

Chapter Fifty-Six

And the violent take it by force.

Matthew 11:12

Natalie was awakened from the fitful slumber she had fallen into while waiting to learn about her mother's condition. The entire emergency room was engulfed in mayhem. Hospital personnel were frantically scurrying around, bumping into one another. Natalie repeatedly heard the words police, gunshot wounds, burns; and *riot.*

It was nearly1:00 a.m. when she phoned Curtis who, in turn said he would send Gwen and Bernadette to the hospital. He agreed that something strange was happening in the city when Natalie described the chaos at the hospital. He said he'd heard an unusual number of sirens and what sounded like guns firing within the past couple of hours.

"I'm glad you're safe inside the hospital, it almost sounds like a war zone outside. I thought I was back in Korea for a minute." He heard an explosion in the distance and peeked through his front window.

"Yup, something is definitely up. I'm looking at what looks like flamethrowers shooting through the air as we speak! It looks like the Fourth of July out there. Somebody must be throwin' Malatov cocktails."

"Sweetheart, I'd better let you go so you can call Bern n'em. I really should let them stay at home with all this mess goin' on out there."

"You probably better let them decide. They'll have a fit if they find out you're at that hospital by yourself. I'm going to go ahead and get in touch with them. Call me when you find out what's going on with Mama Hattie."

The hospital was on full alert by the time the others arrived. Natalie's head was pounding and she felt nauseated. Bernadette pulled a plastic collapsible cup from her purse and sought out a water cooler. Gwen put her arm around Natalie's shoulder and tried to comfort her.

Moments later Bernadette reappeared and handed her the cup full of water and an envelope of Bromo Seltzer. She emptied the contents of the envelope and shook it in a circular motion then gave it to Natalie to swallow.

She rested her head on the back of the chair and started to drift in and out again. She still hadn't told them the details of Hattie's condition. She couldn't make her mouth form the words.

"Did y'all notice anything strange when you were on your way here?"

Gwen answered, "Strange is putting it mildly. Somethin's up. We almost got sideswiped by a speeding police car on the way here."

Bernadette added, "And there seem to be a lot of fires tonight. I don't know what's going on but it don't look good."

She recognized the distinct tap-clip-clop, tap-clip-clop of her mother's post-stroke gait and four pronged walking cane.

"Here comes Mama." She scooted over so her mother could sit next to Natalie.

Baby Sis lowered her large frame onto the seat next to her niece. "Dem folks done started riotin' out there."

Natalie asked, "What folks, what you mean rioting?"

"The news man on the radio said some po'leeses busted up a party over on 12th street and Clairmount. The folks was givin' a welcome home party for some boys who just come back here from Vee-et Nam. Look like them Stress and Big Fo' po'leeses done went too far this time. Peoples is burnin' and breakin' up everythang in sight."

"Aintie, you say you saw black people setting fires in the neighborhood?"

Baby Sis nodded. "Yeah Gwen. I ain't nevah see'd nothin' like it. Folks was nailing up signs that said *Soul Brother* and *Black Owned* on all the stores and shops."

Gwen looked at Bernadette. "That must have been what that couple we saw in front of Feldman's dry cleaners was doing. I wonder if they really think people are stupid enough to believe black folks own that dry cleaning store."

Bernadette gasped. "Nat – what about your shop? You want me to tell Curtis to go down there?"

"No. He'd have to bring the kids with him. I don't want them out there in all that craziness. Anyway, all I'm worried about is my mama. The way I feel right now, that shop can burn to the ground."

Gwen said. "I don't get it. Even if the businesses aren't black owned, why would you set fires and destroy your own neighborhood?"

"Peoples gets tired. Dem po'leeses been arrestin' and beatin' up on these peoples for no good reason and they ain't got nobody to turn to. Sometimes all that sanging' and marching and carrying signs just ain't enough. They doing the same thang dem white folks did when they left out from over in England. That's how this country got started. Only when white folks did it, they called it a revolution – when black peoples gets fed up they calls it a in-suh-rection."

Baby Sis chuckled. "They called it a tea party when dem white folks cut up in Boston 'long time ago."

Gwen said, "Well I know one thing. Mayor Cavanaugh had better get a hold of his police department or there's going to be another civil war! He needs to see to it that we get more black police officers on the force." She turned to Natalie. "Remember when I used to date Raymond? He's on the police force. He told me that for every two black policemen, there's eight white ones. That's a big part of the problem in this city."

A Negro clerk working the midnight shift in the waiting room overheard their conversation. She tiptoed over to Natalie's group. "Excuse me ladies, but I couldn't help overhearing your conversation. I got my radio on at my desk. It's a mess out there. Tanks are rolling down the main streets of the city like they're taking a Sunday drive. If you want to, you can come over to my desk and listen. You have to stand close by though. I have to keep the volume turned down low or else I'll get in trouble."

The group followed the clerk and listened in disbelief as a field reporter described the mayhem that began in a blind pig on 12th Street and Clairmount.

"...Earlier this evening, Albert Crowe, a Black administrative assistant to Detroit's police commissioner, called together several of the city's Responsible Negro Leaders. In pairs, the leaders have fanned throughout the Tenth Precinct to plead with the crowds to disperse. One pair was comprised of Deputy School Superintendent Andre' Johansson and U.S. Representative Bertram Collins, Jr., who is quite popular among his constituents. Here at the intersection of Clairmount and 12th Street, Collins is standing on the hood of the car... He's shouting to the crowd through a bullhorn, "We're with you! But, please! This is not the way to do things! Please go back to your homes!" ...I don't know if you can make out what the crowd is saying but they're chanting. "We don't want to hear it Uncle Tom." ...They're throwing rocks and bottles. One of them just hit a cop nearby. This crowd is getting "uglier." Johansson is motioning for Collins to retreat... Collins reluctantly dismounts the vehicle and the two meld into the sea of rioters...

There is no end in sight. This insurrection seems to be far from over... I've been told that Michigan State Senator Coleman Young is somewhere in the crowd. It's unknown whether he is here to calm the confusion or add fuel to the fire. From his reputation on the Senate floor, the latter is more likely."

Bernadette said, "That Coleman Young is a real pistol. I wish he would run for Mayor! I know he'd straighten this city out."

"I only hope I live to see the day when a black man is running the city of Detroit." Baby Sis thanked the clerk and said to Natalie, "Alright, thas 'nuff 'bout riotin' and all that. What's goin' on with yo' mama gal?"

Chapter Fifty-Seven

...And with his stripes we are healed.

Isaiah 53:5

Talking about Detroit's maladies had given Natalie a brief respite from worrying about her own. She sadly recounted her conversation with Dr. Kleinhauer.

Both Bernadette and Gwen's eyes began to mist. The older woman's face contorted as she forbade her tear ducts.

"Um, hmm. Well what they doin' now?"

"I don't know. I've been here for hours but they won't tell me anything except they're running tests."

"Umm hmm, lemme see what I can find out."

Baby Sis hoisted herself up from the vinyl chair and tap-clip-clopped her way down the hall. Several minutes later, she returned with a young man dressed in medical garb.

"This here is Mizziz Harris, Mizziz Jordan's daw-ter, tell her what you just said."

"Yes Ma'am, first of all, my name is Dr. Maija. I am a resident on staff tonight working with Dr. Kleinhauer." The young doctor extended his hand to shake Natalie's. "From what I understand, Dr. Kleinhauer has already explained to you that we are pretty certain Mrs. Jordan has breast cancer. How wide spread it is and what methods of treatment, if any, have still not been determined. What I can tell you, is that Mrs. Jordan has a very long road to recovery ahead. Eh?" He placed his hand on top of Natalie's hand. "But I am a firm believer that anything is possible as long as there is still breath in the body." He smiled reassuringly at Natalie. "God is in control Mrs. Harris. Let's see what He has to say about the matter - yes?"

Baby Sis grunted and nodded in agreement. "Alright now, when can we go in to see her?"

"I think it's alright for you to visit with her very briefly right now."

"Good, where she at?"

"She has been moved to the intensive care unit, room I-200. Take the elevator up to the second floor then turn left at the first corridor you come to. Mrs. Jordan's room is directly across from the nurses' station."

"Thank you doc-tah. Come on y'all." Baby Sis led the group to Hattie's bedside. "Alright y'all, now we know how to pray."

Natalie winced at the sight of her mother attached to the varied life-sustaining apparatuses. Hattie was heavily medicated with pain killers and antibiotics to treat the open wounds in her breasts and underneath her arms.

Baby Sis ordered, "Pull yourself together gal, your mama needs you strong." The old prayer warrior reached into her purse and retrieved a small vial containing holy oil. She anointed her sister-in-law with the oil and laid her right palm on her forehead. Then she and the others joined hands at the foot of Hattie's hospital bed. She squeezed her eyes together and began to petition the God of heaven and earth.

"Father God in the holy name of Jesus, we come to you right now, 'umbly as we know how... thanking you Lord for your tender mercies and your grace. Lord Jesus, you alone is the author and the finisher of our faith. God, we, your 'umble servants come to you with the confidence of knowing that you is full of wisdom and don't never make a mistake."

Bernadette began to pray in the language of heaven as Baby Sis continued. "Lord you healed the woman who had that issue of blood with just a touch of the hem of your garment. Lord we grabbing a-holt to your garment hem, pleading with you for mercy on my dear sister's behalf. Your word told us that we are healed by your stripes. You said in your word that we could ask anything in your name and it would be done.

Now we come boldly to your precious throne of grace asking for another one of your healing miracles. Lord we thanking you in advance. Believing it is so in Jesus' powerful name. Amen."

The others repeated. "Amen."

Baby Sis looked at her niece's harried face. "Y'all go'on try to make it home now, get some rest. All of you. No sense in all us staying up all night."

"Oh no Auntie, I couldn't leave Mama like this." The aunt pounded the floor with the cane and she raised her voice just enough. "What did I say? Go on home and stay there until I call you to come back. Hear me?"

Natalie looked at the clock. It was after three o'clock in the morning. Gwen and Bernadette stood and gathered their belongings.

Bernadette kissed Hattie's forehead. "Come on honey, Mama will call you later."

"Y'all be careful out there. And Nat'lie, don't worry 'bout yo mama chile." She pointed toward heaven. "Remember, with His stripes, we are healed!"

Chapter Fifty-Eight

Cast me not off in the time of old age;
forsake me not when my strength faileth.

Psalm 71:9

Dressed in a non-descript, terry cloth robe, Albertina sat in her isolated room at Our Lady of Grace nursing home in Baton Rouge. After she was released from a lengthy stay at the hospital, C.J. felt compelled to follow up on her care at the nursing home.

The older woman credited their strange relationship to the fact that C.J. was the only one who could properly identify the cause of the illness that attacked her body and had nearly killed her several years earlier, during her internship at Xavier. She also told C.J. that she felt they had a lot in common.

"My late husband and I attended Xavier's School of Pharmacy back when the dinosaurs still roamed the earth. Our son graduated from there as well."

C.J. snickered, "Oh, Mrs. Baptiste, you're not so old."

The elderly woman continued. "No really, I feel we have… what is it you young folks call it nowadays? Oh yes, kindred spirits."

C.J. simply nodded and listened as Albertina continued.

"You're not going to believe this Dr. Harris, but you look strikingly similar to me when I was a young girl."

C.J. searched the old woman's face and shrugged. "Evidently you're not the only one who thinks so. The staff here is always asking if I'm related to you. People at the hospital used to ask about our being related as well. That's some coincidence, huh?"

Today Albertina would take C.J. along with her on a sentimental journey as she reminisced about the days when she was young, beautiful and powerful.

She and C.J. perused dozens of pictures of herself, Astor, and an array of family photographs.

Astor had spent innumerable hours visiting and catering to Albertina in the hospital and the nursing home until he suddenly died of a heart attack while en route to visit Albertina.

She used to complain to Astor about the food, the drab décor, the doctors, nurses, her medication - and she complained about him. Once, she told him he smelled like an old man. She chuckled as she remembered his response.   "I smell like an old man because I *am* an old man Tina."

For over 50 years, Albertina shot insults and Astor responded with jokes – or retreated behind a newspaper. That was their way.

Gregory made phone calls and occasionally flew in from Detroit for perfunctory visits. She hadn't heard from his ex-wife, Beverly since their divorce nearly a decade ago.

On more than one occasion, Albertina mentioned something to C.J. about being glad she got *Tallulah* back from Beverly. She wondered, but never asked who or what Tallulah was.

"Can you believe that judge awarded alimony to that greedy hussy? He also gave her my son's beautiful house in Rosedale Park, one of his cars, his vacation home in Highland Beach, and half of everything that had a cash value. Why she'll even get half his pension when the time comes – as long as she doesn't remarry. I hear she's been running around with some singer in Detroit these days. It's been rumored that he's with the Temptations or the Four Tops – riff raff I tell you! Dr. Ware would turn over in his grave..."

Albertina paused. "I used to give my husband the dickens about keeping Gregory on as an employee, rather than giving him a proprietary interest in the business. Thank God Astor was wise enough to stick to his guns. That blood-sucking shrew would have gotten half of everything my husband and I built.

She told C.J. that she hadn't seen Gregory's son since she and Astor handed him the keys to his graduation present - a brand new Mustang Mach IV. "His mother never saw to it that he so much as sent us a thank you note."

Sheila lived in Pittsburgh with her husband and sons. "My daughter married a dentist. I believe the boys are right around your age."

Although Sheila's boys spent nearly every summer with their grandparents, last year was the only time she had come back to Louisiana in the past fifteen years - to attend Astor's funeral.

C.J. sat close to the old woman as she reminisced with a faulty memory; and through bifocals and cataracts. She strained to identify a young man in a picture who was leaning against a sports car.

"Nice vintage car. That's your son, right?"

She peered at the photograph. "No. That's not Gregory. I'm trying to remember who it is..." Albertina tapped on the photograph while she struggled to remember the young man in the picture. "Why that's Thomas! My God."

"He looks a lot like your son. He is a relative of yours, right?" Albertina's face darkened. "My husband's nephew. Bad seed. Couldn't seem to keep himself out of trouble." She tsked and shook her head. "It broke his mother's heart when they found him dead. She had a nervous breakdown afterward."

C.J. raised her eyebrows "Somebody found him dead? What happened to him?"

Albertina sighed. "Thomas always managed to get himself into trouble. The family never got the full story but according to the police, his charred remains were found in an alley. Odd thing, that car he loved so much has never been found.

We couldn't even give him a proper funeral. We had to have a memorial service instead. Mr. Diggs, the funeral director, said a casket would have been a waste of money." She sighed. "Poor

Audrey. No mother should ever have to stand at her own child's graveside, but I think even that would have given her some sense of closure. Astor's brother eventually had to put her in a place they call a rest home, but we all knew that was just the genteel way to say he had her committed."

"Oh no. That's awful."

Albertina nodded. "Unfortunately, that was the lifestyle Thomas chose. God knows our family made every attempt to rehabilitate him."

Albertina shut the photograph album and pulled out another one. A loose picture fluttered to the floor. C.J. picked it up and was amazed by what she saw.

"My God, Mrs. Baptiste, if I didn't know better, I'd swear this was one of my own baby pictures."

Without even looking at the photo, Albertina plucked it away from C.J. and stuck it in the back of the picture album.

She smiled absently. "Well, they say everyone has a twin."

Chapter Fifty-Nine

*Rejoice ye in that day, and leap for joy: for,
behold, your reward is great in heaven.*

Luke 6:23

The music ensemble played a pleasant melody as Natalie led the funeral processional into the church. She was flanked by Curtis and Bernadette's husband, the recently appointed Pastor, Reverend C.W. Healy, Jr. This would be the first funeral held in the newly constructed Greater Rose of Sharon Cathedral of Worship.

The sanctuary was packed with Hattie's relatives, friends and other mourners; among them – Freddie, Eddie and Rhoda Feldman, who drug an oxygen tank behind her.

The tone of Hattie's home-going service was exactly what she would have wanted – jubilant. Natalie remembered her mother's words. "I don't want nobody crying and moaning over me. I got somewhere to go, so when the Lord calls me home, make sho' it's a victory service, a celebration!"

After Hattie's home-going service, Natalie changed her clothes and entertained the numerous guests who had gathered at the Linwood house.

She told her guests, "I have no sad song to sing today. God gave Mama several more years after she was first diagnosed with that cancer."

Baby Sis added, "Bless the Lord, she lived to see her only grandbaby grow up to be a doctor." She turned to C.J. "What's the name of that hospital you work at down there in Lou-zee-ana baby?"

"Xavier University, it's a teaching hospital Auntie."

"You some kinda specialiss ain't you?"

"Yes Ma'am. I'm an oncology radiologist."

"Praise God. I guess all that running back and forth to the doctors and hospitals with your gran'mama musta rubbed off on you. Right baby?"

"Yes Ma'am. I decided I wanted to be a doctor when I was quite young. I probably got on Nana's doctors' nerves asking questions and following them around so much."

Bernadette sadly added, "Too bad it didn't rub off on Jamie. He can't stand doctors or hospitals. His daddy would have loved it if he had been a doctor or made something out of himself. He certainly is smart enough."

Baby Sis barked, "I guess Jamie got good reason not to want to be around doctors and such. He'll be alright. Just keep him lifted up in prayer. Yes suh, the good Lord gon' take care of my Jamie. He promised me that this time when he gets out, he gon' give his life to God and make something outta himself."

"Mama, don't get your hopes up. Jamie's been making promises for as long as I can remember."

"You don't nevah give up on your chirrens, Bernie. Nevah!"

Chapter Sixty

And let us not be weary in well doing:
for in due season we shall reap, if we faint not.

Galatians 6:9

C.J. watched the Baptiste family enter the conference room of DeWitt, Nolan and DeWitt, Attorneys at Law, P.C. As she looked around the room, she felt she already knew many of Albertina's family members.

Some of their faces were somber as they filled in the seats around the huge cherry wood conference table. Others seemed curious. The younger ones simply looked bored.

A forty-something-year-old couple entered the room holding hands. A handsome set of young men with bronze skin and dazzling smiles followed close behind. *That must be Sheila and her family.*

Next, a distinguished looking man with thinning auburn hair and graying temples kissed Sheila and bumped fists with her husband and the young men. He sat next to Sheila - facing C.J. *That guy must be Gregory.* Their eyes met. He nodded politely and said "hello." Gregory and Sheila stole inquisitive glances at C.J. Sheila's sons stared and whispered.

A stunning woman with a perfectly coiffed French roll sauntered into the conference room. She wore a navy blue and cream colored Ruth Joyce cashmere dress, three inch navy eel skin pumps and carried a matching handbag. She unashamedly perused the room until she caught Gregory's eye.

With an expressionless gaze, the woman kept her eyes locked on Gregory as she made her way to a seat in the back of the room.

She was followed by a young man with a giant auburn Afro. He was wearing bell bottoms, a colorful dashiki and a peace symbol medallion dangling around his neck. The young man plopped into the chair next to Gregory. The older man embraced the younger, then the two slapped palms. The resemblance between them was unmistakable. *Ok, this must be that spoiled brat of a grandson and I'll bet the glamour girl back there is Gregory's ex-wife, Beverly.*

Everyone in the room seemed to know each other – of course except C.J. The Baptiste family's obvious curiosity about her spread throughout the room.

Finally, she reached across the table to shake Sheila's hand. "You must be Mrs. Baptiste's daughter Sheila. I'm Dr. Christian Harris. I was part of your mother's team at Xavier Medical Center." With just a hint of harshness she added, "I also stayed in touch with her afterward, when she was alone in the nursing home."

Sheila was unmoved by C.J.'s apparent disdain. She smiled warmly. "Yes, I'm Sheila Westbrooke. Mother talked about you often. Thank you so much for looking after her. She was very fond of you."

Sheila's disarming smile put C.J. somewhat at ease. "I enjoyed your mother's company. She told me a lot about your family. I've seen hundreds of pictures of you all. I feel as though I already know many of you. But I have to admit I'm a little confused about why I'm here today."

Sheila's husband stood and offered his hand to C.J. "It's nice to meet you Dr. Harris. I'm Sheila's husband, Barry."

Gregory followed Barry's lead. "It's a pleasure to meet you Dr. Harris. I'm Mrs. Baptiste's son, Gregory. I'm not a bit surprised that you're here. I also heard a lot about you. Mother seemed to think of you as the granddaughter she never had."

Sheila's son Brandon was fascinated by C.J.'s resemblance to his grandmother. "Is it just me, or does Dr. Harris look a whole lot like that old painting of Mimi that used to hang over the fireplace at her and Poppie's house in Detroit?"

C.J. noted that Sheila kept looking at her watch and that she appeared to be agitated. "I wish they'd hurry up. Our plane leaves in two hours. I can't get out of Louisiana fast enough. Hanging around here just gives me the creeps."

Without realizing it, Gregory was staring at C.J. "Hmm, you know Dr. Harris, my nephew is right. Who knows? We might even be related somewhere down the line. Have you always lived here in Louisiana?"

"No. I'm from Detroit."

"That's an interesting twist. My sister and I were born here, but we were raised in Detroit. Maybe I know your parents."

"Probably not. The way Mrs. Baptiste described all of you, I doubt you ran in the same circles as my folks."

Barry said, "One thing is certain. You hold an astonishing likeness to my mother-in-law."

"This isn't the first time I've heard that. People at the nursing home used to ask us if we were related all the time. Oddly enough, I once saw a baby picture in one of her photo albums that looked so much like me I could have sworn it was my own. Strange, isn't it?"

Sheila snapped. "They say everyone has a twin."

"Funny you should say that Mrs. Westbrooke, your mother said that to me not long ago."

Albertina's attorney politely interrupted by requesting everyone to be seated. The remaining beneficiaries crowded into the room and the reading of the Last Will and Testament of Mrs. Albertina LeFleur-Baptiste began.

...I leave equal portions of Baptiste Holdings, Inc. to my son Astor Gregory Baptiste Jr., and my daughter, Sheila Albertina Baptiste-Westbrooke. Namely, the Motor City Pharmacy – East, the Motor City Pharmacy – West, the Motor City Pharmacy Midtown; and the Motown Medical Equipment and Supplies Company.

I leave the sum of $500,000 each, to my grandsons, Gregory Ware Baptiste, Barry Alister Westbrooke, Jr. and Brandon Alexander Westbrooke.

Should there be any minor grandchildren at the time of my demise, the law firm of DeWitt, Noland and DeWitt will establish a trust fund until said minors reach the age of majority. At which time, they will also receive the sum of $500,000...

The attorney continued tediously reading the pages of bequests from Albertina's will for nearly an hour. "Finally, departing from an antiquated family tradition, I leave the Baptiste family heirloom, the three-carat sapphire and diamond ring, also referred to as *Tallulah*, to Dr. Christian Joy Harris..."

Chapter Sixty-One

...But they that wait upon the LORD,
they shall inherit the earth.

Psalm 37:9

Curtis was mowing the lawn in the backyard and Natalie sat on the back porch shelling peas when C.J. appeared at the back fence. "Hey you two!"

Natalie clutched her chest as she ran to her daughter. "Girl, you almost to made me jump outta my skin!"

Curtis idled the lawn mower and rushed toward C.J. "Come here girl, you fixin' to get a whuppin.' How come you didn't tell us you were comin' home?" C.J.'s parents encircled her and gave her a tight hug.

"I have a lot to tell you guys about what's been going on with me lately and I needed to see you in person."

Natalie headed inside for the kitchen. "Sit down, I'll get us all something to drink."

Curtis pitched the patio table's large umbrella. Within minutes, Natalie returned with three ice-filled glasses and a pitcher of cherry flavored Kool-Aid.

"First of all – I've accepted an invitation to work on a research project in London."

"London? London, England? You mean you're going all the way to England?"

"That's right Daddy, your little girl is going to cross the big pond."

"Well congratulations sweetheart. That's exciting news. I'm so proud of you. How long will you be gone?"

"Anywhere from six months to a year."

"A whole year? That's a long time. Are you sure you want to be away from home that long baby?"

"Come on Nat, C.J.'s been away from home for years."

"But then she was only a car ride away - and we didn't need a passport to get to her."

"Wait guys, you're forgetting the point. I said I accepted the invitation. It's all settled."

She turned to Natalie. "I'm a big girl now Mama. I can take care of myself. I'll fill you in on the details about London later. But first, I have a surprise for you."

C.J. told her parents about how she discovered that one of her patients was suffering from a rare disease at the beginning of her internship. She told them that no one else was able to diagnose the woman's near-fatal illness.

Natalie interrupted C.J.'s story to remind her of Mother Winston's prophesy when she was a newborn.

C.J. snapped her fingers. "That's right! No wonder medicine comes as second nature to me."

Curtis said, "Give God the glory for your gift."

"Yes Daddy, I thank Him every day. Anyway, I remembered researching a disease that produced very similar symptoms to what this patient was experiencing back when I was in pre-med."

C.J. excitedly sucked in air and continued. "Well, to make a long story short, one day after we did rounds, I showed the paper I wrote to my Attending Physician. Most senior doctors would never have even looked at the paper - or at the very least they would have tried to take full credit for saving the woman's life."

Natalie interjected. "Only God deserves to get the glory."

C.J. was excited. "Right Mama. Praise the Lord. Anyway, years later, the lady got sick again and ended up in my care when I had just completed my residency.

She hung in there for quite a while but her illness finally got the best of her. Her family didn't seem to care much about her. They rarely bothered to check on her in person – well, with the exception of her husband. But he died last year. So I guess the Lord put me in her life so that I could fill in the gap. She and I got close - to the point where she was kind of like a grandmother to me."

"The Lord will reward your faithfulness C.J."

"He already has Daddy." She waved her arms in the air. "That's what I'm *trying* to tell you guys!"

Natalie and Curtis were awestruck as they listened to C.J. recount the incredible story.

"So Mama, that brings me to this little present I brought you." C.J. handed her mother a tiny antique silver box. "This is for you Mama, thanks to that feisty old lady..."

Natalie gasped when she peered inside the box. "Lord have mercy, if I didn't know better..."

Curtis looked at the ring and teased C.J. "Hmph, that ring ain't no prettier than your mama's wedding ring. Ain't that right Nat? C.J., did I ever tell you the story about how your Grandma Mamie lost your mama's engagement ring?"

C.J. laughed. "Only about a million times Daddy."

Natalie exclaimed, "This is *almost* the most beautiful ring I've seen in ages. But why are you giving your ring to me?"

"It's the strangest thing. From the moment I laid eyes on that ring it just felt like it was rightfully yours. Try it on Mama. We can have it sized if it doesn't fit. My patient said the ring had been handed down for several generations, so I guess only her family would understand the inscription inside. We can have a jeweler replace it with anything you want."

Natalie adjusted her glasses. Her eyes misted as she read the inscription. Then she dabbed her eyes and laughed out loud.

C.J. was bewildered. Curtis reached for the ring and after reading the inscription, he hunched his shoulders and said, "I don't get it. What's so funny? All it says is *Finally Yours*."

"I will surely strike my hands together at the unjust gain you have made
and at the blood you have shed in your midst."

Ezekiel 22:13

*F*orgive me Father for I have sinned..."
As if he expected to hear something different, something
new, Father McClorey listened attentively as Sheila
attempted to purge her tortured soul. The elderly priest concluded the
confession in his customary manner...

"My child, I grant you pardon and peace, in the name of the Father,
and of the Son and of the Holy Spirit. Go now and sin no more..."

For years, Dr. Cartwright, Sheila's psychiatrist, had said her
chronically recurring episodes of neurosis were the manifestation of layers
of deep seated issues that had not been resolved...

Neither half a lifetime of psychotherapy nor innumerable confessions
to the priest had absolved Sheila of nearly thirty years of anxiety and
suppressed guilt that plagued her.

This most recent bout of phobic behavior was triggered at the reading
of her mother's will.

The nightmares had returned with more fervor. Images of that young
doctor invaded her mind day and night. The girl's hands, her eyes and
voice all belonged to Albertina.

Thomas had also resurfaced to taunt her. At night, his mutilated face
and charred body loitered in her dreams. Through jagged, bloody teeth he
threatened her. "Dead men tell no lies."

During the day, he followed her to the grocery store, to restaurants and the movie theatre. She thought she spotted him at the post office and the department of motor vehicles.

He even had the audacity to sit within a few feet away from her family one Sunday during Mass at Holy Redeemer Cathedral.

A handful of prescribed barbiturates, amphetamines and an entire bottle of premium bourbon lured Sheila into an eternal abyss. For the last time, she thumbed through the tattered pages of her family's photo albums. For the last time, she asked herself the unanswered questions that had tormented her for decades...

Why didn't Dennis love her... the way Gregory loved Natalie – even today?

Why had she been insanely jealous of the love Gregory and Natalie had for each other?

For God's sake, why didn't Thomas pay those thugs his gambling debt?

Most of all she wondered, what would life have been like for all of them...

262

...if she hadn't paid Thomas to lie.

Book Club Discussion Questions

1. Near the beginning of the novel, Natalie stated that she was responsible for the perception that she cheated on Gregory. Was she in any way responsible?

2. Prior to reading this story, what was your knowledge about the terms Brown Paper Bag Test, colorism and intra-racial discrimination?

3. Was Sheila spoiled and manipulative like Albertina said; or was she damaged by not knowing the truth about Dennis' disappearance as Astor surmised?

4. Gregory told Sheila that he thought she had a problem with Natalie. Was he correct?

5. Hattie Jordan died of breast cancer in the story. Today's preventive screening and aggressive treatment for breast cancer wasn't available during that era. What measures should today's women take advantage of?

6. Several times throughout the book, Natalie is described as the only woman Gregory ever loved. Based on his behavior, do you think that statement could be true? Explain your answer.

7. What motivated Bernadette's involvement with Dr. Robinson?

8. Who is responsible for Dr. Robinson's death?

9. Hattie and Mother Winston stated that God gives everyone a gift, which is to be used for His glory. Do you know what your gift and your purpose is?

10. If Bernadette was a real person, do you think God would forgive her?

11. Who was your favorite character? Why?

12. What characters would you like to see in the future?

Motor City Trivia

Detroit...

- is home to the Motown sound founded by Berry Gordy, Jr. in 1957

- installed the first mile of paved concrete road, just north of the Model T plant, on Woodward Avenue between McNichols and 7 Mile Roads in 1909

- installed the country's first traffic light in 1915 in downtown Detroit

- built the nation's first urban freeway, the Davison, in 1942

- is home to the oldest state fair in the nation, first held in 1849

- has the country's largest island park within a city – Belle Isle Park

- is home to the world's only floating post office, the J.W. Westcott II, which can be found on the Detroit River

- shares the world's first underwater auto traffic tunnel between two nations – the Detroit/Windsor Tunnel

- is home to the second tallest hotel in North America – the Detroit Marriott Renaissance Center, at 73 stories

- is also home to Vernors ginger ale, Sanders hot fudge, Better Made Potato Chips, Faygo soda pop, and Stroh's Ice Cream

- has more theater seats than any other city, east of the Mississippi River, outside of New York City

Source: Detroit Metro Convention and Visitors Bureau 2006

Recipes

from

Brown Paper Bag

Natalie's Hoppin' John and Black Eyed Peas

1 cup chopped onion

1 tablespoon olive or vegetable oil

1/2 cup chopped green bell pepper, about 1 medium pepper

1 clove garlic, minced

1 1/2 cups cooked field peas (black-eyed peas)

1 teaspoon salt

1/2 teaspoon black pepper

1 cup raw long-grain rice

1 sprig fresh thyme or a pinch of crumbled dried thyme

Heat the oil in a large pot over medium heat. Add the onion, bell pepper and garlic and cook until translucent. Add the peas, stirring to combine. Add 2 1/2 cups water, the salt and the pepper and bring to a boil.

Add the rice and the sprig of thyme; stir once. Bring back to a boil, cover and reduce heat. Simmer for 20 minutes, then remove from the heat and let stand, covered, for an additional 10 minutes.

Uncover, taste and adjust seasonings with salt and pepper. Fluff with a fork and serve. Makes 6 to 8 servings.

Hattie's Biscuits

1 1/4 cups self-rising flour

3/4 cup cake flour

1 tablespoon sugar

3/4 teaspoon baking powder

1/2 teaspoon salt

1/8 teaspoon baking soda

4 tablespoons (1/2 stick) cold unsalted butter cut into pieces

1 1/4 cups heavy cream

1/4 cup all-purpose flour

2 tablespoons melted unsalted butter

Preheat the oven to 475 and position the rack in the center of the oven. Sift together the self-rising flour, cake flour, sugar, baking powder, salt, and baking soda. Work the cold butter into the flour until the mixture resembles coarse crumbs. Add the heavy cream and stir just until the cream and flour come together to form a moist dough, being careful not to over mix. Sprinkle some of the all-purpose flour on a flat surface and place the dough on top of the flour. Using your hands, pat the dough into a 1/2-inch thick disk about 8 inches in diameter.

Using a 3-inch round cutter dipped in some of the remaining all-purpose flour, cut out rounds and place on an ungreased baking sheet.

Hattie's Red Eye Gravy

1/2 stick (1/4 cup) unsalted butter

1 1/2 pounds ham, cut into 1/2-inch thick slices

1/4 cup brewed coffee

1/2 cup boiling water

Hot pepper sauce to taste

In a large skillet, heat the butter over moderately high heat until the foam subsides and in it sauté the ham in batches, turning it once, for 2 to 3 minutes on each side, or until it is browned, and transfer it to a platter. Into the skillet pour the coffee and 1/2 cup boiling water and cook the mixture over high heat, scraping up the browned bits, for 2 minutes. Season the gravy with the hot pepper sauce and pepper and pour it over the ham slices. (If desired, strain the gravy before pouring it over the ham.) Serve ham and gravy with spoon bread or grits.

Gregory's Dagwood Sandwich

1/3 cup mayonnaise

2 tablespoons yellow mustard

10 slices of bread suitable for stacked sandwiches (i.e., white, wheat, rye or pumpernickel)

1/4 pound each of your choice of assorted sliced deli meats
1 medium tomato, cut into thin slices

10 whole green leaf lettuce leaves, washed, patted dry, and stem end removed

3 red cherry tomatoes

3 small pickle slices

3 long metal skewers

Combine mayonnaise and mustard in a small bowl. Arrange 5 bread slices on a large cutting board. Spread 2 tablespoons of the mayonnaise mixture evenly on each slice. Layer the meat and cheeses evenly among the bread.

Fold the meats so that the sandwiches will stack evenly on top of each other. Top each of the sandwiches with tomato slices and the remaining bread slices. Spread about 1 tablespoon of the mayonnaise mixture on top of each sandwich. Carefully build the Dagwood Sandwich by stacking all 5 sandwiches on top of each other. Separate the sandwiches by placing 2 lettuce leaves in between. To keep the sandwich tower from falling over, fit the skewers into the sandwich tower all the way through the center. To serve, pull off the desired amount of bread, meat and cheese.

This recipe serves 3.

Mamie's Chow Chow

4 quarts green tomatoes

1 large head of cabbage

10 medium onions

5 medium green peppers

7 medium sweet red peppers

1/2 cup salt

15 cups vinegar

5 cups sugar

3 tablespoons dry mustard

2 teaspoons powdered ginger

1 tablespoon turmeric

4 tablespoons mustard seeds

3 tablespoons celery seed

2 tablespoons pickling spice

Chop all vegetables; combine in a large kettle. Stir in salt; let stand at room temperature overnight, or at least 8 hours. Drain.

Combine vinegar, sugar, dry mustard, ginger, and turmeric in a large kettle. Put mustard seed, celery seed, and pickling spices in a 6-inch square of cheesecloth or cheesecloth bag.

Tie ends or gather and tie string and add to the kettle. Bring the liquid to a boil and simmer for 30 minutes. Add vegetables and return to simmer for 30 minutes longer. Discard spice bag. Spoon chow chow into hot sterilized jars and seal. Process for 15 minutes in a boiling-water canner. Serve with greens or peas.

Astor's Plantation Iced Tea

12 tea bags

3 bunches of mint leaves

3 cups of sugar

2 cups of lemon juice

1 qt pineapple juice

4 liters ginger ale

Boil 3.5 gallons water. Add the tea, mint and sugar. Allow to steep for 30 minutes. Remove bags and leaves. Refrigerate. Just before serving, add lemon juice, pineapple juice, and ginger ale. Pour over ice.

Mother Winston's Sunday Company Pound Cake

3 sticks unsalted butter

3 cups of sugar

3 cups of flour

6 eggs

½ teaspoon of vanilla

½ lemon or almond extract

½ teaspoon of baking powder

½ teaspoon of salt

½ cup of orange juice

Cream together butter and sugar. Add eggs one at a time, then add the extracts. While butter, sugar and eggs are creaming, combine dry ingredients. When butter mixture is creamy, gradually add dry ingredients. Add orange juice last.

Bake in prepared tube pan at 350 degrees for approximately one hour or until toothpick comes out clean. Allow pan to cool just enough to hold in bare hands. Turn out on cake plate and drizzle with powdered sugar. Serve with fresh berries and whipped cream.

Coming Soon!

A Long Time Coming

Prologue

For there is nothing hid, which shall not be manifested;
neither was anything kept secret, but that it should come broad.

Mark 4:22

1990 ~ Detroit, Michigan

Gregory Baptiste stood there dry mouthed and dumbfounded. Plain as day, real enough to reach out and touch, he saw a ghost. Right there in front of his cash register. He stared at the ghost and the ghost stared back at him.

The unwitting patrons in line behind didn't notice him. They flipped through magazines and read labels on packages while the ghost taunted their favorite neighborhood pharmacist.

The little girl behind the ghost couldn't wait much longer.

"Mommy, I have to pee pee." He turned and looked down at the girl, then smiled at her mother.

"Miss, you can take my place. Looks like you need to hurry." Without looking at him she said. "Thank you."

Gregory didn't see the exchange between the lady and the ghost. The embarrassed mother moved to the front of the line; and unpacked the basket containing a jar of Vick's VapoRub®, a box of tissues, and a bottle of cough syrup.

He swiftly tallied the items, collected the money, made change, thanked her for shopping at the Motor City Pharmacy and invited her to come again.

The ghost had moved out of the line and propped himself against the wall to watch Gregory work. He smiled as he observed Gregory alternate between filling prescriptions and cashing out orders for candy, reading glasses, newspapers and sundries.

Gregory watched the ghost watching him. He wished he could slap that insolent smirk right off the ghost's face. He certainly couldn't say anything to him. Surely no one else in the pharmacy had seen him. People would think he had completely lost his mind.

He had seen the ghost all around the city... driving down Jefferson Avenue, eating at restaurants, and at Cobo Arena during a Piston's basketball game. He even thought he caught a glimpse of the ghost on the campus of the University of Detroit during his son's graduation. Now the ghost had the audacity to show his specter face at Gregory's place of business.

He continued pouring liquids into brown plastic bottles as he watched the ghost slowly walk toward him. Even dead, he still walked with that cool-cat limp. Finally the ghost came right up to the counter and spoke to him. "Boo!"

Gregory jumped straight in the air. The potion he was mixing spilled all over his smock and shoes. The bottles he had neatly assembled in rows of six fell in domino-like tumbles, and one by one rolled off the table, sending each of them crashing to the floor. The ghost crossed his arms over his chest and belly laughed hysterically.

The ghost was still laughing as the terrified pharmacist clumsily struggled to clean and reassemble his work space.

"Man, Eddie Murphy ain't got nothin' on you. You need to come from behind that counter and take your show on the road."

Gregory had had enough. He confronted the ghost. "Who are you? What do you want? Why do you keep showing up everywhere I go?"

"Man, how you gon' ask who I am? I know it's been years 'Cuz, but I ain't changed that much."

Gregory took several horror-struck steps backward. "Tom? You can't be Tom!"

The ghost roared with laughter. "Man, you look like you just seen a ghost."

A quick survey of the pharmacy assured Gregory that he and the ghost were the only occupants at the time. He took off his soaking wet smock and eased in front of the counter.

He walked right up and stood face to face with the ghost-man. He cautiously reached forward and touched his face.
Flesh, muscles underneath the flesh and a scratchy five o'clock shadow. "Thomas? Is it really you?"

The ghost stopped laughing. "Yeah 'Cuz. It's really me. Alive – and well."

Dear Reader:

Thank you for reading my debut novel, Brown Paper Bag. While it was meant for your reading pleasure, I also hope that you were encouraged to deepen your relationship with our Lord and Savior, Jesus Christ.

If any of you are in an abusive or otherwise unhealthy relationship, understand that you are a marvelous, glorious reflection of God's love. You were not created to live in fear, intimidation or squalor. I encourage you to ask God for the strength and the resources to love and esteem yourself enough to find permanent safety. Talk to someone you can trust or contact the following national organizations for help. Know that God loves you and even though we may never have met... so do I.

Please take care

- Scrutinize relationships – Do the people in your life add value or drain you of energy and enthusiasm? What do you bring to the table?
- Visit your doctor often. Get health screenings that are appropriate for your age and lifestyle – encourage everyone in your circle of influence to do so as well.
- Bask in the love of friends and family.

Finally, if you haven't already done so, discover your God-given gift and walk in the greatness of your purpose.

Love,

Venus

Domestic Violence Information

National Domestic Violence Hotline
www.ndvh.org
1-800-799-SAFE (7233)
1-800-787-3224 (TTY)

United States Domestic Violence Hotline
1-800-799-7233
TDD: 1-800-787-3224
Spanish Language: 1-800-942-6908

About Venus Mason Theus

*That [the older women] may teach the young women to be responsible,
to love their husbands to love their children, to be wise, chaste,
keepers at home, good, obedient to their own husbands,
that the word of God be not blasphemed.*

Titus 2:4-5

In 1997 while still raising her children, she relinquished her corporate job as a paralegal to assume the role of full time *family manager* and caregiver for her mother; and both her maternal grandparents. Venus attests that through God's grace, her family has emerged victoriously through a myriad of heartaches, tests and trials, which prepared her to accept the assignment to serve as Christian Marriage and Family Consultant.

In her workshops, books and blogs, she uses real life experiences, humor, and the Word of God to edify the body of Christ, evangelize to the unchurched and to entertain the masses. Her workshop titles include *"Living Well, the Sweetest Revenge"* (Conquering Bitterness After Breakup), *"Can You Hear Me Now?"* (Communication in Marriage)" and *"Your Slip is Showing"* (An Empowerment Workshop for Women). Venus is the author of the novel *Brown Paper Bag*, and an eBook entitled *Pearls of Wisdom for Wives: How to Have a Joyfully-Ever-After Life.*

Venus is married to Jerome Theus and has five children and 15 grandchildren. She and her husband serve as the Co-Directors of the marriage and family ministry at their home church, Greater Grace Temple in Detroit, Michigan.